# Too Loud a Silence

# Too Loud a Silence

# Jo Jackson

*Cover image by Catherine Downes*
www.catherinedownes-artist.co.uk
*Cover design by Isobel Bushell*
www.aardvarkid.com

ISBN: 978-1-326-86566-5

PublishNation
www.publishnation.co.uk

*For the twins*

# Acknowledgments

I am especially grateful to Writers on the Edge for their encouragement and uncompromising feedback as chapter by chapter they watched this novel evolve; also to Maggie Bardsley, Brenda Carter, Margaret Cannon, Paul Francis, Olga Levitt, Lorna Taylor and Kathy Watson who read and reread my manuscript.

Thank you to Susan Davis for her professional editing and constructive comments and to Colin Taylor for his generosity and his meticulous attention to detail in copy-editing and proofreading my manuscript. Kate Innes, Ina Taylor and Heidi Robbins patiently guided me through the intricacies of the publishing process. Catherine Downes painted the beautiful picture for the cover which was designed by Isobel Bushell.

This book is for my children, Matthew, Olivia and Tom – who make everything worthwhile – and for their families for the joy they bring. Lastly, thank you to Andy my husband for his unstinting love, and for not minding all those nights when I've crept out of bed before dawn to write this book.

# Prelude

**Cairo 1980**

She watches her mother from the darkest corner. Her small brother and sister lie asleep on the cardboard beside her. She pulls up a corner of their shared blanket but still she shivers in the night cold.

A sound pierces the black, like the whine of the hot wind which coats everything with sand in the spring. Her mother is making the noise, biting on scrunched-up cloth until she becomes quiet again.

She wishes her big brother was here. He is nearly eight; he'd left before the day had begun. Usually he comes back with bits of food he's found in the bags on the roadside; sometimes he brings pieces of broken bread, still warm from the oven, thrown out by the bakery.

She creeps across the space and touches her mother's hot, sweaty face but is pushed away, told to go and look after the little ones.

Her mother is grunting now, long drawn-out moans getting louder.

She holds her hands against her ears and sees her mother pull a small, pale shape from between her legs. Water spreads across the tiles. It runs into the cracks and drips down the step, darkening the compacted dust. Her mother screams, bangs her fist into the floor, arches her back to reveal a sliver of light. Another pale shape appears and the tiles become red, dark-red like the sky when the sun has disappeared. The red spreads across the floor.

Her mother is still now, lying with her head pressed against the wall. She can't see Mama's face but she never lets her eyes move from the black curve of her body.

Light has squeezed past the blanket that hangs across the entrance to their shelter, a crumbling tomb amongst the many other tombs. Her mother calls her name and makes her stand still as she winds a piece of blue cloth around her, securing the awkward bundle onto her back. She is told what she must do and she slips out, silent as the shadows.

This is el-Arafa. The City of the Dead, but home to the living. They have been here since last summer, after her father was killed by a truck

1

and there was nowhere else to go. Then it was hot. Flies fed on the rubbish and dogs scavenged the rotting food; the children threw stones at them.

Now it is winter and the nights are cold until the sun rises with the morning. Rain, when it comes, runs in muddy rivers and she, her brothers and sister press the mud through their fingers and put out their tongues to catch the raindrops.

She dodges between the hooting cars and lorries, used to the noise and the chaos. Gold and purple outline the Mokattam Hills as they turn from black to dusty brown. The bundle is heavy but her back is warm where it lies against her.

She knows she is nearly there because the stench from the rubbish mountain blots out the smell of fumes from the traffic. In the narrow, winding alleyways, she jumps the donkey shit deposited by the beasts in their endless pulling of carts from the city. The *Zabbaleen*, the rubbish collectors, in dirty *gallabayas*, beat the animals with sticks, opening sores on the donkeys' sides where their ribs ripple below the thin skin.

Already the mountain is alive. Women and children crawl over it, their eyes hunting out anything to eat or to sell. She waits until no one is near, then unties her bundle and lays it on top of the rubbish. A green flip-flop with a broken strap lies next to it. She picks up a watermelon skin and sucks, but it is dry and sour.

With a quick tug, she pulls back the corner of the blue cloth. She sees two crumpled faces and a fist clenched against black hair. There are small mewing noises reminding her of the kittens she once found before her brother drowned them in a barrel. She brushes away the flies and pushes the cloth back. She can see a chicken carcass a few feet away and knowing Mama will be pleased she scrambles to collect the bones.

She hides behind an oil drum, waits until she hears a woman shriek and sees a small group gather around her bundle. Then she is gone.

When she gets back her mother is on her knees scrubbing at the floor with a filthy cloth. Her mother looks at her and nods faintly. Then she returns to her task. The child takes the cloth and rubs hard at the tiles. The red stain dissolves in the water and swirls in rainbow shapes until it disappears into the earth.

When the floor is scrubbed clean she squats next to her mother and holds her hand.

# Chapter 1

**England 2011**

'I'm going to Cairo, Mum.' The words invade the space.

It wasn't meant to be like this. Maha had rehearsed it differently. It was to have been quietly said, in a gentle moment when the two of them were comfortable again, when the strangeness of having been apart for a few weeks had evaporated.

Pippa, her mother, sat on the sofa, hands clasped tightly, white against her red skirt. She stared out of the window, her eyes fixed somewhere beyond the garden and the blue outline of the hills. A tractor rumbled on the road and a sheep bleated in the evening air. Even the breeze had died. The leaves on the birch hung silently waiting for the night.

'Well, say something, anything. I wanted you to be pleased but even anger or tears would be some sort of response.' What was wrong with her mother? Usually so attentive, creative, always supportive. Now only this suffocating silence. 'I've made up my mind. I'm determined to go.'

Her mother went to stand by the window, gripped the sill to steady herself. Still slim, narrow hips, young-looking for sixty-three, her hair fashionably cut. She turned a geranium around to face the light and took off a brown dead leaf, which crumbled to pieces in her hand.

'Is this about Robin? I thought you were over him.' Her mother's voice was cracked.

'No, Mum, it's not. You know our relationship finished two months ago. His newspaper is commissioning the assignment, that's all.'

She addressed her mother's back. 'Mum, I was born an Egyptian, but I don't know what it's like to feel Egyptian. Always it's a closed

3

subject. I need to go there, to know who I am. I want to go.' She had expected her mother to be anxious, to tell her not to go, to tell her she was being reckless especially now with all the rioting, the violence of the Arab Spring. She thought she had all her arguments prepared. She didn't know how to deal with this void. 'I'm thirty, I'm a journalist; I have a mind of my own. I'm not asking your permission.'

The light in the room faded and a dying sun painted the fields with a muted wash. The sky was cherry-silk, shot through with mauve.

She watched as her mother wiped a wet cheek with the palm of her hand and rested her head against the windowpane. Her breath made patterned rings on the glass. They heard the farmer in the field beyond, whistling as he always did, calling in the cows for milking. Her mother turned and collected up the cups. She whispered, 'Darling, I'm sorry.'

Unable to sleep, Maha lay in the familiar bedroom with its teenage wallpaper. She had begged her parents not to change it when she left home. The photograph of her in the school hockey team still hung on the wall. Beside it there were pictures of her friends, pulling faces and laughing, their arms around each other, taken on her first holiday without parents when she was in the sixth form. A lot of growing-up happened on holiday in Newquay. Even now, when they all meet up, they laugh about what they got up to.

She wandered around the room touching her books and rearranging the sports trophies on her dressing table. She will pack them away, help her mum to redecorate, move on. Wearing an old T-shirt, she sat down by the open window and stared at the dark shadows of the trees. The wings of an owl loomed in silhouette. She had brought Robin here once. He said it was mind-numbing, too far from anywhere. She loved it. The undiluted sky pierced with stars, the wind in the trees. Until her dad died it was always just the three of them, Mum, Dad and herself, this house. 'Safe,' Mum used to say.

She wasn't travelling to Egypt on a whim. The desire had been growing for months since before the revolution began. She told herself her job was providing her with the opportunity but was it more of an excuse. Her mother had seemed shocked. No, not shocked, more frightened. Maha peered into the night, saw only the look on her mother's face. It had been deeper than anguish, a cocktail of emptiness and loss. She knew she had touched an indefinable loneliness. A small voice asked, is it hers or yours?

Maha heard the sound of a footfall on the stairs and the click of the latch as the kitchen door opened. Her mother was awake too.

*

'Only one, only one.' I hate those words going round and round, a motorbike riding the wall of death. I don't want to hear them but I still can. The intervening years haven't dimmed his tone or blurred the sight of his rheumy eyes. I still want to cry and plead or scratch his face and kick and punch. Anything to make him say something different.

I knew I wasn't going to sleep tonight. I'm too familiar with the routine, the fierce anger followed by the tide of hopelessness and exhausting defeat. I watch the night clouds move like drifting smoke backlit by the moon. I like going to bed with the curtains open especially since Gareth died. I like to think of all the people in the world who can see that same moon, a common thread linking us to each other.

I flinch as the stair creaks. It sounds so loud in the quiet of the night but Maha will surely be fast asleep. I don't want to waken her.

I wish tonight had been different. Her announcement had come as such a shock, so definite, so final. I should have hugged her; we should have discussed it but instead I froze and when she needed my support and encouragement, I let her down. It was easy when she was small. I could sit her on my knee, give her a hug and make things better. Now she's an adult, I've had to learn to let her go, to accept she doesn't need me now. That's not true: it's more that she needs me in a different way. We have always been able to talk but…the secrets are there. I don't want her to go to Cairo.

I pour the boiling water into the mug and swirl the teabag around. Through the decades, how many cups of tea in the middle of the night? How many books read? Temporary fixes, a time that's mine but never a peace.

The breath of night wafts over me as I step into the garden where the faintest hint of light outlines the Edge. My mug of tea warms my hands and I watch the steam curl upwards.

I shouldn't have spoken about Robin as I did. I always found him difficult to like. There was a hard edge to him. When he'd come to stay for a weekend he'd been restless, eager to get away, hadn't tried to hide his boredom. Maha too had changed – become more brittle. Never time to talk and her conversation was peppered with 'Robin says' or 'Robin thinks'. Things are better again now, as if her confidence is returning.

*

Out of her bedroom window Maha watched her mother walk slowly around the garden in her dressing gown. She saw her pause to smell a lily and to deadhead some phlox. She was a dark ghost moving silently between the flowerbeds and the shrubs.

Maha held back the curtain, tried to let go her feeling of hurt and confusion. She thought back to how her mum had coped when Dad died. How she'd nursed him at home and how she had read to him when he no longer had the strength to hold a book. All his favourites like *Anna Karenina, Frankenstein* and the novels of John Steinbeck. She had seen her mother struggle through *Ulysses* knowing it was this time together that was precious, not the words on the page. They had lain together on the bed at the end. Her mum, her dad and her, separated by this new intruder called cancer but bound by a history shared, a hundred moments so special they didn't even need to be recalled.

Her mother had been so quiet and dignified at the funeral. It was she who had found Maha's hand as the coffin had slipped from view, had held her when the tears came. It was her mother who had pushed her gently back to London, to Robin and to her freelance work; it was her mother who had always been at the end of the phone when she was homesick or lonely or when the grief was too raw and bewildering. Her mother's strength and focus had been a surprise. Within their altered relationship they had moulded around each other in the way a tree heals the wound of a broken branch. Experience had made Maha sensitive to sudden silences, slow withdrawals and her mother's need for space when sorrow crept in like an autumn mist.

Now her mum was walking around the garden in the early morning. Why? Thinking about what?

She took her bathrobe from the hook behind the door and went downstairs to join her. She didn't want her own decisions to push her mum into one of her downward spirals, into an empty space beyond reach.

'Mum, whatever are you doing out here? You'll get cold.'

'No, it's lovely. I needed to sort out my thoughts, Maha. Night is like a photographer's darkroom, nothing to see at first, then an image gradually emerges until the picture makes sense. Look at how the white roses show up in the dark. Come and sit beside me on the bench and you can share my cup of tea. You used to when you were little. You would let me hold the cup while you took a mouthful. I don't think you liked tea but you thought you were such a big girl.'

'Mum, I'm sorry I said those things earlier.'

'We do sometimes, hurt each other when we don't mean to.'

The arc of light, more like a halo now, was spreading above the hills, illuminating the mist trapped in the valley. Maha rested her hand on her mother's arm, all their anger blown away with the night clouds.

What was her mum trying to say? Was she making it easier for her to go or more difficult? Maha didn't know.

# Chapter 2

'Bye, Mum, don't worry, I'll be fine.' Her mother was biting her lip, her eyes creased shut. 'Mum, what is it? What am I not understanding?'

'Go now, Maha.' A whisper squeezed out to keep back the tears. The station had been so bleak. She'd waved until her mum was a small figure on the concourse. She told herself she would only be away for a short time. Her mum had been well for years now. She would be all right.

Maha peered through the train windows, drawing circles in the condensation as the rain raced down the glass, pushed in horizontal lines by the speed of the engine. 'A coffee, please.' The man turned to Maha. 'Can I get you one too?

Milk?'

'Me? Oh...yes. Thank you.' Maha pulled back from her drifting thoughts to look at the person who had spoken. She was momentarily surprised to find herself in a railway carriage, rattling its way to London, full of business people, shoppers and day-trippers. Whispered conversations between fellow travellers and loud telephone talk surrounded her, mixed now with the aroma of coffee and the bored voice of the trolley attendant and his repeated questions: black or white, with sugar, diet coke or ordinary?

'I thought a drink might help to calm the nerves,' the man said with a smile. 'What is it, an interview or an important meeting?'

'Sorry, am I so obvious?'

'No, not obvious, just distracted. I couldn't help noticing you've been reading the same page since we left the station and you have shut the book and reopened it at least three times. Either it's not very good or your thoughts are somewhere else.'

Maha took the lid off her coffee and felt the hot steam touch her face. She wrapped her cup in the serviette and dabbed at the stain on the table. She traced the rim of the cup with her finger.

The man watched her, alternating between concern and amusement. He had a modern face, short hair, a slightly long nose and the faint white line of an old scar above his eyebrow.

'I've just been back home for the weekend and sometimes conversations occur that leave you with more questions than answers.' She was surprised to find herself sharing her thoughts with this stranger, but something about him made her want to offer an explanation. 'I expect I'm making a big deal out of nothing. Anyway, thank you for asking. The coffee is great.'

'Families, huh,' and they both laughed. 'Tell me,' he said. 'What do you think about whaling? You come as a welcome distraction.' He waved his newspaper. 'I was reading this article and becoming increasingly incensed. Editorials can be so biased, don't you think?'

'I'm a freelance journalist,' Maha told him, 'so don't get me going on the subject of editors.'

'Freelance. I guess that means you get to do what you want. Your own boss.'

'It sounds romantic but it's hard graft and poorly paid.'

'OK, let's start with the state of the British press. Good or bad?' They moved onto jobs versus countryside, their conversation punctuated with laughter. She found him easy to talk to, funny and interesting. The journey was passing too quickly.

'What brings you to London? Is it work?' she asked.

'Why am I on my way to London?' He pondered the question. 'Well,' he said, and tapped the briefcase between his feet, 'in here is an important piece of work. I'm an author. I'll say it again because I like how it sounds. I am an author and today I'm meeting the publisher who has accepted my first novel.'

'Wow, that's exciting. It makes my job seem ordinary. How long did it take to write your book?' 'My whole life, all thirty-three years of it. It would be difficult to describe me as an overnight success.'

'So what kind of book is it, a crime novel, travel, a psychological thriller? What name do I have to look out for on the shelves of Waterstones?'

'I would describe it as almost a crime novel but more as a case of deception. As to the name – a difficult decision. Should I have gone for the ordinary James Reid or the more flamboyant pseudonym, maybe Ashley McGregor Moore? What do you think?'

'I think you have cheered me up and I'm glad you sat next to me today.'

'Pleased to be of service. The pleasure has been all mine. You looked so pensive and upset before.'

'James.' Maha tried the name. He lifted his eyebrows and inclined his head. 'Are you teasing me?' Is that not your proper name?' She wasn't sure how to take him but he no longer felt like a stranger. 'Do you mind if I ask you a question?'

'Go ahead.' His tone was light but she knew he was listening.

'Do you ever feel someone's not told you everything?'

'All the time,' he said. 'But we all have secrets.'

'I don't mean little things. This is something important.' She looked at his face to see if he was laughing at her.

'Certainly. I think one day they'll tell me I'm not just a boy from a semi-detached in Aylesbury, I am the heir to a castle in Scotland. I own hundreds of acres and all this working for a living has just been to develop my character.'

Maha laughed. He said, 'That's better, and what about you? Without wishing to be too forward my observation is you are much too beautiful to be English and there is a touch of the exotic about you.'

'You can't make such outrageous comments.' Her smile wound its way into her voice and he smiled too.

'My name is Maha. I am English.' She never knew how to describe herself. 'But my… Well, I was born in Egypt.'

'Ah, so there's the secret. In fact, you are a reincarnated pharaoh's daughter banished to these damp and dreary northern climes. Scottish laird meets and falls in love with an Egyptian princess courtesy of Virgin Rail. It could be a plot for a book, don't you think?' He raised his empty coffee carton and Maha solemnly raised hers so the paper cups came together in mock celebration.

A small laugh burst from her lips. 'Now you are making fun of me. It's odd you should say that because when I was seven I told a boy at school I was a pharaoh's daughter, to stop him bullying me. Ethan his name was.' She paused. 'Now I've told you, it all sounds rather ridiculous and not worth worrying about.'

'As I said, Maha, I'm glad to be of help and I like your name.'

Too soon the train pulled into Euston station. People squashed into the aisles wanting to be the first off. James turned to her. 'Sheep and sheepdogs come to mind,' he said with a grimace. 'By the way, because I have to live with myself and because I'd like to see you again, I have to tell you; I *am* an author, but for now I'm a boring accountant.' He slipped a business card into the pocket of her jacket. She found him one of hers and handed it to him as they were bustled off the train.

An elderly couple, fumbling for their tickets, stopped suddenly on the platform and Maha banged into the wheels of their trolley. The crowds streamed either side of them and when she reached the barrier she heard James's voice above the noise. 'Hey, I'll ring you.' He waved, blew her a kiss over the moving heads and disappeared into the tapestry of colour. She watched him go, wondering about him – a genuinely nice guy or a chancer? She'd probably never know.

# Chapter 3

The effort of pretence makes me rest against the station wall for a minute. I had seen her searching my face, her own screwed up with anxiety. 'I'll be back before you realise I've gone,' she said. 'We'll have so much to talk about. I'll be fine. Don't worry about me.'

She'd hugged me, her black hair blowing across her face. Then there were those few minutes when I didn't want her to go but wished she would because there was so much to say but we were unable to say any of it. I'd waved as she headed onto the platform, her red scarf bringing brightness to the overcast day.

I am getting used to living on my own. I find my small routines a comfort but Maha's visit has disturbed and frightened me. My thoughts refuse to be ignored – like smudges on a window, exposed by a low sun.

The thought of going straight home does not appeal. I stop the car in a lay-by and walk along a favourite track into the woods. It's raining now and the leaves are a vibrant green against the pale sky. Ridges of earth outline the path and broken twigs lie strewn by summer winds. I love walks on my own, the space, the peace. The rambling group is fine but it's more about chattering than admiring the countryside. My friends are good to me. I have my painting and my garden. I've enrolled on a craft class, to learn to quilt. Perhaps I'll make a little quilt for a cot.

'So stop feeling sorry for yourself.' My shout rebounds off the trees. Please don't let her...

Getting older is about aches and pains, stiff backs after gardening, loss and fear and sometimes loneliness. What no one tells you is the secrets you hold build up like the years. The cupboard that houses them becomes too small and the lock begins to weaken. Occasionally one slips out, floats gracefully like a piece of paper disturbed by a breeze. Sometimes it doesn't matter. The secret crumbles, becomes the cobweb on the wall or the dust in the corner behind the dresser and for a short time the cupboard seems secure again.

What's the difference anyway, I wonder, between a secret and a lie? When do you know to stuff it into the cupboard? I remember Gareth's sixtieth birthday. I lied to him for weeks about us going away for a weekend break and I kept the surprise party a secret. A secret to be giggled over with Maha, sudden changes of conversation on the telephone and the admiration of everyone on the day that we had managed to keep the secret so completely from him.

What they didn't know was they were talking to an expert, to the secret keeper extraordinaire, to the top of the class. How did I get to be so good at it?

It is beginning to rain more persistently, decorating the Edge with its own colour palette. The sky is a soft grey with brush strokes of a darker hue above the hills. I enjoy a walk in the rain. Just me and the trees, the leaves shaking themselves like a wet dog. The sound is all in the canopy and only droplets of water seep through to remind me it's raining.

I suppose the first secret I can remember being put into store was when my brother and I stole a shilling. Our mother was upstairs making the beds and we went into her handbag and found her purse. It was black with a silver clasp, which snapped shut with a click. The click had sounded so loud. I had jumped up and down wanting to go to the toilet.

We took the money to the shop. My brother was older than me but he made me carry it. I remember clutching it inside my glove and the silver circle becoming warm. I imagined the Queen's head rubbing off in my palm. We bought a packet of opal fruits, the ones that stick to your teeth and give an explosion of taste in your mouth. Bizarrely I was at a restaurant recently and instead of mints after the meal that's what they gave. It took me straight back to the swings where my brother and I sat and ate the whole packet. We fell out over the last one. He said he should have it because it was his idea. I said it should be mine because I took the money.

I don't know if Mum ever knew; she never said but we didn't get any pocket money that week, I still remember. I nearly told her, I wanted to tell her but my brother stood on my hair until I promised not to. I think it's when I learned the rules around secrets. We have laughed about it since but we never told Mum.

The bench I usually sit on is wet today but I sit on it anyway. Only seed heads visible now where tiny orchids, like wax specimens, once pushed through the grass. The view across the plain to the Welsh hills is interrupted by swirls of rain-soaked mist, like memories, forming, changing, receding and clearing. It's too hard to think about those other secrets today, the ones that were never meant to be kept but somehow kept themselves.

When we adopted Maha we gave her love, a home, opportunities but she gave us so much more. I had also made her watchful, an ability children acquire when depression lurks in a household. I can name it now but it wasn't always so. The scars of infertility, my scars.

'Go well, Maha, go well.' I say it out loud so the wind will pick it up and take my words to her.

# Chapter 4

'May I sit beside you?' A lady wearing a purple bobble hat with a pompom that matched her snow-white hair eased herself onto the seat beside Maha. She pushed her rollator to one side.

'You're looking at my hat,' she said. 'My granddaughter knitted it for me and she said I have to wear it when I go out because it will keep me warm. A strange choice for a lady of eighty-five, but she's right. It does. I walk along here most days; the ducks know me and the pigeons too.' She threw some crumbs onto the ground and Maha watched the mallards waddle nearer and a sparrow take its chance, hopping on thin legs.

'This bit of sunshine's nice, isn't it, after this morning's rain?' the woman said, and Maha nodded, startling the birds. 'Are you out for a walk too, dear?'

'No, not really. I think I'm just wasting time. I need to go into the office, in the building over there. I have to make some final arrangements – I'm travelling out to Egypt. The trouble is, it means seeing someone I once knew quite well but don't anymore so I'm sort of summoning up the enthusiasm.'

'Oh, I think I understand. I'm sure it will be all right. Do you want to go to Egypt? It's an awfully long way to go, especially at the moment.'

Did she want to go? Maha watched a small boy kicking a ball across the grass. She turned to the old lady. 'It's what I want to do most in the whole world. I want to go back to where I came from. I've never admitted that to myself until now.'

'Then you must do it. You young women, you're so lucky. You get to make up your own mind about your life now. Not told what to do or what to think as we were in my day. My Tommy used to say I itched to be a rebel but he didn't mind. I think he was quite proud of me. "Jean," he used to say, "you were born thirty years before your time!"' She smiled to herself, the brown spots on her face creased like corrugated paper. She patted Maha's hand. 'Well, I best be getting back. It's been nice to have a talk.'

The old lady put her glove to her lips and touched the small brass plaque on the back of the bench. 'Don't waste a chance, dear; you make the most of it. Bye-bye.'

Maha watched her go and felt quite bereft. She read the plaque: 'In Loving memory of Thomas (Tommy) Bartlett who loved it here'.

The water on the canal rippled gently, throwing up arcs of silver, and the ducks came closer hoping to be fed. Maha stared at the huge glass skyscraper that was the newspaper office. She saw a million shafts of sunlight reflected by its windows. The canal boats moored in the basin were dwarfed by the structure like toy boats in a bath.

She sat for a few more moments. The old lady was right. This was a chance she wouldn't let go to waste. She clapped her hands, and sent the birds into flight.

She walked towards the glass building. Robin would be at his desk absorbed in his work.


'That's too bloody late. I want it by the end of the afternoon.' Robin was in his office. He had the phone crushed into his shoulder as he scowled at his computer screen.

He was a tall man, slightly stooped from too long spent at a desk. It was his energy Maha had been attracted to. 'Let's go for drinks after work,' he'd say, and they'd join the group of journalists in whichever bistro pub was the 'in' place. There amongst the sanded wooden floors, white walls and pine furniture they'd all stand in groups shouting at each other, friends on one level, fierce rivals on another. Halfway home on the tube Robin might jump up and pull Maha by the hand. They would squeeze off the train just before the doors shut and race up the escalator to emerge into the buzz of London before running to a cinema to catch the last showing of some must-see film. It had been fun while it lasted. They had been together for almost two years but the relationship had drifted. Maha was relieved when he moved back to his own flat. She was disillusioned with the fast, ego-driven media set and bored with him. They had parted before the rows became bitter. It was right for both of them at the time.

Robin fiddled with his sub-editor's nameplate, stood it on its end, then repositioned it; he traced the brass letters with the end of a pen. He looked up briefly and waved his hand at her, the person on the phone still commanding his attention. She watched as the words on his computer tore up the screen as he searched for a vital piece of information. A paper cup of coffee stood on the corner of his desk half drunk, its contents cold, the colour of dung.

He put down the phone. 'Hi. Good weekend?' His eyes flicked to her then back to the screen.

'OK. I've been home. I wanted to see Mum before I went to Cairo but she was really strange about it.'

'Well, you're not going anyway so it doesn't matter. You're off the job. I'm sending someone else. One of the guys.' Robin pushed some papers onto the floor so she could sit down.

'What do you mean, off the job? I'm going, Robin.'

'I decide, remember? No contract. My choice.' He thrust his nameplate towards her across the desk, its corner digging into her arm before it landed on the floor.

'No, that's not how it is.' She lifted her hands, hoped Robin might pause for one moment and listen. 'Just to remind you, I'm freelance. That means I go anywhere, do anything, a free spirit.'

He leant across the desk, his face inches away from hers. She could see the long hair in his nostril, the one she used to cut for him.

'I won't buy your copy.'

'Well, other papers will. I won't change my mind, Robin.' She tried to keep her voice low.

Colleagues looked up, paused at their work. 'Hey, you two. Cool it,' Simon shouted across the room. He was big, scruffy and gentle, always the peacemaker. 'My head hurts and my body aches. Sex on

17

Sunday, peace on Monday, remember the rule. I can't cope with too much aggravation.'

'Bloody idiots.' Robin stretched across to kick the door shut, knocking the cup off his desk; its contents mapped a pattern on the floor.

'Robin, it's not what we agreed. You're making this personal, not professional.'

'So what if it's bloody personal.'

'This matters to me. Each night I watch Egypt on the television. You know it's where I was born...'

'Don't give me that. You think you're going to swan into Egypt and everything will fall into place. You're an outsider, Maha. You're no more Egyptian than I am.'

'I'm also a good reporter, Robin, and I speak Arabic. Three years studying the language gives me an advantage over Simon or Jake or anyone else you send.

'I need to go – to get it out of my system.' She stood up. 'Robin, stop what you're doing and look at me. This is your country, Robin; you were born here. There isn't a blank space for you. I want to touch Egyptian soil, to see an Egyptian sky, to connect, and right now to try and tell the stories of its people. I was adopted by the best mum and dad in the world, but I was adopted, so I've always known there was once something else somewhere. It never mattered before but now it does.'

Robin stared at her. 'Here comes the sob story. Adopted, so you're bloody adopted. So are hundreds of other people but they're not making a big drama out of it like you are all of a sudden. Your excuse is you're there to report on events when really you're looking for a mummy and daddy who threw you away in the first place. Grow up, Maha. Get real. History is just that, history. Leave it there.' He picked up the phone again and shook it at her. 'And do you know what? You're too prissy to make a good reporter.'

'Sod you, Robin.'

She headed towards King's Cross and mingled with the other commuters, her mind detached, empty as though she'd been a spectator to the event, an extra in the scene. First her mother, now Robin. She felt like a boat tossed by a spring tide. What was it they didn't understand? How could she explain this compulsion, this need to go to Egypt? It had overwhelmed her quite suddenly and unexpectedly, as though it had been sitting there, waiting for its moment, hiding in her clothing, under her skin, in her mind. It was a missing piece, an absence, a shadow always moving just out of reach. Did Robin's decision change anything? Should it? No, she decided, remembering the old lady in the purple hat. She would go it alone.

She spent the rest of the afternoon at home, on the computer. She purchased airline tickets and arranged insurance. She could do this, make it a personal crusade, use some of the money her dad left her and fund it herself. He would approve she felt sure. Once in Egypt, she would meet up with press from all over the world – if she wanted to.

She looked at the Foreign Office site: *advise against all non-essential travel to Egypt: there is serious risk of violence and sexual assault at demonstrations. There is a high threat from terrorism. Westerners may be targeted or caught up in such attacks.* Maha read it and a knuckle of apprehension lodged in her throat. Was she a westerner? She wasn't sure. She would not be put off. She would make it a success.

She pulled out her old battered rucksack. It had accompanied her on many good trips. She fingered the clips. It had been with her when she interviewed tired and frustrated travellers grounded by a volcanic ash cloud; at the student protests in Parliament Square; amongst the rioters in London. She had made her mark, against the background of violence and looting, and buildings in flames. Her name had become known from articles on economic unrest, a frustrated generation and underlying inequality. It had all seemed so exciting then. Could Cairo be so different?

On impulse she ran down to the luggage shop on the corner and bought a bright red rucksack; the newness of it added to her mounting excitement. When packed and ready, it was a full stop in the whiteness of her bedroom.

She was curled up on the sofa, a guide book to Cairo open on her lap when the text came through.

*Hi,*
*I don't want to drink champagne on my own. There's an Italian restaurant just off Piccadilly, Casa Cacciatore. It's pretty special. Please say you'll come and celebrate with me. I'll tell you all about my meeting with my publisher. James*

He was waiting for her, smiling a greeting, his jacket slung over a blue shirt and jeans. He took her hand and pushed open the door. 'Shall we?'

# Chapter 5

I was in the garden when the phone rang. Isn't it always the way? I had been waiting for a sunny warm day to tackle the job and this was it. I had on my old clothes and my wellies and was knee-deep in the pond pulling out weed when the familiar ring tone interrupted the birdsong. I slithered to the edge and squelched into the house. As I put the phone to my ear the earthy, muddy smell of my wet hands made me think of tiddlers and jam jars.

'Hullo,' I shouted hurriedly, and hoped my voice would stop the caller putting the phone down.

'Hi, Mum, it's Maha.'

'Oh darling, how nice, I was in the pond so now I'm dripping onto the floor.'

'Sorry, there's a lot of background noise here. Did you say you were in the pond, Mum?'

"Yes, just clearing it and pulling out the leaves. It's great fun on a nice day. Where are you? It sounds like you're at a station or somewhere.'

'Mum.'

The cold water trickled down my arm.

'Mum, I'm at the airport. I'm on my way to Cairo.'

I caught my breath, my hand swiped at the telephone table. Must dust it. Those flowers are past their best. Must pick some more. Don't speak, don't say the wrong thing.

'Mum?'

'So soon, Maha, I didn't know it would be so soon, that's all.'

'I have to go there now. Now is when it's happening, news doesn't wait around. Anyway, it means I'll be back sooner. Back for your birthday and we'll have a weekend in London. I'll tell you all about the modern Cairo, although it seems a pretty mixed-up sort of place at the moment.'

'Yes, yes, it does.' My finger made bigger and bigger circles in the dust. 'Maha, be careful.' I should have practised what to say. What is a mother supposed to say when her daughter goes off to a conflict zone?

'I'll be all right. I'll try and ring but it's not always easy. I can't believe I'm leaving for Egypt…at last.'

Her words tailed off. I couldn't speak. I wanted to be near her.

'I just wanted to say cheerio, Mum. I must go, I love you.' Her voice was wrapped in a sob.

'Maha, wait. Have you got a pen? Since you told me you were going I've been thinking. Maha, can you write this down? 188 El-Horeya.'

I sat down on the stair as suddenly a smell of boiled cabbage engulfed me and my skin felt dry as dust. Down the phone I could hear a tannoy call for passengers.

'That's the address of the orphanage, Maha; it has huge green gates and a big tree, a flame tree. Why am I giving you the detail? It probably isn't there anymore; I haven't heard for…' The late sun broke free and slanted through the window, defining a straight line across the wall. 'Well, it's probably not there anymore.' I leant my head against the shaft of sunshine and closed my eyes.

'Maha, go well, I love you too.'

'I know. Thanks, Mum.' Her whisper was softer than the flutter of a moth. Then the phone was quiet, just a lump of plastic and a set of numbers.

Eventually I go out to the garden but sorting the pond no longer interests me. In my absence the pond skimmers have reclaimed the water and are skidding along the surface in frantic circles.

Maha's Egypt adventure is just beginning. When had mine begun? I knew the answer. It screamed in my head.

# Chapter 6

*Don't go through to departures just yet. I'm on my way. I'll be with
you in five minutes. J. xx*

And he was. James arrived breathless with a big grin on his face,
his light brown hair dishevelled. 'I couldn't let you go without seeing
you again. I wanted to wish you bon voyage.' He wrapped his arms
around her and pulled her face into his chest. Hands touching, they
sat and talked, drank coffee at a table sticky with scattered crumbs,
as easy with each other as they had been that first night in the
restaurant.

'I wanted to share these last few moments with you,' he said.
'Take care, and come back soon.' He leant forward and kissed her;
his hand brushed back her hair. She watched him, tall and lanky,
lope away from her. She wanted to run after him.

How different from Robin. She didn't want to think of them in
the same moment. She tucked away her thoughts of James. 'For
later,' she said, hugging herself.

She leant on the railings of the terminal and watched all the
people coming up on the escalator. A small excited boy jumped off
as he reached the top. He tripped and fell backwards, prevented
from further harm by the volume of passengers. People squealed,
jostled, then picked up their cases and walked by, glancing at the
embarrassed mother and the now crying child. All of us here today,
we're a swarm, temporarily thrown together, Maha mused. But
where will we be in twenty-four hours? Thousands of miles apart.
Some will be in hot countries, some in cold, some returning home
and some leaving. She was off to Egypt. The knowledge spread
through her head, down her arms to her fingertips: a tingle of
delight.

The plane was delayed, first for two hours, then extended to four. A technical problem. She just wanted to be off. She was scared the whisper, the other voice that said 'Are you up to this?' would become too loud. The whisper that kept her walking around the airport and wouldn't let her sit and relax as so many of the other resigned travellers were.

Maha wandered through the duty-free shops. She found a silk scarf and draped it over her arm. It was soft and smooth. The splashes of colour, orange and pink and vibrant yellow, were glaringly bright under the subdued light. An assistant, with impeccable make-up and a bored expression, hovered in hope; black, manicured nails made small gestures in Maha's direction.

Maha looped it loosely around her neck. It was as gentle as a caress. Her olive skin and dark eyes calmed the colours and she let her black hair fall across its folds. Do you know what you are doing? She addressed the tall, slim young lady in the mirror. In a few hours she would be there. What if she's disappointed? What if she doesn't feel anything? What if it's as foreign as any other country? Did she have to care if it's tearing itself apart? Stop it. She knew she had to go. She wanted to go. She covered her face with her hands to hide the one that stared back at her.

'Oh I don't know. I don't know.' She shouted at the mirror.

'Madam, honestly it looks beautiful. It's just right for you, it's absolutely perfect.'

She was jolted back to the present, the assistant's cool touch on her neck as the scarf was rearranged.

She pushed the hands away and unwound it. She screwed the scarf into a ball and tossed it onto the counter. 'It's only a stupid scarf, for goodness' sake, it's not important.' She rushed out of the shop.

She had been unfair, she thought later as she watched planes like grounded dragonflies manoeuvre into position. The woman had only tried to help. The beleaguered assistant had let her go and then, with a shrug of the shoulders, had picked up the scarf, refolded it and placed it back amongst the others.

Maha woke; she felt stiff, hot and uncomfortable. The plane had eventually taken off near to midnight, the last slot out. Tired adults and fractious children had collapsed into their allotted seats and fallen asleep. She stretched her cramped limbs and removed her eye shade. The plane's engines droned in a monotonous hum. The lights in the cabin were still low and the window blinds drawn.

She pulled the folded piece of paper from her pocket. 188 El-Horeya. The address had seemed to pour from her mum like water released from a dam. Of course, Maha had known about the orphanage but she'd never heard the address before. Even as a small child she'd learned not to ask about Egypt – not because she had been told not to but through the furtive looks, the short replies to her questions, her mum leaving the room suddenly and Dad finding a game to play or producing crayons to draw with. Children learn the rules; they don't need them to be spelled out.

There was that time she'd come home from school. There had been no drink of juice or cake for her as there usually was. She'd found her mum, still in her nightclothes, in a chair at the window, just staring. She'd been given a fierce hug that hurt. Her mum wouldn't speak. Maha had fetched her favourite book, *Topsy and Tim Go on Holiday*. She had read it to her mum over and over again, making up the words too big for her to manage. She'd curled up on her mother's knee and when Dad returned from work he'd found them both fast asleep. She hadn't known what was wrong but she had known not to ask. She would check out the Cairo address, so she knew where her story had begun. Robin was wrong. She wasn't looking for her birth parents – impossible anyway – but a building, a street, something to remember, would feel good.

She could hear other passengers beginning to stir and the stewardesses moved down the aisle to offer tea and coffee. Despite the restless night her anxiety had gone, left behind in London. Breakfast was served and cleared away. Dishevelled travellers stretched their limbs and headed for the washrooms, clutching toothbrush and paste.

Maha opened her blind and watched the night give way to day.

The plane banked and the sun streamed into the cabin, enveloping her in its brilliant light. Shadows coursed across the aisles chased by beams of yellow. Through the window she could see an orb, red as a blood orange, sitting on the horizon. It rose slowly like a helium balloon. Far, far below she could just see the Pyramids, three-dimensional triangles holding off the city. And beyond, there was sand that stretched to infinity. She had never seen anything so beautiful.

As they queued to get off the plane an Egyptian lady who was struggling with her bag asked her, 'Are you going home for a visit or do you live in Cairo?'

Surprised by the question she said, 'I'm a journalist.' Then a realisation dawned. She was recognised as belonging. It was a new feeling, a nice feeling and Robin's cruel words came back to her. 'You are no more Egyptian than I am.' Yes, I am, Robin, yes I am.

If Cairo from the air had looked amazing with the Nile curved like a plait through the city, the atmosphere in the airport reminded her it was a country in turmoil. Police in green uniforms used their rifles to herd the crowds of people behind barriers. There were men and women, some in the western uniform of jeans and T-shirts and others in *gallabayas* and colourful headscarves. They jostled and called as they spotted relatives. Children clung to their mothers' clothes, others pushed to the front only to be hauled back into line. As they disembarked the passengers were scrutinised by police officers with guns. Soldiers stood menacingly at the exits.

It was early morning, but the hot air had already lined the walls and dampened armpits. It welcomed the newcomers and garlanded them with its taste and smell. Long queues formed as papers were stamped and passports were studied. She showed her press pass but the officials were not interested and she moved forward slowly in the line of people.

She emerged into the sunshine, stood still and took a deep breath. She looked down at her pink sandals; was she really here, standing on Egyptian soil at last, her joy, her relief, and a thousand emotions escaped in a tear. She could see the waiting transport assigned to the press, more of whom seemed to be arriving with every plane. Journalists and cameramen shouted greetings to each other whilst they lugged all their equipment towards the bus. There were faces she recognised, a hand raised in acknowledgment. 'What a bloody fiasco this is.' The language coarse and their manner bullish. She had almost reached it too when on impulse she turned away and sat on a dusty bench, not yet ready to be part of the brash, beer-drinking, chain-smoking and all too familiar crowd.

*James, I'm here. I am in Egypt. I can't quite believe it. xx*

She fumbled as she typed the text.

She began to walk away from the airport terminal, stopping to run her hand down the rough bark of a palm tree. The sun was getting hot; dust on the side of the road was thrown up by the lorries and cars that chased each other in a mad procession.

She hailed a black and white taxi that flew past but which then executed a smart U- turn on the dual carriageway and came back for her. Horns sounded and cars screeched; a mangy dog acknowledged the manoeuvre with a bark.

'Hi, thank you,' she said as she climbed in.

'Where to, madam?' the driver asked as he pulled across the stream of traffic, making her shrink from the window. 'I don't know,' she said. 'Do you know any reasonable hotels?'

'No problem.' He turned to look at her. 'You have no luggage?' His accented English was quizzical. 'Do you want big hotel, medium hotel or little place? Hosni, he knows them all. You are very lucky to stop the best taxi driver in all Cairo.'

The 'best taxi driver' accelerated through the traffic at an alarming speed. He had one arm on the steering wheel, the other dangled out of the window. Wavy dark hair fell across his forehead and a birthmark like a tea stain ran down from below his ear. He's probably early thirties, Maha thought, but it's difficult to be sure. He kept turning his head and grinning, amused at the way she clung onto the door strap.

A sudden desire to sleep swept over her. She longed to close her eyes against the bright glare, to hide the green and orange fluffy toys that hung from the driving mirror bobbing up and down, up and down. 'Maybe for tonight, a big hotel,' she said, afraid of the quiver in her voice.

Hosni grinned. 'You a tourist? You want to see the Pyramids; you want to see the museum and the souk? My friend he has a *felucca*, he take you down the Nile. Hosni, he will look after you. All very safe. Egypt a good place to come, you tell your friends.'

She felt a pang as his words placed her again as an outsider and her fragile raft of confidence lurched. Tears wet her cheeks and her tissue crumpled into pieces as she wiped them away.

'No, I'm not a tourist, I have come here to work. I'm a journalist. I just can't face it yet.'

The taxi stopped in front of a smart hotel. A concierge stepped forward to open the door and a group of soldiers with rifles on their shoulders shifted their position and stared intently into the taxi.

Hosni had stopped grinning. He said quietly, 'Missy, be careful. Cairo very bad at the moment, very dangerous. Many bad people. Tell your country how it is.'

'Hosni.' Maha touched his arm. 'Will you come for me tomorrow and take me to Tahrir Square?'

A look she couldn't interpret refigured his face. She was reminded of Chinese artists who perform with rapidly changing masks. He took the money she proffered and in a voice she could barely hear he said, 'OK, I will come. What time? Eight o'clock before it gets too hot?'

She nodded and he drove off.

She brushed away the porter's offer to take her rucksack and went inside. The soldiers nudged her as she passed. It was easy to ignore them but she felt their stares on her back.

In the foyer, quiet music played and a fountain decorated with flowers splashed gently as it cascaded from level to level. For a moment she wondered where she was. New York, London, Singapore? This hotel could be in any of those places. A cold drink was put into her hand and she sank gratefully into an ornate armchair.

Refreshed but still weary, she collected her key, found her room and opened the door. The curtains were closed and only a teardrop of sunlight lit one wall. The stale smell of hot breath assaulted her. She stepped backwards, her rucksack banged against a chair. Three soldiers were sprawled across the unmade double bed. Their rifles lay amidst the bedclothes. They were all asleep. The nearest soldier groaned, clasped the butt of his gun, then turned over and lay motionless again.

The hotel manager was apologetic, shrugged his shoulders and spread his hands in a gesture of resignation. He showed Maha to another room opposite. As she lay fully clothed on the bed she heard shouts and scuffles from across the way. An object hit the wall with a dull thump and raised voices retreated along the corridor. Then there was silence.

Crazy taxi drivers, soldiers in her room. She was too tired to be amused. 'So this is Cairo,' she said to the unfamiliar walls.

The day passed slowly and night fell early. She went outside and lay on a sunbed beside the deserted swimming pool. It was a warm, noisy darkness. Horns still sounded and planes circled as they waited to land. She could make out the familiar tailplane of a British Airways jet and she thought of long, cool, late summer nights left behind in England.

A man was watering the gardens; the fragrance of frangipani perfumed the night air and mixed with the music of the frogs and the cicadas. She took a picture and sent it to James.

She knew by coming here, to this hotel, she had created a space for herself. She was avoiding what she had to face. Here was a lush green oasis, a place to pause but not a place to hide. Tomorrow she would be a journalist, impartial and professional. Tonight she just wanted to be here, under a million stars.

# Chapter 7

*September 22nd*

*Dear Maha,*

*It is the middle of the night. All I can hear is the clock ticking. This one has a deep tone, serious and profound. I remember another time, another clock, light and tinny, the second hand dancing a monotonous tap dance as I counted the minutes. There was also that other clock, the stopped clock, the one that hadn't moved time on, the one that had proclaimed that's it, that's how it will be.*

*As soon as you told me you were going to Cairo I knew it was time to tell you something, to explain. I could no longer hide. I have to write this letter. You will see why. I hope you will understand.*

*I am staring at a screen, Maha, willing the right words to come. Words that will make sense of it all. I will write it as it was. Forgive me. Remembering is so easy.*

*I was lying in the bath; the room was steamy, filled with the fragrance of bath oil. Your dad sat on the chair. He didn't say he was watching me but it's what he was doing. Watching to make sure I didn't just sink beneath the water and stay there with my hair flowing like seaweed in a rock pool. I remember seeing the clots and small circles of blood float up from between my legs, make patterns like paper doilies. I had just come home after suffering my third miscarriage. I could still hear the doctor, 'No more. Each one gets more dangerous; it wouldn't be wise to try again.'*

*I hated that man and I hated your dad for squeezing my hand when those words were uttered. I wanted him to tell the doctor we would be the ones to decide.*

*Can someone else, someone disconnected, who doesn't know you, give an opinion on something so personal? I knew it was a professional decision but I guessed too he would go home at night to his wife and two or three children. He would probably help to put them to bed and read them a story, their newly bathed little bodies cuddled up close to his, their sleepy kisses leaving a warm spot on his cheek as he put out the light.*

*Your dad lifted soap bubbles and blew them gently into the bath. 'I was asked today if I would like to work out in Cairo for two years. Instead of having to travel every six weeks or so, would I like to base myself there? With you, of course. I turned them down.' He said it so quietly. 'I said I didn't think you could cope with such an upheaval at the moment. It's a dirty, chaotic place; I'm not sure you would like it.'*

*The water in the bath was cooling. I told him I would go anywhere to escape a cold British winter. Over those past few days it seemed to have licked my skin and woven its greyness into my own dark canvas.*

*'Gareth, I'm frozen from the inside out.' I begged him. 'Let's go. Please let's go to Egypt.' I wanted to run away. 'Can you tell them you've changed your mind?'*

*Your dad hugged me. We cried for the baby we had just lost and the one before that and the one before that. And I sobbed inside for what I had never told him.*

*Have never told anyone, Maha, until now.*

*I was seventeen, halfway through my A level course. Much more importantly I was in love. Miles was a year older than me and for months we had been inseparable. I was at the girls' high school and he at the boys' boarding school in the town. We would meet on Saturdays and spend hours hiking, finding hidden places away from prying eyes. We mapped each other's bodies as we mapped the hills. At night we would enjoy the warmth and darkness of the cinema or go to a local hop and cling to each other in a sweaty morass of gyrating bodies. Everything about life was good and I never supposed it would change even when I guessed I was pregnant.*

*'Miles, I think I'm pregnant.' I had been excited all day about telling him. I put my arms around his neck and hugged him. I pressed myself against his shirt, putting our baby between us.*

*He hugged me too, held me in a tight embrace. My head was on his chest but I could imagine the smile on his face. I heard his voice, high-pitched as though being strangled.*

*'OK, OK, I'll fix it. Don't worry, I'll fix it.'*

*'What do you mean, you'll fix it? What are you talking about?' I pulled away from him. I remember his face was pale and his top lip*

31

shone where he had licked it. I tucked his hair behind his ears as he loved me to do, but he pushed my hand away.

'Aren't you happy?' I said as I tried to retrieve a mood that had evaporated like steam.

'Don't be stupid, of course I'm not happy, but I told you I'll fix it.'

He'd gone then and left me to stare at the wallpaper in my bedroom, hating the pink and white stripes and the ridiculous border and the baby-pink curtains.

He did fix it. We were to go to his aunt's house in Edinburgh. I told my parents it was for a holiday, an opportunity to go to the festival.

By then I knew nothing would be allowed to stand in the way of Miles's university place and the career path as a lawyer his parents had set out for him. Nor would he disagree with them. It's been fun, he'd said, still could be. But I had to be reasonable. Surely I must see it was for the best.

I was frightened, naive and alone. I stared into the future and was silenced.

Miles's aunt was not unkind, just curt and matter of fact. 'We'll get the business done, then it will give you a couple of days to recover.' She never addressed me by name and never told me hers. Her brief, clearly, was to extricate Miles from this inconvenience and he was patently happy to let her take charge.

She took me to the door of a doctor whom she knew. It was a blue door in a grey tenement building. She rang the bell and left. The door opened and I was faced with grey concrete steps with instructions to go up two floors. I was shown into a room by a nurse wearing a mask, told to undress and lie on the bed.

The room was bare except for a clock. The tinny sound echoed around the walls and the second hand moved persistently round the face like a donkey working a well. I watched its every movement. I counted down the minutes of the 'before'. Later I watched it again incessantly, obsessively. Now it registered with accurate monotony every second of the 'after'. It also deadened the screams of the ghosts that clung to the window-blind and stared at me from the ceiling.

His aunt took me back to her home. Edinburgh, I remember, was softer in the evening light, a setting sun touching the castle, long shadows streaking across Princes Street gardens. I saw people talking together, laughing and happy as they made their way to concerts and *other Festival events. Miles wasn't at the house. He had gone to the Fringe comedy show that everyone was raving about.*

*I went to bed. I hurt and I bled and the room moved in circles. My temperature soared; the sour smell of infection surrounded me. If I opened my eyes the light fitment swayed and the door post wouldn't stay upright. If I closed them I heard murmurs and saw tiny coffins in rows along a road. For five days I hid. Miles was the scalpel. Miles was the clock. Miles was the hint of light behind the curtains. People came. They gave me injections and went away. My pillow was my only comfort. It absorbed my tears and stifled my cries.*

*On the sixth day the raw air of morning woke me and I could see the tepid glow of the sun stretched across the bed. I got up. I went home on the train. Miles tagged along like a stray dog. I never spoke to him again and I've never, ever, been back to Scotland.*

*It's how something becomes a secret I suppose, something you know, a taste, a smell, a colour, a shadow, buried under layer upon layer of other experiences, still raw and hard and there, but hidden. Like in your favourite story, Maha, the Princess and the Pea. We used to read it all the time. Do you remember?*

The moon has almost disappeared. It has slid behind a cloud outlined in gold. It's now that in-between time when dawn creeps into day, conjuring softness, blurring the edges. I can hear the woodpecker's knock as he hammers at the birdfeeder. I would like to paint the scene, capture it on canvas.

*Where are you? Will you be in Egypt now?*

33

# Chapter 8

An apricot dawn sweetened the sky as Hosni drove Maha towards the centre of Cairo. Already the heat was making the plastic seats of the taxi sticky. Outside, the backdrop of minarets and domes stood half-dissolved in the light of the new morning. Hosni kept looking at her through his driving mirror. She shuffled across the seat to avoid his gaze. He was quiet, his lips set in a grim line, a strand of damp black hair falling onto his forehead. He flicked at his phone repeatedly before he threw it down onto the passenger seat.

The traffic was snarled up and drivers swerved across lanes to take advantage of any available space. Lorry wheels loomed alongside their taxi, so close Maha could have touched them; a smell of hot rubber seeped into the interior. A bus swung around a corner, a person clinging to the outside hit the wing mirror so it snapped and flopped like a hanged man. Hosni cursed loudly and banged the windscreen with his fist.

'Is this because of the protests?' she asked, in an attempt to lift Hosni from his sullen mood. In front of them, a woman pulled a small child and wove between the vehicles. The woman's black *abaya* pressed against the contours of her body and her red scarf made a cameo of her face.

'No, this is Cairo, it's always like this, all day, every day but yes, it is worse. People are angry and now they are less afraid to show it. Maybe I take you back to the hotel?'

She said nothing at first. 'No, Hosni. This is what I have come for.' She coughed to cover the catch in her voice.

He screwed his head around to look at her and their eyes met, identical pools of black. 'You have family here, sister, cousin maybe?'

'No, no one, Hosni, I don't know anyone in Cairo.'

'No one, you are sure?' He stared at her and shook his head. 'OK, Hosni will take you to the square.' The decision seemed to have the effect of cheering him up and he waved his arm and squeezed his nose. He pointed towards the line of carts taking rubbish to an enormous tip. 'The Smellies, a tourist once called it. Good name.' He laughed and she felt a tip of fear receding. The taxi pulled up in front of a hotel; she could see men and women in press jackets milling around. 'Where is this, Hosni?'

'The place for the Press,' he said with deliberation, not looking at her. 'What do you say? Safety in numbers.'

He turned and opened her door from the inside so it bumped against a cameraman carrying equipment. She knew the man. In London a few months ago, fuelled by drink, he'd shouted along the bar. 'Hey, Maha, you're Egyptian. This Arab Spring – in the name of God what's their bloody game?' He and several of the others had seemed to find 'in the name of God' to be particularly funny and had laughed raucously. Words of abuse now came from that same person. She pulled the door shut. 'Hosni, take me round the corner, I will walk from there.'

The taxi lurched forward, throwing her across the back seat, but Hosni did as he was asked and she got out a few streets away. She paid him and called her thanks as he pointed past the buildings and said, 'Be careful.' He watched her go.

It hadn't been necessary to show her the way because crowds of people were moving in the same direction. She pushed her way up some steps in front of a building where a young man sat with his head in his hands, blood seeping through his fingers. Others looked on and their rapid, loud speech gave way to anger as they remonstrated with security police who just stood and watched.

She had seen all this on the television back home, followed it on the blizzard of social media. This is what had made her want to come, but nothing had prepared her for the reality. There were thousands upon thousands of people stretching as far as she could see. Like a river in flood, they moved as one. They streamed past parked cars or climbed onto them, sliding down the bonnets to be swallowed up again.

Dust stirred up by the crowd hovered over the panorama like pollution above a city. It blurred the outlines and softened the scene so it resembled an impressionist painting. Everywhere flags were waving. The horizontal lines of red and white and black were splashes against the intensely blue sky and the seething masses. The buildings, some old and mellow, others burnt, gaunt as though in shock. They stood like sentinels, haphazard in height, herding people into the confined space.

Maha jostled her way into the throng. A man in a red bandana made the victory sign with both hands, his elbow pushed her forwards. Beside him was an older man who shook his stick in the air. Their hot breath brushed her face as they screamed out words she couldn't make sense of. Most of the protesters were men but there were women too and children. There was no opportunity to stop. The crowd swayed in waves, rolling like a relentless sea. The smell of sweat and deodorant swirled in a potent potpourri.

'Allah, Allah.' A group of women shouted, their voices shrill and piercing. They pumped their fists in the air, faces contorted with passion. Maha's throat was tight, her breath came in short bursts as she struggled to remain upright. She scrabbled to keep her feet on the ground. Her vision narrowed to a tunnel. 'Help me.' Her voice banged around her head. No one heard, no one cared. Was she shouting out loud? She didn't know. She pushed her way towards the women. Bright headscarves bobbed like corks and a young woman in jeans and T-shirt, her head uncovered, was hoisted above the others. She could see the mass of brown hands supporting the girl. Where nothing else made sense she fixed her sight on the intricately painted nails of one of the thrusting hands, like a Michelangelo picture in a Salvador Dali exhibition. Here was her story, her focus – young women of the revolution.

She stumbled sideways against a door jamb and was steadied by an old lady who pulled her into the doorway. The woman was dressed all in black, her head no higher than Maha's elbow, her face lined like sand after the tide's gone out; an open mouth showed toothless gums. She lifted her hand so that Maha stepped back, but the woman wanted only to touch the material of her white shirt. The old lady's lips moved but the words were lost as she disappeared into the morass.

Doubled up, Maha allowed her heart to stop thudding. A spider had made a web across the corner of the doorway. She stared at the filigree of threads woven into its own unique pattern. Incredibly it hung there, unbroken, moving gently in the air made restless by the crowds. The spider moved across its surface, sensing prey, but found nothing and scuttled back into the dark, patiently to wait.

She took photographs over the heads of the women; a kaleidoscope of chaos, images like beads that arranged and rearranged themselves. This could be mistaken for a festival, a melee of colour and excitement; she needed their faces, their raw emotion. Her breathing steadied, a frisson of excitement grew. She surrendered to the thrill coursing through her veins. It was a hidden undertow, sucking her in, squeezing her lungs and occupying her head.

The chants were much louder now: 'Ash-sha'b yurid...' The people want to bring down the regime was what she thought they cried. She thrust forward, her raised voice a surprise even to her own ears, 'Ashsha'b yurid isqat...' She used her elbows like weapons and the crowd parted only to wrap her in a tighter cocoon.

Everyone was surging forward towards the government building. Years of pent-up frustration and anger fuelled their behaviour. She needed to remember the taste of it, the smell of it, its colour and its mood. 'Wow.' A surge of adrenalin made her whoop and she linked arms with those around her. 'Ash-sha'b yurid...' She joined in the chanting, the Arabic words coming easily.

A thought from nowhere made her laugh out loud. She remembered one of her Arabic teachers at university. He had stood out from the other professors. He had carried a briefcase and was always so properly dressed in a suit and tie, worn with an immaculate white shirt. Whatever would he have thought if he had known the first time she would use her Arabic for real was with a crowd of millions in Tahrir Square. 'Look at me, Mr Samy,' she yelled, causing those around her to stare.

She ebbed and flowed with the other protestors, men and women, teenagers and children. The sun paled the sky with its heat as the day wore on. Her shirt was damp and she needed water but no one else paid heed to the stifling conditions. An intensity drove them on. Muslims, Christians, it wasn't always possible to distinguish and it didn't seem to matter. They were in this together. They had deposed a president. Now they demanded choice.

Her head was yanked back. Hands twisted her hair. 'Get off. Stop. Get off me. Leave me alone.' Her cry pitched high like a cornered rabbit. Men, eyes dead with hate, tossed her around like a ball. Her cries spurred them on. Shock magnified the pain. They *wanted* to hurt, to hurt *her*. Fists punched. Clawed at her breast. Saliva hit her cheek. Her shirt ripped as a button was torn off. They reeked of violence. A man picked her up, putting her over his shoulder, his hand between her legs. She bit his ear, kicked out, scratched at his face, pulled at his rough and greasy beard. Feeble, so feeble. She screamed for someone to notice. The jeers of others circled her in stereo. The man fell forward and she was falling. She hit the ground, grit tearing her skin. She lay winded amongst a forest of legs, pain thumped her as a shoe was thrust into her ribs. The yells were becoming faint, everything turning navy blue. She was hauled to her feet and dragged along. A fist pressed into her back, her arm twisted and pulled. She was swept stumbling from the crowd.

The bright sunlight disappeared and she slid down a wall in the shade of an alleyway, gasping as water was thrown in her face, its coldness running down her neck. She saw Hosni's face swimming before her, so close she could see the pigment of the mole beneath his eye.

'Hosni,' Maha croaked.

'Get out of here,' he said and pulled her roughly to her feet. They ran down narrow passages, stumbling over a dead dog on which a horde of flies feasted. She vomited against the wall but Hosni pushed her on, the sour taste of bile in her mouth. He bundled her into his taxi; she was sick again as it lurched off.

He said nothing to her and she kept herself awake by concentrating on the bobbing toys. His good-luck charms he had called them. Hot shame like a scald spread within her. Her body hurt, only shutting her eyes eased the pain.

*

Maha guessed she was in Hosni's house. The shutters on the window were almost closed, shadow and light played together in the room. A fan moved the hot air around but gave no relief. There was a small sofa in one corner and a square, woven mat in the centre of the floor.

She was sitting on a wooden chair at the table and above her a dim candle flickered in a recess. Hosni had left her with his wife who was making short clicking noises with her tongue as she dabbed at the cuts and grazes on Maha's face and arms, the pungent smell of disinfectant stinging their eyes. Maha sipped a glass of water slowly to wash away the taste of dust and blood. Her body was still shaking and she fought to hold back the tears. Hosni's little daughter looked on. Her head was a mass of matted curls and her faded dress reached almost to her ankles. A pink sash was all that gave it colour. Maha could hear a high-pitched bleat and someone walking backwards and forwards on the balcony. The little girl abandoned her watching vigil only to reappear with a kid goat. Its legs stuck out below her thin arms and its nose lay across her wrist. The kid was the palest grey with a black stripe down its back. She held it tightly and it was quiet. Now two pairs of eyes stared at Maha.

'For Eid,' Hosni's wife ventured timidly indicating the goat.

'*Shukran*,' Maha murmured. 'You are very kind.' She hoped her Arabic would be understood; the woman rewarded her with a smile before she removed the bowl of water and went out of the room.

She was left with the little girl and the goat. They watched as she eased herself down beside them on the mat and put out her hand to stroke the goat's soft coat. The child passed the kid to Maha and the three of them sat there in peace.

Hosni came into the room but was shooed out again when his wife brought in a loose top, its whiteness glowing in the gloom. She held it out to Maha and then spoke hurriedly to her daughter. The little girl took back the goat and played with its ears as Maha stripped off her blood-stained shirt, 'What is your name?' Maha asked Hosni's wife.

'Chavi,' was the soft reply.

'Thank you, Chavi. *Shukran.*' Maha felt the softness of the thin cotton and traced the embroidery with her finger. 'I'm Maha.'

They both smiled and each knew the other understood.

'And your daughter's name?'

'Her name is Kamillah.' The tentative exchange of Arabic began to feel more comfortable. 'It means perfection.'

'And your name, what does it mean?' Maha asked Chavi.

She screwed up her eyes and said, 'Female child.' She gestured with her hands and shrugged. Smiling together they shared the joke.

Hosni came back and sat on the sofa. He dragged at his cigarette, then ground it out in the ashtray.

Car horns sounded outside and somewhere close by *Allahu Akbar, Allahu Akbar*, the call to prayer, sank into the heat. Hosni flicked his face in the direction of the sound.

'There are things you don't understand.' They listened to the tinny recording rasping out the words.

'Hosni, I'm sorry. I don't know how or why you were there, but thank you. Perhaps after today I will understand just a little bit better.'

He looked at Maha where she still sat on the mat. 'We are protesting for hope.' He walked to the window and opened the shutters just enough to let the sun filter in and for Maha to feel the warmth of it on her skin. 'For hope. There has to be an end to this. We've had enough of the state of emergency and prices going up and up. Hungry people are angry people; bread, it used to cost five piastres, now it is seventy piastres.'

She could see the intensity on his face; she acknowledged him with a slight movement of her head. He must have noticed because he said, 'Forgive me, my English, it gets very bad when I am cross.'

'No, no, it's good. Tell me.'

Hosni hesitated before he continued. 'Unemployment, it goes up too so more people need subsidised bread but there is less of it. The food of the poor, no more can they get it. Last year half the country's stockpile, it was crawling with insects. Tell us how we say that to our starving children.'

He slammed a shutter back. 'Mubarak.' He spat out of the window, adding to the graffiti and leaflets littering the streets. 'Twenty per cent, that's how much food has gone up, twenty per cent.' His words were shouted across the roofs of the passing cars.

Chavi came and stood beside him and put her hand through his arm, leaning into him. They stood in silhouette, parting the rays of sunshine; it felt like they had forgotten she was there. It brought back the moment when she had made the announcement at home, about coming to Cairo, when her own mother had stood in silence by a window. She had felt excluded from something then and she felt the same now. Hosni lit another cigarette, its smoke shaping his sigh as he sat back on the sofa. Chavi left the room and Maha could hear water being boiled in the kitchen. Her head ached and her body had stiffened after her fall. She winced as she rose from the floor and sat on the chair by the table. She smoothed the gaily-patterned plastic cloth.

'You have a lot to be angry about,' she offered into the silence.

'Being angry doesn't feed my family. I need to work. At first the protests were peaceful. They called for Mubarak to step down and for new elections. You want to hear this or your head, it is too sore? Chavi, she says to stop talking now.'

'I do want to hear. My head is all right.' She was determined to ignore the throbbing behind her eyes and the feeling of nausea caught in her throat.

'OK, what do you say? Okey dokey.' His attempt at a refined British accent made them both laugh. Then his face was serious again. 'We knew what to do. Tunisia, they showed people across the Arab world, not just political activists, that popular protest can bring down a dictator. But here, the police, they responded with tear gas so the crowd began to throw stones. Many people, they get hurt.'

He thumped the arm of the sofa. 'One man, he was dragged from an internet cafe by the security forces and beaten to death; others, reporters too, arrested by plain-clothes police and hit with steel bars.' He drew on his cigarette then stabbed it out only half-smoked. 'We slaughter animals with those bars. These were ordinary people, all kinds, their religion wasn't relevant. We were all together, we wanted change, an end to corruption.

'I followed you today. I was worried. You were too new, too, how shall I say it, obvious. Maybe you behave different. Always bad people, they make use of a situation. Anger, protests, war; it makes men high, worse than drugs and they think women are their spoils, especially western women. They are weak men but it makes them feel strong.'

Chavi brought in three small glasses of tea and handed one to Maha. A few tea leaves spiralled in the amber liquid and it was thick with sweetness as Maha drank it.

'Have your tea and I will take you back before the curfew,' Hosni said abruptly. Chavi clicked her tongue and looked at him.

'Violence, extremism, it's not the way,' he said. 'It will spread until no one trusts anyone else. Violence destroys.' He looked straight at Maha. 'I didn't always want to be a taxi driver you know.' Chavi spoke softly to him and lifted a finger. His head sank into his hands and he ran his hand through his hair.

'Thank you again and thank you for talking to me.' Maha's words faltered; she knew they were not enough. Kamillah ran in and took her hand, pulling her to where the goat stood munching some dusty, dried leaves. They all stood and watched it for a few minutes, letting the tension subside.

Hosni stopped to pick up two other passengers as he took her back to the hotel; he hadn't done that before when she was in the taxi. The new passengers openly stared at her; the woman pointed to her grazed face and cooed in sympathy. Maha smiled back and grimaced, then shut her eyes and leant against the window too tired to try and converse. The couple got out at a busy junction and joined the crowds of people who still streamed in all directions despite the approaching curfew,

'Hosni,' Maha said, talking to the eyes that regarded her through the driving mirror. 'Do you know of an apartment I can rent – maybe for a few weeks? I don't want to stay in a hotel any longer and I certainly don't want to move into the press hotel. I would like to live properly...in Cairo.' Her words tailed off. 'To feel the city.'

He nodded slowly and she knew he understood.

Keeping one hand on the steering wheel he picked up his phone and spoke quickly into it, then gave her the thumbs-up sign.

'In two days, at breakfast time, you meet my friend Masud. He will show you a small apartment. He is a very good man and fair. He will meet you at Le Cafe here in Heliopolis. You ask everyone, they know it. You can walk there.'

'Hosni, you are wonderful, my own Mr Fix It. What time shall I meet him?'

'For breakfast. Maybe eight o'clock or nine o'clock, *inshallah*.' She had begun to recognise the shrug of the shoulders that meant 'whenever, no problem'.

'Back in your house, Hosni, you said...' She stopped, suddenly unsure of an invisible boundary. 'I was wondering, what did you want to be before you were a taxi driver?' Their eyes met and held each other's gaze.

'Another time, another time,' he said as he stopped in front of the hotel and opened her door with a grand gesture. 'Tonight it is for sleeping, no more talk.'

# Chapter 9

Men's faces, purple and mean, visited Maha in unguarded moments. The memory of hands on her body made her scream. She didn't want to see anyone, even the sun was filtered out by the thick, closed curtains of her hotel room. She lay in bed for twenty-four hours, the sheet wrapped around her like a shroud, before she forced herself to get up. She had to meet Hosni's friend.

A bright red canopy hung gaily above Le Cafe. Maha pushed open the door and was enveloped by its cool interior. Her palms were sweating and she pushed her hair behind her ear as she scanned the faces. There were a few people already having breakfast as the aroma of coffee percolated the air. No one looked like a Masud so she found a seat in the open area at the back where she could watch the door but avoid the stares of other diners. Creepers in hues of green fashioned a roof of leaves that poked between rusted ironwork; chairs were comfortable with cushions in vivid reds, oranges and yellows and a bird of paradise flower stood in a vase on the table, its exotic shape seeming too defined for this chaotic colourful space.

Swiss pastries, each one lavishly rich and inviting, lay in rows behind the counter. Maha guessed it wasn't the kind of place Hosni could afford to come into and she wondered what Masud would be like.

She had already drunk one cup of coffee when she heard a loud 'Ah, mademoiselle, you must be Maha. I am Masud; it is my pleasure to have breakfast with you this morning.'

A tall man of about fifty approached the table. He wore dark trousers and a crisp white shirt. Suave and cultured was Maha's immediate impression. He extended his hand and she felt the firm grip of his handshake.

'More coffee and your very best croissants,' he called across the restaurant, making other diners look up. The staff obviously knew him well and had begun to prepare a tray.

'Thank you for agreeing to meet me. Hosni said you might know of an apartment I could rent for a few weeks. I'm not...'

'Stop, stop.' Masud put up both hands. 'Mademoiselle Maha, in Egypt first we eat and drink and make friends, then we do business.' He laughed so his eyes danced. She found it so easy to talk to this engaging man, although they were frequently interrupted by other men who came to their table and greeted Masud with a loud slap of hands.

'You have many friends,' she remarked and Masud became serious.

'Right now, it is good to have many friends for you don't know who might be your enemy tomorrow.' They finished their breakfast; the tables were filling up. 'So I will take you and show you this apartment. It is the place of my friend but he is away at the moment so it is empty. He has asked me to look after it and what better way to do that than by filling it with a beautiful woman, a beautiful woman with an Egyptian name.' Masud tipped his head to one side and looked at Maha, his eyebrows asking the question.

'I was born in Egypt, but brought up in England. This is the first time I have been back.'

'And look how Egypt has greeted you,' he said, tracing her cut face with his finger.

She pulled away from him, still unused to Arab intimacy. She screwed up her napkin and dropped it into her empty cup. 'It was horrible and frightening. I was stupid. I don't want to think about what might have happened.'

'I am sorry. Hosni told me. He is a good man.'

'That's what he said about you too.' Maha forced a smile.

Masud drove her to the apartment in his silver Mercedes and on the way they 'talked business'. The flow of conversation was interrupted only when he slowed down to sound his horn and shout to a small figure who stood on the side of the road. The little boy was wearing maroon shorts, a striped T-shirt and a blue denim hat that sat askew on his head. When he saw Masud he began to wave with both hands and jump up and down.

'Hi, Tom,' Masud called out of the window and waved back. 'Tom is my friend too; he is a little English boy but soon I think they will have to go home. Cairo is a difficult place for them now. I think it must get worse.'

The apartment was on the first floor. A man wearing the traditional striped *gallabaya* sat cross-legged on a blanket beside the stair and a woman squatted in the shade. Masud explained the man, Mohammed, was the *boab* and he and his wife looked after the building. Masud shouted a greeting and they acknowledged it with a nod. He indicated a small room to the side where they lived. Outside a fire was burning, cobs of sweetcorn charred in the embers, smoke wrapped around the discarded cans of ghee. 'Mohammed will watch out for you,' he said.

The apartment seemed to be suffocating in its own heat and as Masud opened the door hot air rushed out in a frenzy to escape. He opened the doors onto the balcony and Maha looked down into the street through the pinnate leaves of a mimosa tree. Lantana flowers in shades of pink and apricot spilled over a wall, splodges of colour making a Monet painting of the sepia scene. 'It's perfect,' she said, 'just perfect.'

'You are a journalist,' Masud ventured as they both leant on the balcony rails. 'Are you a good journalist?'

She looked down into the street where a car stirred up the dust. How did colleagues used to describe her? Sensitive, clever, intense. She had been proud of those traits. 'What is good? What is the measure? Editors used to tell me I was good but now I'm not sure. My planned assignment is to interview the young women caught...' She stopped, and slowly shook her head. 'But I've begun to think words aren't real; people are real, like those in Tahrir Square. Words are read today, tomorrow they will be in the recycling bin or lining the cat's litter tray. Being a journalist doesn't seem important anymore. I used to think having the opportunity to tell a story made it an obligation? Now I don't know.'

'Then I wonder why you have come to Egypt? Perhaps it is not to tell the world about what is happening in Tahrir Square. Maybe Maha is looking for the story of herself.'

A man selling food from a cart called up to them. 'That's *ful*, best street food in the Middle East,' Masud mused. 'Made from fava beans. Another time we'll try some.'

'You may be right, about me, I mean,' Maha said. 'I was only a baby when I left. Am I reaching back to those few brief months when this was my homeland? Maybe I am. There is no story about me, at least if there is, it's only a short one,' she added, laughing. 'But it feels right to be here and when it's time to go home I will know.'

Masud's eyebrow arched. 'Home?' he said.

'My adoptive mother and my gran, they are all the family I have now, but they are the reason I call England home. Conflict on this scale is new to me. The rapid spread of the Arab Spring across North Africa, the number of people involved. I've never experienced similar in my country. Yes, the government may change but the people simply carry on, in a sort of apathy, I suppose. I've only been here a short time but already, what fascinates me, is the individual stories, the passion. Hosni, Chavi, the man selling *ful*, the little English boy even, what's going to happen to all of them? If anything, that's what I want to write about. What will be the impact for you, Masud? What do you hope for?'

He sat down on a dusty plastic seat. 'Always there needs to be honesty. There will be elections and the people will vote for change. The Muslim Brotherhood will fill the void but it won't be the moderate men who take charge. No, it will be those thirsty for power, those who grow big on the feeling of power and so corruption starts again. When the people realise they have been duped then I don't know what will happen. I have fear in my heart.' His eyes conveyed the gravity of the words.

'Mademoiselle, here is the key. When you need to pay again or you need anything at all you will find me in Le Cafe. I think you are a good person. I want you to be a good journalist.' He placed the key in the palm of her hand and was gone, leaving the air to settle in his wake.

After she had paid her bill at the hotel and retrieved her belongings Maha came back to the apartment. Her apartment.

*Dear James,*

*I have an apartment, my own address in Cairo! I've been in Egypt for such a short time yet already it has touched me. Something frightening happened but I am all right. The people, the honest people in Tahrir square, their cause, their determination, all make my purpose feel shallow and meaningless. Telling their story for them is the most valuable contribution I can make, but I don't want to report it, I want to be part of it. Being a journalist doesn't seem to matter to me anymore. Does any of this make sense? I wish you were here to talk to.*

*Maha xx*

She wandered through the rooms. She knew her words were meant but other thoughts rattled around in her head. Dislocated thoughts that distorted her perspective.

She found a small kitchen with a fridge and an ancient stove fed by a gas bottle. The sink was green where water had dripped; dust lay like a mantle. She turned on the tap, it spluttered noisily before relinquishing an intermittent stream of brown water that eventually began to run clear. In the bedroom the walls were muted mustard-yellow and it was bare except for a double bed and a wardrobe. Her red rucksack lay against the pillow; it looked small and as bright as a poppy in a field of corn. Next to the bedroom was another door but it was locked. She rattled the handle – the noise echoed in the airless, tiled hall. It was where the owner was storing his possessions, she convinced herself.

In the lounge she tried the upright furniture reminiscent of the Victorian elegance of grand English houses. Its elaborate woodwork was painted gold and small flakes lay on the olive green upholstery like tiny flowers. She ran her hand along the cool, marble-topped sideboard, feeling the roughness where it had been repaired. Lying face down was a photograph in a silver frame. She lifted it and wiped away the dust. It showed a young man standing between two people who she supposed were his parents. The woman was looking away from the camera; her hand rested on the young man's arm. Maha stood it up and just that small ornamentation made the room come alive.

She took off her shoes and wiped the floor with an old mop. It made her feel the place was hers. The touch of the black and white tiles, deliciously cold to her feet made her skip along the hallway. 'Mum, be happy for me,' she said into the space. 'I've come home.' She didn't know what she meant but the words seemed to fit.

The memory of her mother's anxious face when she had left her at the station hadn't gone away. She could still see her waving bravely. Was she feeling better now? She hoped her mum's normally busy life would make the worries recede. 'What are you doing now, right now, at this moment?' She knew her mum would be wondering the same about her.

She sighed. When she was a child, her mum's friend would come to the house to be with Mum. 'To cheer her up, they'll natter together,' Dad used to tell her. He would then pack up a picnic and they would go fishing, just the two of them. Long days beside a river, sometimes lying on a rug, sometimes huddled under a big green umbrella. She hadn't much liked fishing but she always took a book to read and she had been in charge of the chocolate. A whole block had to be divided up and shared out, in pieces, throughout the day. She loved to spend time with her dad and she forgot how sad her mum was – at least for a little while. As she got older Maha had learned to look for signs. Quietness, easy tears, a slow withdrawal. She hoped her mum's friends were there for her now.

A knock on the door disturbed her reverie; she opened it to find the *boab*, Mohammed, holding a brown parcel tied with a beautiful purple ribbon. He thrust it at her, his lip curling away from his teeth. '*Salaam aleikum*,' Maha greeted him. 'Is it for me?' she asked in Arabic, pointing at herself. He pushed it into her chest, then turned and walked away, the echo of his footsteps resounding in the stairwell.

'*Shukran*,' Maha said, calling after him, puzzled by his hostility.

She turned the parcel over looking for a name but there was nothing. She took it into the lounge and carefully untied it. The ribbon was made of net, in shades of purple, the colours of a pansy. She knew a little girl who would love this. She would give it to Hosni for Kamillah. A papyrus card was slipped between the folds of the tissue paper; she read the crafted, handwritten words.

*For you – to say a proper welcome to Egypt.*
*Masud*


She lifted the dusky-pink headscarf and let the material slip, like silk, against her skin. She draped it over her head and wrapped it around her chin, the ends falling down her back. For many moments she looked at herself in the mirror before the tears moistened her cheeks. She whispered 'hello' to the young Egyptian woman who looked back at her.

# Chapter 10

*24th September*

*Love you lots, Mum. Such simple words. Maha, I am reading your text again enjoying the sound of them, adding them to the fabric that defines me. Out of the window I can see my pheasant strutting across the lawn pecking at the grass. I think of him as mine because he's almost tame. Turquoise, orange, blue, his plumage is as bright as Egyptian fabric.*

*You made me a mother, with the right to be called one. Before then I was Pippa or Gareth's wife. We always had lots of friends. Life together was good. I had my teaching and I was well respected. I loved my job but my pupils, they were other people's children. They called me Miss, no one called me Mummy.*

*I always planned to tell your dad about the abortion. It wasn't as though either of us pretended we hadn't had previous relationships. Somehow, though, it was never the right time. When we met at university we were so wrapped up in each other I didn't want anything to spoil it, not a rainy day or a bad film or even study. Everything was bright and light and wondrous and we bathed in the warm pool of new love as the rest of the world slipped by like water off a fish.*

*Slowly of course it became too late to tell; too much time had passed, so it was difficult to talk about. Why hadn't I just come out with it? Did it matter anyway – except to me? It did when the consequences became apparent, difficulty in conceiving, miscarriages one after another, doctors' questions and the guilt that, like a moth, fluttered around in the dark. Tears, sadness, bereavement, all making it too huge to tell and so we had gone on, my secret locked away so it couldn't hurt or destroy.*

*Your adventure has just begun, mine began in 1980. I remember packing up to go to Egypt. It was exciting, frantic and exhausting, a house to let; possessions to go into store, some to take with us and for me a job to leave. Family and friends to say goodbye to, with promises made, to come and visit us in Cairo.*

*As I recall it, Maha, the years seem to slip away like a mudslide. I am back there, holding your dad's hand as our plane takes off, scared because it is my first experience of flying, apprehensive of what lies before us.*

*I remember we flew out of the night into brilliant sunshine. The delta of the Nile lay like outstretched fingers reaching for the Mediterranean Sea.*

*'It's so exactly like looking at a map,' I said. He laughed and squeezed my hand. He had seen it many times before but it was all so new to me.*

*'It's going to be all right, isn't it? There's a lot to look forward to now.'*

*He smiled. 'Yes, it will be all right.'*

*I stared out of the window at the grey river below with its strip of fertile land bounded by desert. I let the grief of the past few months stream off the plane's wings. Could all this upheaval fill a void? Could Egypt embalm me like some ancient pharaoh and offer me safe passage into the future? I was full of doubt but still I held onto the small hope it would. As we circled over Cairo, the Pyramids tipped to impossible angles and I made out the Sphinx standing guard before the tombs. Streaks of light and shade played 'catch' across the desert that stretched from the city to the horizon.*

*Maha, I wonder if the intensity of the heat took you by surprise as it did me. I remember stepping from the plane and the hot air blasting my face. In the airport terminal a smell of rancid sweat made me cover my nose and it seemed all the city's inhabitants were there. So many soldiers everywhere. Young men with guns, impatient with the crowds. I hung onto your dad and squealed as one of them stepped close.*

*The luggage carousels were littered with belongings spewed from cloth bundles. Electric fans, flip-flops, undershorts and cooking utensils. They circled endlessly before being pulled off by a bored worker and heaped in a corner. It smelt of dirty washing.*

*People shouted, waved to relatives. Ill-disciplined children climbed through barriers to be prodded back with the butts of rifles.*

*Ahmed, the 'Mr Fix It' from the office, steered us through the chaos to a waiting car. He wore a blue anorak and he rubbed his arms. 'Cold,' he said. 'For me, not for Missy.' He grinned and watched me wipe my forehead and take off my jacket. 'Nearly winter.' He swept his arm towards the grass and the bougainvillea that trailed over a wall. 'Good. Egypt very good. Yes?'*

*I felt sick. Choking, I turned away and left your dad to talk to him.*

*All these events seem so long ago and yet I can remember every detail. It's as though your dad is standing next to me as I am writing to you. I put out my hand but there is no one.*

*Words seem so inadequate. How to describe how events unfolded? It's so difficult but I must, this time I must. I have made a promise to myself and to you. I won't give up.*

*My pheasant has just risen, screeching into the air. Something must have frightened it.*

*My darling...*

# Chapter 11

*Dear Maha,*

*What happened to you? You don't say. Are you all right? I scour the news every day and search for your face amongst the crowds I see on the television. I try to imagine what it must be like. Already you've been gone too long!*

*Tell me about Cairo. Is it what you hoped for? Is it a city of minarets?*

*Take care and most of all be safe.*

*Love*

*James xx*

His caring email soothed her and she replied immediately. She wrote of how kind Hosni had been when she was hurt, described the chaos and the noise but skipped over the horror of the assault. She didn't want to relive it in words. Her face was almost healed but for the shadow of a bruise; her body less sore.

She had tried to phone Hosni yesterday to share her excitement about the apartment. She had put the phone down before she'd finished dialling his number, wanting to be ready but knowing she was not. Today she was determined. 'Hosni, I'm better. Tomorrow I want to go back into Cairo. Please will you take me?' She heard his sharp intake of breath, the click of his tongue. 'Hosni, other women find the courage to demonstrate every day. If they can do it so can I.' There was a long pause before he answered.

'You must stay on the edge, not go into the square; if you do not promise, then Hosni will not take you. There is a burned-out building nearby – it will be safer for you. Please stay around there.'

'Thank you, Hosni. I will be careful. You are a good friend.' She stood in front of the window and heard Mohammed calling to his

54

wife. She unlatched the shutters one at a time and let sunlight illuminate the room.

*

Her pink headscarf gave her confidence but still her chest felt tight. She hovered on the edge of the crowd, only her face visible, her hair more contained, less free. She could see there were even more people than before and dozens of tents, some newly erected, some in pieces where they had been torn down and left to flutter like flags. The mood of the crowd fluctuated with the heat of the day; chanting erupted in waves that rolled across the square, dissipating into the surrounding streets and dark alleyways. Panic threatened to make her run, but she concentrated on writing notes and taking pictures as she tried to capture the atmosphere of hope and fear, blended like colours on a tie-dyed cloth.

She caught glimpses of other members of the press, even colleagues she knew vaguely through nights out in London. She felt distant from them, not part of the pack. Once she had wanted to be a war correspondent, admiring of their ability to deal with situations, to cope with the horrific sights they saw and the mayhem they reported on. She wasn't sure anymore.

'Hi, is there room for me on the step? I've been here so long I just need to sit down for a while.' The young woman, who looked like a student, spoke to her in English. Hosni must be right, Maha thought, feeling disappointment, she must stand out in some way. The girl was also wearing a headscarf and when she sat down she pushed it from her head. 'That's cooler,' she said and shook loose her black hair. 'Have I seen you here before, with the other women?'

'You may have done. It's possible, but there are so many people. I was here for only the first time a few days ago. It wasn't a good experience.' Maha offered the girl her bottle of water and initially she shook her head, but then took it and drank several mouthfuls.

'Yes, it can be rough but I won't stop coming, not until conditions in the country get better. See what the graffiti says on the side of the building: "Enjoy the revolution". Huh, well, this is our chance to improve the lives of women. Some fathers and brothers, they say this is not the time to bother with women's issues but they are wrong. Now is the time. Everything must change together. My father, he is not like other fathers but he would still prefer me to stay at home.'

The girl finished the water and when she realised what she had done she handed back the empty bottle to Maha. 'Sorry,' she said. 'Now I've drunk all your water and talked too much.'

'That's all right. The passion, it's tangible. What brings all these people here? The same cause or different grievances? Back home I'm a journalist.' It sounded like an apology. 'I'm Maha,' she said, offering her hand.

'Wahida.' The girl put her hand lightly into Maha's. 'For a while it was better, not all this rubbish and debris and tents in tatters. The people, they came out and cleaned up the square and the chants then were: "We build Egypt". But the mood is changing again as we talk about elections. Some parties, the militants in them, they see a chance to take control.' She looked at Maha. 'Maybe we can be useful to each other.'

Their conversation was drowned by a noise at the end of the street, followed by what sounded like gunshot. Instinctively they shrank back against the wall. The crowds parted, and people ran to the sides of the road, trapped there by the buildings. Wahida grabbed Maha's hand, squashing her knuckles.

'Turn away, don't look at them,' she hissed, pushing Maha's head down.

'Please not again,' Maha cried, but nausea drowned the words.

Clinging to each other they rolled into a ball. Sour breath and body odours swept around the two women.

Men, maybe fifty of them, stampeded past, a pack of wolves hunting. Most carried bars or sticks, some waved rifles in the air while others hurled stones and cobbles towards the buildings; the sound of shattering glass fuelled the panic. People were knocked aside. A young boy, barely a youth, crawled on his hands and knees towards Maha and Wahida, to lie at their feet clutching his head. They hauled him up so he wouldn't be trampled on. He looked at them with wild eyes then ran off crying.

The rampaging men passed like a freak wave and headed towards Tahrir Square. They left chaos in their wake. When their coarse shouts began to grow faint the panicking people stopped, righted themselves and began to walk again, reclaiming the middle of the road. Maha thought it was like drawing a line through sand – for a brief moment it exists then more sand fills it in again. The beat of her heart returned to normal, but she could feel Wahida still trembling, her ring cutting into Maha's palm. They sat, without speaking, their arms around each other. A man was struggling to push a motorbike through the crowd. He stopped to wipe the top of the petrol tank so its colour shone through, then he wiped his forehead with the same rag and moved on. 'Scenes within scenes,' Maha said out loud.

'Thugs,' Wahida growled. 'Thugs, thugs, thugs. Not him,' she said, pointing towards the man with the motorbike who had been joined by others helping him to push. Wahida's shaking stilled but her face was ashen. 'I'm sorry. I hope I didn't crush your hand.'

Maha smiled. 'I am only beginning to appreciate what you are all fighting for. To defy your father must be hard.'

Wahida looked up at the pure blue sky where a plane was leaving a vapour trail. 'Look at that, isn't it beautiful? Despite all this. Sky art,' she said with a laugh. 'Yes, it is hard. There is only me and my father. My mother and my brother both died when he was born. All my life I am a good daughter and I try to please. My father is angry right now about so much. He is proud of me attending university. He wants women to speak out, to fight for their rights but he knows the danger. He is afraid when it is his daughter. I don't always tell him that I come – sometimes I have to lie.'

A woman selling herbs pushed a pitiful bunch towards them before she shuffled on.

'Wahida, what are you studying at university?'

'Fine Art.' Then she added, 'And English, so I am practising my English with you. I love beautiful pictures and sculptures. I want to go to Rome and Florence, London and New York. To see the churches and the galleries. I don't want to deal with all this, then one day to wake up and find I am old.' Wahida's sigh reached across the space between them. She sought Maha's eyes. 'Do women in the UK know about women in the Middle East, or Africa or anywhere else? Do they care what goes on?'

'Do you want them to know?'

'Yes, of course. We may be from different cultures and we may have different religions but we are all women. I was wondering...' Wahida, still sitting on the wall, was making circular movements with her foot. Her sandal fell off and she picked it up, twisting it around in her hand.

'I've only just met you, I have much to learn,' Maha said. 'You seemed scared. Those men? What was it all about?'

'I was scared.' Wahida put her sandal back on and tied the leather strap around her ankle. 'This conflict has robbed me of my freedom, my safety and my dignity. I am young and I am resentful.'

They sat for a while, watching, their words drowned by the siren of a police car.

'Would you talk...? I have a friend. If I can get her to talk to you... Will you...?'

'Will I tell her story? Yes, and yours too if it's what you want. I can't promise it will be published but I will try. I admire you. You are so full of life and energy and yet so caring. A young woman with the courage to stand in the crowd and protest despite the challenges and the fear it evokes, to risk even your relationship with your father. I can make all the notes I like but a few minutes talking to someone like you tells me more than I could ever glean on my own. I'm glad you have a dream.'

Wahida closed her eyes for a moment; her long, straight eyelashes lying like a fringe on her cheeks. 'Today feels like a lucky day,' she breathed. 'My friend has hardly been out for weeks. Her family won't allow it but tomorrow or the next day I will say I am taking her to Al Azhar Park and perhaps they will let her come. Can I ring you? I will show you how beautiful Cairo can be. It is not all shouting and placards and rubbish. We will go when it is cooler, later in the day about four o'clock. It's near the Citadel.'

'I'll find it; I have a wonderful taxi driver, his name is Hosni, he will know where it is.'

Wahida jumped off the wall and embraced her, giving her a kiss on both cheeks. 'My friend, her name is Salma – I know you will be gentle with her.'

Maha sat on the steps for about another hour. She kept her promise to Hosni to stay on the periphery. Without Wahida beside her the sound of chanting from the square became sinister. People moved in all directions. Women carrying children, women on their own, some fiery and determined, energised by the atmosphere, others who looked exhausted, their weariness apparent in their bodies and their faces. The men the same and the children, crying in confusion, empty stares, faces frozen in fright.

All around her tension fizzed, erupting in squabbles where the crowds pressed in on each other, anxiety, tension, excitement, hope, a cauldron of emotion barely contained.

She took photographs with her phone and texted James. She wanted him to see what she saw: an old lady scrabbling in the dirt, picking up her shopping scattered by a running youth; a child, no more than four, who sat on his father's shoulders waving a stick.

Let it all be worth it.

# Chapter 12

*25th September*

*My darling Maha,*

*Today I have been painting. I took my easel into the garden; I wanted to capture the magic of this beautiful autumn day. The soft light was just touching the white hydrangea blossoms. I will finish it and give it to you as a memento of the time you were away.*

*As I was sitting there enjoying the sunshine I was imagining you flying over Europe into Africa's embrace. I remember it all as though it was yesterday.*

*Your dad found a villa. The owner wanted to meet us for breakfast to settle the deal. He wore a grey linen suit and scratched at his crotch, squirming to adjust his trousers. I didn't trust him. When I asked him about the accommodation he wouldn't answer; he ignored me as though talking to a female was beneath him. It was at least half an hour before rents and terms were even mentioned. Your dad proposed a lower figure but then capitulated; the man was obviously exploiting us and getting away with it.*

*'Why didn't you barter? Isn't that what you're supposed to do in these sorts of countries? I haven't even seen the inside of the place yet. What if I don't like it? Don't I have a say?' I fired the questions at him and saw pain flit across his face.*

*I remember he was patient with me. He held my hand. 'We have to do it their way. We are visitors in their country. It's no good trying to steamroller them. It doesn't get you anywhere, it just takes longer. Trust me.'*

*We lay on opposite sides of the bed that night, not wanting to touch, unable to comfort each other. I lay awake in the dark of the hotel room, the thick curtains blacking out the rest of the world. Maha, it felt like I had nowhere to go.*

*The villa as it turned out was all right, at least the top floor was. Downstairs the sitting room was vast and formal and dark. Mr Bolbol, the landlord, wouldn't allow us to open the shutters for 'security reasons' so the room was stuffy and unaired. Upstairs there were two bedrooms and a bathroom with an old bath and a shower that dripped continuously.*

*I moved the furniture around to make it feel homelier. We also lugged a high-backed settle up from downstairs, we whispered like naughty children in case Mr Bolbol, who lived in the back, heard us and disapproved. Giggling, we put it at the foot of our bed – we hadn't laughed much in Egypt up until then. Still our favourite place to sit was on the balcony where we could look down on the road below and watch the people pass.*

*Of course I didn't recognise it then, Maha. It was new to me. I know it now as depression, grief, whatever you want to call it. My slow acceptance there would be no children; the giving-up of an expectation, a right, a dream. It's a numb, dragging feeling that sits on your shoulder or deep in your gut, gnawing away. It can be given many names. It's the rat in a sewer. It descends without cause, triggered by a word or a memory. Insidious, slow, a walking backwards from the world instead of towards it.*

*Depression was, probably still is, a coping strategy. It has helped me to hide on the dark days; at times it has been my friend. It has rescued me.*

*The anniversary of the October day we brought you out of Egypt. We should have made it into a celebration, eaten chocolate cake covered with Smarties or something – anything to stop us reliving what happened. I always dreaded that month. It was the worst time. The approach of the date.*

*You were my cure. No, not cure. Depression will probably always be lurking but you are what pushed it away. It was afraid of your love, it didn't like laughter and giggles and joy. It didn't like light and fun, running down hills into bracken or toasting marshmallows on a bonfire in the garden. Long chats into the night as you got older, our shopping expeditions, and those stolen luxurious days we had together at a spa after you left home – it ran from those and its power was diminished.*

*I am getting too far ahead, jumping about. None of this will make sense to you at the moment, Maha. Let me tell you what happened to make us stay in Egypt.*

# Chapter 13

The smell of warm bread and pastries greeted Maha in Le Cafe. 'Excuse me, I'm looking for Masud.' The man behind the counter flicked his head towards the open area at the back. Masud was with a group of men. Numerous coffee cups cluttered the table, cigarette smoke tainted the air and voices competed to be heard. She wanted to thank him for the scarf before she went to the park to meet Wahida and Salma. Now she felt unsure of the situation.

As she approached, one of the men, much younger than Masud, saw her coming. He jumped up, scraping his chair across the tiles. He pointed at her, dragged his hand down his face. He fired out indistinct Arabic words.

Masud stopped talking and lifted his head; he put his hand on the man's arm and pushed him back into his seat.

'*Sabakir.* This is Maha.' He said it loudly and no one else spoke. 'You are welcome. Is everything all right?' He smiled warmly. 'These are my friends.' He swept his hand around the circle of men. 'Maha is our British journalist with the Egyptian name. Perhaps our very useful journalist.'

All their eyes were upon her. She moved away from the table. Her skin prickled. The man who initially had seemed so panicked still stared and muttered to himself.

'I'm sorry, I am interrupting. I just wanted to thank you, Masud, for the gift. It's lovely.'

'And it makes you look beautiful. I am pleased you like it. Anything you need, you must let me know.'

She raised her hand in a small wave and left them, aware of the murmur of low voices behind her.

She had a while to wait for Hosni, busy on another fare. She didn't want to stand right outside the cafe. She didn't want to encounter any of those men if they came out. She shivered, trying to shake free from the undercurrents she had felt. Was it because she was a woman, an outsider? In sensitive times who to trust must be crucial.

Maha began to wonder about Salma. How old would she be, twenty, twenty-one? What had she been doing at that age? Experimenting with life, steeped in the culture of a student. She'd worked hard but also had fun. Her friends were all-important. At weekends they'd piled into a minibus, off to climb in the mountains with the university club. The feeling of exhilaration afterwards, nights spent in wind-battered tents, each moment relived, chewed over, exaggerated. Males and females together, sexual tensions sometimes breaking through. She hadn't needed her parents' permission to do something, go somewhere. Mostly they had no idea what she did except in the broadest sense.

How different would Salma's story be? Maha was curious. She took a deep breath. Perhaps this opportunity would rekindle her love of journalism.

She wandered along the street, stopping at a tiny open-fronted shop that seemed to sell only ribbon and sewing materials. The interior of the shop was dark and full of shadows but brightened by the strands of colour that hung from the ceiling and covered every surface, like discarded rainbows. A rhythmic clicking sound came from the furthest corner where a wizened old man sat hunched over an ancient Singer sewing machine. His bare leathery feet worked the treadle, his face so close to the needle Maha feared his skin would be sewn into the material. The ribbons were so gorgeous it was hard to choose. She eventually settled on scarlet with white spots and sugary, pink gingham. She also picked up a hair slide, three painted flowers set side by side reminding her of her mother's garden with all its blooms. The man put the ribbons in a paper bag for her. His eyes were watering and red and he wiped them with a bony hand but he smiled and nodded before his feet restored the machine's hum.

She had brought the purple ribbon with her, from Masud's gift; she added it to the bag. When Hosni arrived she gave it to him for Kamillah.

'She will love these,' he said. 'She keeps asking when the poorly lady is coming back; she says you have a kind face. Children, they notice these things. You have been keeping out of the way of trouble?' he asked with a grin.

'I have, but I have been working too and today I am meeting a girl in Al Azhar Park, a new friend I have made.' She was reluctant to tell Hosni more. 'One week in Cairo and already I have friends.'

'You must be careful all of the time. For women it is more dangerous. I will not always be there.'

'Hosni, you are a gem.'

'A gem. What does that mean?'

'Wonderful, like a diamond or an emerald or a sapphire.'

'Yes, I like that. Hosni is a gem; I will tell Chavi.'

He dropped her at the park and she said it before he did, 'I know, be careful.' He gave her the thumbs-up sign.

Her first impression of the park was one of tranquillity. Everywhere there was green, in so many different shades, from the brightness of the grass to the sage of the palm trees. It was quiet and peaceful and ordered. Shaded walkways beckoned her with the sun sprinkling its light through the leaves, and she found a secluded niche where she could sit and wait. The chaos of Cairo was a faint and distant hum drowned out by a bumblebee foraging on the flowers beside her. It pressed open the petals with its body and eased itself inside, to emerge, dusted with pollen, before alighting onto the next flower. Persistent and focused.

She needed to be the same. She had written about Tahrir Square. She had struggled to put herself back there, to capture the smell, the colours, the intensity. She addressed the bee. 'People, everyday people, impassioned, driven. Is their passion real, or are they coerced, caught in a maelstrom of excitement disguised as a cause? History has shown it happens. Hitler, Communism.' The bee wasn't listening. She remembered what Hosni had said, his quiet determination. His feelings were real. She was ashamed of her doubt. She envied them their singleness of purpose, the willingness to cast aside normal life, the togetherness. She had never felt that way about anything, never felt the need to, her life had been too easy. In the West, people were cocooned, suffering sanitised, something that happens on the television. It had helped to write the article but she wasn't ready to send it off as copy.

She sighed, so caught up in her thoughts she didn't see the two young women approaching until their feet appeared in front of her. Wahida spoke quietly, 'I hoped you would be here. This is Salma. Her mother has let her come but her brother will meet her at the gate in one hour. They think we are walking in the park. I didn't tell them about you.'

Maha's greeting reached only Salma's eyes. No more of her face was visible but she raised a finely boned hand, small and pale against her black *abaya*.

'I can see you are surprised.' Salma's hand touched the *niqab* that covered her face. 'I did not always wear this, but now, they are scared for me, and I understand.'

'I am sorry. Yes, it was a surprise but it shouldn't have been. I feel privileged you should want to talk to me. Everything is a surprise today, all this, it's so beautiful and so peaceful.'

'The park was a gift to the city in 1984 from the Aga Khan but it took many years to build. For five hundred years it was a rubbish tip, a mountain. I will give you another surprise later and show you what they found underneath.' Wahida linked arms with her two friends and together they walked beneath the palm trees.

Salma's voice was hushed. 'I want you to know what happened to me and to others and what is still happening now. The law, it must be changed. If we stay silent we will continue to experience all the discrimination of the past.'

'Shall I begin, Salma?' Wahida asked as they reached a citrus grove and sat on the grass. The air was perfumed by crushed leaves. 'This is just one time, there have been many. We were women, protesting, because we thought Egypt would improve but it is

65

changing in a way which excludes us so then what is the point? Where is the democracy? They say a woman cannot be the president. That it is against Islam. Some men, protestors, they were polite but many were aggressive. They were shouting, "Go home, wash your clothes," and "You are not married, go find a husband."'

Salma nodded, 'They hurled many insults and we shouted back, "Shame on you."' She paused. 'It was very noisy.'

Wahida laced fingers with Salma. 'Yes, suddenly there was a lot of yelling and many men rushed at us and pushed through the rows of women. They were violent; they spat at us and pushed us to the ground. We all scattered and I lost sight of Salma. We all ran in different directions to avoid the blows. There were shots fired into the air. It was very frightening.'

Maha watched a young couple walking in the distance, hand in hand, laughing together. Such a different scene to the one being recounted. Salma lifted her head and looked at her. She heard Salma's intake of breath. 'Men surged forward. Some of us were rounded up and detained by the soldiers and the security forces. We were taken to a military establishment. We were put into a room; it was hot. The walls were brown and dirty and flies buzzed against the glass.' Salma's voice faded. 'They made us take off all our clothes and we were strip-searched. It was a female guard but male soldiers, they walked past the window and looked in. Some they took photographs.' Salma plucked at the coarse grass and twisted the blades into small rings. Wahida drew up her knees and hugged them.

'Then those of us who were not married were separated. We were examined in turn; it was a man.' Salma stopped speaking and fragile remembrances swarmed in the space. 'They wanted to know if we were virgins.' She bowed her head. 'It took five minutes.' Salma's words rose from the citrus grove, across the formal gardens and up to the dome of the Citadel, a distant backdrop, hazy in the dust.

Maha touched Salma's hand. She wanted to tell her how brave she was, not just then, but now, in the retelling of the story. Words

66

seemed inadequate, so instead they sat there, three different young women.

'They said it was so we could not say we were assaulted in custody, but it was just using our bodies to intimidate us.'

'And you?' Maha asked Wahida gently.

'I was not caught; I ran away and was not followed. I was very angry. Back in January, when the revolution began, the role of women was remarkable. We marched side by side with the men. We can't be ignored now; we are half of the population and we cannot be denied a place in the future.'

Salma nodded. 'On television they said the girls who were detained were not good daughters. They said we had camped out in tents with male protesters and they had found Molotov cocktails and drugs. It was lies. My family, they were scared for me but most of all they were ashamed.'

'Now,' Wahida said, 'We use Facebook and online protest but we still come onto the streets and we will carry on doing so. We want you to tell our story so the world will know and the government will be forced to ban virginity tests and those who carry them out will be brought to justice.'

'I promise I will try,' Maha said, and for a while they were quiet, content just to be there together.

'We must walk back to the gate. We must be there before Salma's brother comes.' Wahida broke the silence.

'I should stay here so as not to cause any trouble,' Maha said.

'No, no.' Salma's voice was strong. 'If he asks we will say you are a friend, in your *hijab* you are an Egyptian woman like us.'


Maha watched Salma leave, walking a few steps behind her brother. 'Until now I would have said a person's face, their expression was important in order to read them but I feel I have learned so much about Salma and I've never seen her face.'

'Who we are is in our actions as well as in our words. Salma is an intelligent, brave young woman. She is also respectful.' Wahida took Maha's arm. 'Now I will show you the surprise.'

They walked through a grassy meadow and into an orchard, catching glimpses of a cluster of white pavilions that appeared to float on a lake. Built in a style reminiscent of traditional Islamist architecture, they were luminous in the softening light. 'It's beautiful and so joyful,' Maha whispered.

'It is beautiful but it is not what I want to show you. Come and see.' An ancient wall with rounded towers almost intact curved around the park. Beyond it flat-roofed buildings jostled and minarets punctuated the sky. The crenellated wall soared above them decorated with arrow slits. It was weathered and mellow, with flakes of stone at its base. 'It is called the Ayyubad Wall and it was built in the twelfth century,' Wahida said proudly. 'For five hundred years it has lain under a mountain of rubbish, such a long time that no one remembered it was there. Isn't that wonderful? They only found it when they began to clear away the garbage. Inside there are chambers and walkways and now it links the park with Darb al Ahmer, the district we can see over there.'

'All of this, a rubbish tip?' They stood in the wall's shadow and Maha gazed up its height into the cloudless sky. She whirled around trying to imagine what it must have looked like.

'It was,' Wahida said. 'Imagine the horrible smell when they were clearing it.'

'A rubbish tip.' Maha grasped Wahida's arm and sat down suddenly on the ground.

'Are you all right?' Wahida put her arm on Maha's shoulder and squatted down next to her.


*I am fifteen and sitting at the kitchen table sobbing. 'On a rubbish dump!' I am shouting. My mother is hugging me; Dad is wiping my tears with a handkerchief smelling of him. 'Darling, it's because they loved you that they left you there, they knew you would be found quickly and taken care of.'*


It was so long since she had thought about that moment but the memory rubbed at her mind. She needed to regain her composure;

she picked up a handful of fine dust, letting it cascade like a waterfall to the ground.

'Sorry. Yes, just give me a minute. It was something I remembered.' She swallowed her sob. 'When I was a baby I was adopted from an orphanage here in Cairo. My English parents took me back to the UK. They told me I had been found on a rubbish dump.'

Wahida stood up, turned away from Maha and stared across to the wall. 'I'm...'

'It's all right, Wahida. Please don't be upset. Sorry to have given you a fright. We have a saying, "someone walked over my grave". It means a creepy feeling. I'm much better now. Listen, why don't we go and have an ice cream?'

They sat beside the lake, beneath a green umbrella. Shadows danced on the surface of the water as they talked and the sky turned a fuchsia pink. She told Wahida about London and the exquisite art galleries where sometimes there might be only one ceramic piece displayed on a plinth in a room. 'One day, you must come and I will show you the Tate Modern and the National Gallery,' Maha said.

'I will come.' Wahida clapped her hands. 'And then maybe we can go on to New York and see the Andy Warhol.' They laughed as they lived the dream and scraped the last of the ice cream from their bowls.

The streaked pink sky turned burnt orange. 'I have many friends who are all fighting for the same thing. One day perhaps you can meet them too,' Wahida said. 'Some of them are students but many are older women, also men. It is important for all of us.' They made plans to meet up again before embracing as they parted.

Maha waited at the gates for Hosni to come and take her back to the apartment. She could have taken other taxis but she preferred to wait for him. She felt exposed, alone; she saw the faces of her attackers in those passing by. She clutched her scarf – she wouldn't allow herself to be intimidated. Paper blew around her feet and a plastic bottle rolled across the pavement to lie against a pile of broken glass, the words Coca-Cola shining out.

She looked back through the railings at the soft green outline of the park and conjured pictures of a huge sprawling rubbish tip, imagined a stale, rancid smell drifting in the air. She lifted the ends of her headscarf so it covered her nose.

Opening her purse, she took out the piece of paper tucked into its pocket; 188 El-Horeya she read, and remembered her mother's anxious words, 'but it probably isn't there anymore.' She folded the piece of paper to hide the writing, and put it away again as Hosni drew up.

'You liked our park, magnificent, yes? For me too, it was a good day, very busy, make lots of money. Soon I will be rich. Then Hosni will live in a big house, drive a big car and take my family to the Red Sea.' He was happy, singing away to the strident music emitted from his radio.

'You are quiet today. You have nothing to say to me. Perhaps you just like my singing?'

'I do like your singing, Hosni, but I have so many thoughts all competing for space in my head. I've had a strange, disturbing day. I've just met a student, her identity concealed but for her eyes and hands. I was wondering, who is she? Who is she first: a student, a protester, an Egyptian?'

'I think all of those. Why not?'

'She is loyal to her family. She obeys their wishes, but her sense of duty means sacrificing what she has been fighting for. You see, so many questions, Hosni. This young woman now lives with the aftermath of her experiences, abuse committed in the name of Allah. She is brave enough to tell her story for the sake of others. She wants justice to be done.'

Hosni wiped his forehead with a handkerchief. 'There are many brave people, some they are loud and make their voices heard, others stay in the background. They are all good, Maha. You are kind. You listen to them.'

'I wonder what she dreams of now – for herself? I want to do more than just listen. What were your dreams, Hosni? Will you tell me what you wanted to be instead of a taxi driver? Can you still make them come true?'

Hosni's face in the mirror became serious. 'OK, OK. You will not let Hosni be. I think it is because you are a reporter.' He tried a half-smile.

'No, Hosni, I'm sorry. I don't want to pry. I promise I wasn't even thinking like a reporter. But being with Wahida and Salma today...it has made me think. I'm sorry, please forget it.' She leant forward and touched his shoulder.

'We will stop and I will tell you.' He pulled over to where a couple of rickety tables and chairs balanced on a crumbling pavement. As they got out he shouted into the dark interior and pulled a table into the shade. A man appeared with two glasses of orange juice filled with cubes of crackling ice. Maha sipped hers gratefully, relishing the sweet citrus taste on her tongue.

Hosni stirred the ice with his finger. 'I told you before, violence, extremism, it is not the way. What happened to you the other day, what is happening now. The protest, at first it was good. It brought change but now we have to find a political solution. No more killing.'

He paused. 'My father – he died – it is a long time ago now.'

'Was he killed by extremists?' She let the question sit on the stained table.

'No.' Hosni stared into the distance. 'No, he wasn't killed by extremists.' She had to lean closer to hear him. 'He was one.'

The sun shot an oblique shaft of light between the clouds.

'We didn't know, none of us knew, not me, not my mother, not my uncle.'

Pain seared through Maha's chest. This ordinary man, this kind and gentle man, sitting beside her. His father was an extremist.

'A terrorist, that was how he was branded,' Hosni said, feeding her shock. 'And that's what he was.

71

'I was eighteen, had just gone to university. My father, he was Professor of Science there.' Hosni cupped his glass with both hands. 'I wasn't interested in his kind of science; I was going to be a doctor. I wanted to help people and to make Egypt a place where people didn't die because they couldn't afford medicine.

'See what I mean.' A man was scuffling along the roadside, carrying a straw basket on his shoulder, oblivious to the cars that brushed past him. His neck was contorted, pulling his head backwards as though he was permanently looking at the sky. He stopped at their table and put out his hand, curled like a claw, knuckles swollen. Lines furrowed his face and his moustache, flecked with spittle, partially covered his cracked lips. Maha turned her head away. Hosni threw a few coins into his palm and he shuffled off, no response in his empty eyes.

'Everywhere.' Hosni's gesture took in the street in front of them as a man with no legs propelled himself across the road on a hand-made trolley.

'Do you want to know the rest? Maybe when you have heard it you won't want to associate with Hosni anymore.' She hated having let her hand fly to her mouth. She wanted to find the right words but instead just nodded. '1997. How you say in English?' Hosni struggled. '11, 17?' He looked at her for confirmation. 'That's a bit American. We would say the seventeenth of November,' she replied, wondering why she was correcting him. Did it matter? Perhaps it did; it was a way to delay the knowing. 'Six men with guns and butcher knives.' Hosni swirled his drink around in the glass.

### 17th November 1997 – Eyewitness account

*Four of them were playing on the steps. Dark-haired Egyptian children in shorts and scruffy T-shirts. A pale-skinned child looked on. Waehid, itnyn, talaeta they counted, one, two, three, jumping down each step in turn, their excited voices a chorus to our guide who recited the story of the female pharaoh. They stopped jumping and passed round a bottle of lemonade which each sucked at* through a blue straw. They offered it to the other child; he shook his head but carried on watching.

'The name itself means "Foremost of Noble ladies" and she reigned...' I picked up their discarded ball and kicked it in their direction. 'Mister, Mister, Manchester United,' one of them shouted while another said 'David Beckham' and danced about with his hands in the air. They all collapsed in a heap, laughing, rolling about in the sand.

One, two, three, the couple beside me fell to their knees, then lay down, embracing the dust. My arm left my side and formed a perfect arc before coming to rest, its palm upwards several feet in front of me. There was no pain – then.

### News Report

Fifty-eight tourists are known to have died today and many are injured after a massacre at the Temple of Hatshepsut in Upper Egypt. Amongst the dead are a five-year-old British boy and several honeymoon couples from the Far East. A survivor states the attack was sustained and lasted for about forty-five minutes.

Details are still unclear but the attack is believed to have happened at around 8.45 this morning and to have been carried out by an Islamic group, Vanguards of Conquest. Six gunmen armed with automatic weapons and knives and disguised as members of the security guards overcame and killed two armed guards before opening fire on tourists visiting the Temple. One terrorist was wounded but the rest fled into the hills. A search for the killers has been launched.

'My father was the leader.'

The boy from the cafe came and wiped the table with a grubby cloth; Hosni asked him to bring more juice. A small herd of goats were being shepherded through the traffic and a young girl in a bright dress whacked at those who stopped to grab at the dry grass that grew between the paving stones.

'They found them, days later, in a cave. They had committed suicide. I had to identify my father's body. It was his face but it was crawling with flies. We had to leave our house, go where no one knew us. My mother, she never spoke again and after six months she died.

'I had to look after my sister and my brother. My sister, she was thirteen and my brother, he was ten. I had to get a job to buy food and no longer could I study.'

Maha wanted to tell him to stop, that he didn't need to go on, but it was as though Hosni was somewhere else and would only stop when the story had been told.

'My sister, she became a woman too fast. Now she is in America, married to an army officer. My brother, he was too young to know and we became close. I made him go to school. He was very clever. He followed me everywhere, he tried to do what I did but at night I was the one who would bring him into my bed so the dreams wouldn't come.

'Then I got a job as a taxi driver and he, my brother, would sit in the front and ride the taxi. He made the passengers laugh with his impersonations. When he was twenty we had saved enough money and he went to university, I wanted him to go. He was a student of chemistry and I wanted him to find a cure for something important like cancer.

'When he was twenty-two he began to skip classes and would disappear for many days. He lived with Chavi and me; his room it was always filthy; he and his friends sat there talking all the night. In the end I told him he must go and I haven't seen him for two years.'

Hosni pulled at a quick on the side of his nail making it bleed. 'But I know what he has done, he is with the Muslim Brotherhood, he has become an extremist like his father. He *is* my father. I don't know him anymore but I love him. Yes, I love him. He's still my little brother. I wonder what will I do if he is hurt and he comes to me.'

Hosni smeared a drop of blood down his thumb. 'I know what I will do. I will be there for him like I've always been. But, if he, or one of them, causes my wife or my daughter to be hurt then I will kill him. Not with a gun, that is a coward's tool, but with my own hands.'

'Now I understand why you say violence isn't the answer, Hosni.'

They sat for a long time without talking. A dog snuffled at a scrunched piece of paper which rolled along the pavement. It pushed it with its nose but found nothing to eat, so curled up in the gutter and slept.

'So that is Hosni. Now you will want to find a new driver.'

'No, Hosni. Never. I feel honoured you have told me your story.'

'Today has been a big day for you and now I have made you sad. You must not be sad. Hosni, he is fine. All will be good.

'Come on.' Hosni jumped up, scaring the dog. 'I will take you to the pastry shop, we will buy some sticky, sweet almond pastry, make you into a big fat Egyptian mama.'

'Oh yes, let's. Could we take it to your house and share it with Chavi and Kamillah?'

'Chavi would be pleased. She says we must make Cairo a happy memory for you,' he said as, now back in the taxi, they headed for the city. 'She says I am always work, work, work, and we should take you for a picnic on Saturday. Kamillah, she is already jumping up and down and has pulled out her best dress. Will you come?'

'Hosni, that would be wonderful but you must let me pay the proper cost of the fare.'

'But this time you are our guest, I would not want you to and Chavi, she would kill me.' He drew his finger across his throat and stuck his tongue out.

'OK, you win. I'll bring some goodies for the picnic; something Kamillah will like. Where will we go?'

'I will take you to see the Pyramids. No one can leave Egypt without seeing them.'

'Thank you, it will be lovely.' The thought of leaving Cairo made her sad. She was missing it even before she'd left. She wasn't ready to go yet.

El-Horeya, she whispered to herself.

# Chapter 14

'It took five minutes.' Salma's words, loaded with meaning. Maha sat in the warm darkness and made notes on her iPad about all she had discerned that day, the areas she wanted to think further about. Empowerment or condescension? Not the first time women have played an active role in an uprising only to find their rights disregarded when the revolutionary fervour subsides. Sexual harassment at pre-protest levels. The military, society, the prejudice against women. It felt like Salma was watching her as she wrote. It was the young woman's quiet dignity Maha would remember. Her determination that her experience would be challenged, seen in the wider picture of the denigration of women.

A country, its people, must believe in gender equality not just pay lip service, Maha jotted down. Women need to be represented on the committees responsible for constitutional revision but so far that's not happened. She began to compile an article. She used to love writing print stories, interviewing people, sometimes famous, more often not. Ordinary people, the father who had lost his son to drugs, the cancer survivor who beat the odds, lives that had become extraordinary sometimes because of what they had done but more usually because life events had catapulted them into the limelight. Playing with words, giving them form was what had shaped her professional life since she had finished university. She wanted to use those skills now. To do her best for Salma, for Wahida and for all those other women whose names she didn't know.

Later, she wrote a long letter home. She knew the pleasure it would give her mother when she saw the foreign stamp amongst the post. She told her about Salma and Wahida but spared her the details of their story. She tried to describe the afternoon's sense of peace, the serenity of the park and how her teenage memory of a long-ago conversation had flooded back to her; its clarity taking her by surprise.

'You are sweeter than all the chocolates in the whole wide world, even sweeter than your favourite strawberry creams,' her dad used to say. She'd always known she was adopted. She grew up being told she was special. She smiled as she thought of the time when she had run home from school in tears because a girl had told her she was borrowed and would have to go back one day.

'She's just a silly girl,' her mother had said, giving her a cuddle. 'You're not borrowed, darling, you're adopted, and that means you're ours for ever and ever.'

'Tell me. Tell me who I am, who I was,' she used to cry as her teenage self emerged, fragile as a butterfly. She wanted to know the detail but it seemed there was never much to know. She would pore over photographs of her parents' time in Cairo but there was only one of herself as a baby in Egypt – taken on the day they left. Mum and Dad standing in front of a stretch of water; Dad with his arm around Mum's shoulder pulling her in to him. They looked serious, as though the photographer had caught them unawares. She was asleep, tightly held.

In her head there was also that other story to write. Hosni's story. Growing, forming, embryonic. Untold and dramatic. Exactly what she was looking for, part of why she had come to Egypt. She was a journalist, she reminded herself, and all the phrases banded about in the pub on a Friday night in London now bounced along this dusty Cairo street: 'In the public interest, a human story, great copy, a scoop'. They all sounded hollow, meaningless and brutal.

Hosni, Chavi, Kamillah, they were real people who had let her into their lives – more than that they were her friends. Her professional self screamed: be tough, ruthless, write it, send it off. Could she do it? Could she be so driven? The thought squirmed behind her closed eyes, lodging in her head as an ache.

Why was she tortured by all this tonight? The pain of Salma and Wahida's story was raw. Hosni had trusted her.

77

*Dear James,*

*I met two amazing women today. They made me feel so humble and so profoundly grateful for the life I am free to lead in the UK. Their plight is horrendous but their courage and determination to improve their lot makes me equally determined to help them. Why does conflict always seem to bring out aggression in men, and particularly sexual aggression? When I reflect on history it has always been the same – rape and pillage are considered to be the spoils of war. Here, abuse, under the guise of legitimacy, is being used to subdue women's voices. I want to be part of ensuring it doesn't happen. Perhaps that will be as a reporter or perhaps there are other ways to make a difference. Women must have the opportunity to empower themselves. I am on a cultural learning curve. There is so much to absorb. I go to sleep with my mind racing.*

She and James had taken to making contact each night unless frustrated by the internet being down. For them both it had become a special time. Tonight she wrapped herself in a sheet and curled up on the high bed. She wanted to tell him about the riots and the politics, the big issues but also to share the little things, the colour of Kamillah's ribbons, the taste of the ice cream, the dog curled in the gutter.

*Hi Maha,*

*What a privilege for you to be able to touch these people's lives. What you are seeing and doing will become part of you – I wish I could share it in person.*

*Don't you think we all live cocooned in our own worlds? We are probably afraid to try and live in another man's shoes for fear we disturb our own equilibrium. We are hardened to what we see on television – it's happening over there – allows us not to have to get involved. I'm proud of you and so glad we met.*

*Sleep well. My thoughts are with you.*

*James x*

He encouraged her, was warm and interested. He could also make her laugh. She liked to picture him, his tousled brown hair, his nose a little too long, his tall lean frame that he seemed to occupy so comfortably. She wanted to know about his house, his job and his book. They were beginning to know each other, beginning to care. It felt special. She lay and hugged her pillow, looking through the window at a sky littered with stars.

Pangs of homesickness spilt over like boiling milk.

# Chapter 15

*Darling Maha, you say in your text, 'it's special to be here.' I think I know what you mean but for you going back must be even deeper, another layer that I can only guess at.*

*By now you will have been in Egypt for several days. I am afraid being there will make you angry with Dad and me for uprooting you from the country of your birth. I worry you will think differently of me. Perhaps it is payback time, perhaps Egypt only lent you to us and now she will reclaim you. I wish I could come to you.*

*I wonder how you are feeling. Is the atmosphere tense? What are your first impressions of Cairo? I have so many questions. I hope it will be better for you than it was for me – at least how it was for me at the start.*

*Back then I was anxious, confused and sad. I was running away; I was recovering from my third miscarriage. Recovering, that's the term they use, isn't it? Patching over, sticking down the corners, anything but recovering. I was running away from my own guilt, the pain of loss and a reality I wasn't ready to accept. Running felt like a solution.*

*Maha, it was hard. Your dad was out at work; his long days started at seven. He was often not home until after dark. At first we were in a hotel, a big international chain where I could have been anywhere in the world. I used to stare out of the window from the fourth floor and watch a man water the grass on the central reservation. Sometimes he hitched up his gown, squatting to relieve himself. I thought he was disgusting. Your dad just laughed, 'Wait till you see the real Cairo.'*

*He kept bringing home invitations from other expatriates or colleagues from the office. Would we like to go round for dinner? Join the tennis club? Would I like to go to a coffee morning, meet some of the other wives?*

I scoffed at him. 'Since when have I ever been the coffee-morning type, a load of women sitting around and talking about nothing in particular?'

But, Maha, I was afraid and the longer I sat by myself the more afraid I became. It got so your dad and I didn't talk much. Whatever he did or said I criticised. He started to go to events on his own. He tried to include me, to tell me about people he'd met. I wasn't interested. I turned away from him. I saw his pain but I didn't have the energy to care.

One night he came home and said he would take me to the Khan el-Khalili, Cairo's souk. I protested, but he refused to listen so two sullen, unhappy people set off that night.

I think he was trying to cheer me up; to let me feel the buzz of Cairo after dark, watch the local women shop, hear the stallholders call to one another and see the men smoke and drink tea in the cafes. Instead I smelt the stink of urine in the doorways, saw the dirty pavements, the water in the gutters, the decrepit buildings, the ragged children with unbrushed hair and the chaotic traffic that showed no respect for other road users. I hated Cairo. I slept on the settle and cried myself to sleep, a bottle of pills clutched in my hand.

Maha, I have begun to read what I've written so far. Should I put this in a letter or should I wait until you come home so I can tell you in person? My finger is hovering over the delete button. Do you need to know all of this? Is it that I just don't want to get to the part of the story that involves you?

# Chapter 16

It was early morning when Maha awoke, and the air was fresh. Her longing for home was the ache in her head but it no longer possessed her. The marble tiles were cold as she made a cup of tea in the tiny kitchen, then tucking her feet under her she sat on the balcony and watched the city wake up. A bird hopped around in the tree. It snatched at grubs on the leaves. A yellow American-style bus pulled up at the corner where young people waited. They jostled, eager to jump aboard, the closing doors fading out their chatter.

'Madam, madam.' A young man had stopped and shouted up at her. He had a basket over his shoulder and held two pigeons together by their wings. They squawked and flapped frantically as he lifted them above his head to show her. 'No,' she said and waved him away. She didn't want to look at the birds. He walked further along the street, calling to other people.

She worked all morning, drafting and revising her article about Salma before she sent it off to her previous contacts in London. At the last minute, out of loyalty, she also sent it to Robin; after all they had enjoyed good times together in the past. That life all seemed so distant, the frantic deadlines, the long hours, the zany culture. She didn't miss any of it.

She would go and buy some nice things for tomorrow's picnic. She nodded to Mohammed as she left the apartment. He was breaking wood whilst his wife was shaking rice in a shallow dish, the chaff thrown over the lip. Maha was excited about the outing and particularly being with Chavi and Kamillah again. Hosni's story about his brother surfaced in her mind. How, she wondered, does Hosni's brother regard Chavi, how do women fit into his ideology? She remembered Hosni's pledge and felt cold.

She walked to the market where lots of people were buying fresh vegetables and bartering for scrawny chickens that pecked about in cages. Wilted leaves lay strewn across the road and over-ripe tomatoes were heaped onto shaky stalls.

'Come, see, I have good tomatoes, I have saved the best for you, look, here, round the back.'

A woman, her hair tied up in an orange scarf, beckoned her over. Maha peered under the table and saw the bright, firm tomatoes piled onto a piece of cardboard. A skinny dog followed them but the woman shouted '*Imshi*' and threw a rotting piece of fruit in its direction. The dog devoured the food and skulked off. The woman lifted the hem of her dress and wiped her hands as she put some of the tomatoes in a bag for Maha.

'You come to me next time; I save you the best always.'

Maha gave her some money and said in Arabic, 'You speak good English.'

The woman laughed, her whole face smiled. 'Yes, many English people come to my stall. You will teach me the English, I teach you the Arabic.' She touched the sleeve of Maha's blouse, the rough skin catching on the light material. 'Very pretty.'

Maha bought a watermelon after she watched a man coax a donkey to pull a cart that was laden with them. She had never seen so many watermelons and thought about the pale, watery slices, wrapped in cling film, she used to buy in the supermarket at home. The wheel of the cart caught on the kerb and watermelons bounced off, rolling along the road like green footballs. People rushed to retrieve them and piled them back into pyramids on top of the cart. There was lots of shouting and noise and the carter laughed; he split one of the fruits open with a sharp, curved knife, cut it into pieces and handed it around.

She found something else she felt sure Kamillah would like. The shopkeeper had called it 'dog bone' and had lifted it to his mouth pretending to gnaw on it. He had given her a little bit to taste. It was melt-in-the-mouth Turkish delight but packed with nuts. He carefully placed it in a white box and tied it with multi-coloured string. He bowed as he handed it to her. She was pleased with her purchases and when she returned home Mohammed's wife was squatting on the ground prodding at wedges of sweetcorn on the fire. She held up a piece for Maha who winced as she tried to hold the hot food, but it was delicious, smoky and sweet. She took out a few of the tomatoes she had bought and gave them to the woman who smiled through crooked, stained teeth. Just at that moment Mohammed appeared from around the corner of the building; he shouted at his wife and kicked at the fire, tossing embers into the air. The woman struggled to her feet, rubbing her back. She kept her eyes lowered and retreated into the darkness of their small room.

Maha let herself into her apartment. She had enjoyed her foray to the market and was pleased with what she had bought, unpacking it carefully before she checked her emails. She whooped with pleasure as she saw she had already had a response to her article from one of her colleagues. She couldn't wait to tell Salma and Wahida that at least they had shown an interest. There was also one from Robin.

*Women's rights. Really? Get a new angle, Maha, and I might give a fuck.*

She stared at the words. She wondered if Salma and the other women would regard it in the same way. She deleted his email with the press of a button, then found his number on her phone and did the same. 'Goodbye, Robin,' she said loudly, her voice splintering over the walls and furniture.

A noise made her jump. The squeal of brakes and the smell of burnt rubber, thick in the heat. An object was flung onto the balcony where she sat. It bounced against the window with a loud crack and rebounded. 'Aargh...' she cried at the burst of pain as it hit her on the ankle. Doors banged and a car sped up the road. It mounted the pavement as it rounded the corner sending up clouds of dust.

It was all over so quickly, her heart only began to thump after the car had gone. She picked up the missile, now lying wedged against the table leg: it was a large stone, jagged and broken as though it had been smashed apart. Mohammed came out into the road and raised his fist in the direction the car had escaped. He looked up to where she stood. He stared but said nothing, then returned to the shade of the stairwell. The window wasn't broken but there was a jagged crack across its corner. Had it been meant for her or was it something to do with the apartment's previous occupant? She could see people walking along the street and a maid hanging out washing on the balcony across from her own. If it wasn't for a stinging ankle and the missile, now sitting like a paperweight on the table, she wouldn't believe any of it had happened.

She went inside and shut the doors to the balcony. She was sure Mohammed knew something but doubted he would give her any explanation. She needed to tell Masud about the cracked window – she would talk to Hosni or Masud tomorrow. One of them might be able to make sense of it.

# Chapter 17

Hosni arrived on the day of the picnic, tooting his horn. He leapt out of the car with a smile so wide Maha laughed out loud. He wore dark trousers and a bright orange shirt.

'What a perfect day,' she said, pointing to the wisps of white cloud feather-painted into the sky.

'In Egypt, always perfect. Today I go on a holiday. See.' The inside of the cab gleamed. It was decorated with a silver fringe that danced like a chorus line. 'Kamillah helped me,' Hosni said, the pride in his voice catching in his throat. 'I think she will die with excitement if we don't get there soon.'

'Me too,' said Maha as Hosni opened the door for her and she climbed in.

'Now you sit in the front seat. Today I am not a taxi driver, I am a tourist.' Whiffs of aftershave filled the car and she realised what a special day this was for the family.

'First I want to show you something on the way, and then we go to pick them up.' Hosni had the windows down; the hot wind tugged at her hair; he was singing a song, the words floating away to be drowned by traffic noise. She had been going to tell him about the incident of the stone being thrown but decided not to. She didn't want to spoil a moment of this day.

'Where are you taking me?' she asked, as the streets became narrower and Hosni wove through crowds of people. Men and women bought flat bread from the back of an open cart. A man on a bicycle rang his bell trying to get past. He had a huge block of ice strapped to the back of his bike, the drips like a small waterfall fell on the road as he stood off the saddle trying to pedal faster.

'It's for the drink stalls,' Hosni explained when he saw her surprise. 'All day they ride around to bring fresh ice.

'This is what I want to show you,' he said, parking the car in the shade against a cinnamon-coloured wall. From the street she could see a tall dome, every surface elaborately carved. Long walls joined the porticoes; a slender minaret with its three storeys pointed to the sky. Hosni showed her the steps that would take her to the top of the wall before he crossed the courtyard into the body of the mosque. She climbed the narrow stairway and wandered along the walkway. On every side, Cairo spread out below her. Minarets and domes stretched away in the distance and a soft haze was the city's shroud. When Hosni joined her she was standing beside one of the stepped crenellations looking down into the narrow alleyways and the teeming streets below.

'Those are tombs, aren't they? Is this what they call the City of the Dead?' she asked. A woman with a large metal basin balanced on her head walked between the crumbling structures, a small child clutching her loose robe.

'Five million people live there now and always there are more coming. Most are poor but they have nowhere else to go, not enough houses and no work.' 'What must it be like to live there, I wonder? What about the children, don't they get sick?'

Hosni nodded. 'Yes, many children, lots die; no sanitation and no electricity but they say it is a good place to live, they look after each other. I don't know. We all want change, you see, but these people they still need the simple things like clean water.'

The sun was colouring the polluted air a soft orange and streaking the buildings with gold. 'I brought you here to see the view. This is my Cairo.'

'Thank you, Hosni, it is truly wonderful.'

She turned to take a last look at the maze of mausoleums. Three children held hands and danced in a circle around a small girl in a red dress. Their singing reached her ears; her breath knotted in her throat. 'I hope something good happens for you,' she whispered.

Choked-up traffic made their journey slow but Kamillah was sitting in her doorway drawing patterns in the dust when they arrived. She jumped up and came running to hide behind her father's legs.

'You look so pretty, Kamillah, let me see.' Maha offered her hand and the little girl peeped out before putting her own small brown one into Maha's. As Kamillah lifted the hem of her white dress and shook her head, the spotted ribbon in her hair flipped from side to side.

'A little princess,' Maha said in Arabic, which made Kamillah smile.

Chavi too was shy at first but soon began to talk to Maha and help her if she struggled with the language. She pointed out all the sights as they made their way slowly across the city along the clogged roads. They were all glad to arrive.

Maha's shirt was sticky against her back when she got out of the car. In front of her were the Pyramids. Before she even had time to absorb the scene a camel driver in a spotless grey *gallabaya,* his white headscarf looped around his head, approached her and pointed to the camel lying on the sand. In contrast to the man, it was decorated in a rainbow of colours. A headdress of pompoms wound around its ears and down its neck and a rug, woven in red and orange, covered its back. The camel chewed rhythmically, displaying yellow stained teeth.

'Please, what is your name?' the camel driver asked as he bowed his head.

'Maha,' she replied, amused by his formality. Kamillah had run across to hold Maha's hand. She stared at the camel, their eyes at the same level.

'Maha! My camel, it is called Maha also. It will give you good ride, see the Pyramids. I give you good price.' Kamillah looked up at Maha. Her small hand tugged urgently and she hopped from foot to foot. Hosni joined them and exchanged words with the driver as they slapped hands. 'Can I take her, Hosni? I've never been on a camel.'

Hosni looked at the two of them. 'OK, OK, we will wait for you here.' He took a picture of Maha, Kamillah and the camel using Maha's phone. She sent it to James and her mother.

*Me with my friends at the Pyramids!*

Kamillah's shriek, as the camel rose to its feet, was a mixture of fear and delight – first they were tipped forwards as the camel uncurled its long back legs then backwards as it stood up. Maha could feel Kamillah shaking and the little girl turned to her, her curls bobbing as she screwed up her face in excitement, Maha hugged her, her insides twisted with the strength of longing.

The camel turned and the Pyramids were silhouetted against the aquamarine sky, standing proud, majestic, ancient, and oblivious to the bustle and chaos beneath them.

'No get too close, all the soldiers, now they guard it since the Revolution.' The camel driver threw up his arms in a gesture of disgust and delivered a noisy burp in their direction.

The camel ambled along. Maha and Kamillah were gently thrown from side to side. It stopped to let them look at the worn face of the Sphinx. Kamillah jumped when the camel gave a loud fart and they both held their noses and dissolved into giggles.

Hosni and Chavi sat close together in the shade of a wall and watched them. Maha felt again an ache of loneliness.

After the ride, with Kamillah's help, she chose two postcards, one of the Sphinx for her mum and one of a haughty-looking camel she thought would make James laugh. They took their picnic beyond the Pyramids away from all the people. Maha draped her pink scarf over her head and put up her hand to shade the glare, bright even behind her sunglasses. Only desert stretched before her, endless miles of sand with shimmering mirages smudging the horizon.

'It is a sea of sand,' she said. 'It makes me feel very small.'

They ate fresh, soft *baladi* bread and goat's cheese along with Maha's tomatoes. Hosni cut the watermelon into wide slices. The juice ran down their chins as they bit into it and Maha picked out ten of the black seeds and counted them, first in Arabic then in English. Chavi and Kamillah joined in, Kamillah's high voice rippling across the hot sand. The 'dog bone' was the final treat and they all enjoyed the sweetness and the crunch of the nuts.

'We used to go on picnics at home,' she told them. 'My dad loved it. We would play hide-and-seek in the trees. Sometimes it rained and we had to sit under a sheet of polythene, squealing when the drips ran down our necks.' In her head she could see the intense green and feel the coolness. *One day she would have to go home.*

Chavi and Kamillah wandered away; they were watching a beetle scurry across the sand.

'Hosni.' She took out her purse and pulled out a folded piece of paper. 'Do you know this street?'

'Perhaps. El-Horeya, it is in Maadi and maybe Zamalek and one near Heliopolis, maybe others too.'

'Oh dear, so many,' she said, refolding the paper.

'No, not so many. Why do you want to know?'

Kamillah was now playing at being the beetle, walking along on her hands and feet, her bottom in the air.

'My mother gave me this address before I left. As a baby I lived in an orphanage. This address is where it was, where my adoptive parents found me. It's probably long gone but I just wondered if I could find the street.'

'Who are you looking for?' His voice was sharp.

She took a moment to answer, confused by his tone. 'I'm not looking for anyone. There is no one. I just wondered if the place was still there.'

Hosni gazed into the distance and kicked at the sand with his foot. 'No one. Of course. No one.' He was nodding his head.

'Being here today, with you and Chavi and Kamillah – seeing you together – a family. It has made me want to touch my roots even more than before, Hosni. Can you understand?'

He flicked at the sand. 'OK. I keep telling you Hosni is the best taxi driver in Cairo. I will take you if you really want to go. No problem.'

'Yes, I do. Let's start with the one nearest to where my adoptive parents used to live. My mum said she used to come to the orphanage and take me out for the day, so I think, given Cairo's traffic, it was probably somewhere nearby. When they adopted me they left and took me to England.'

Kamillah slept all the way home. Her head rested on Maha's knee, her hair wet against her forehead.

'Thank you, it has been a wonderful day,' Maha said as they dropped her off.

'For all of us,' Chavi answered. 'It is good sometimes to forget the troubles.' Mohammed came out to the pavement. Maha greeted him and he inclined his head. Slowly, slowly, were they becoming friends? She decided not to mention the incident with the stone. She watched Hosni's car move away, Kamillah's sleepy face framed in the back window.

'I want a child.'

# Chapter 18

*Sometime after our dismal excursion to the souk I ventured to the local food market. I needed vegetables for supper. Often your dad came home to find nothing to eat but this day I had made an effort and cooked a tagine. I wanted some salad to go with it. What I really wanted was to make your dad smile again.*

*I bought lettuces and stubby cucumbers, gagging at the smell from discarded leaves that rotted underneath the stall. I asked for tomatoes and held one up from the front of the pile. The man put all my purchases into paper bags and wrote down a figure for me to pay. It seemed a lot but the money was still unfamiliar and by then I just wanted to go back to the villa.*

*At the corner of my street there was a cart laden with pieces of furniture. Wardrobes and chests of drawers stacked high. A settee, balanced precariously, a cooker on top of it. A chair lay broken on the side of the road. The donkey pulling the cart had fallen onto its front knees and the owner was beating it with a stick. The animal was so thin I could see the outline of its ribs and blood ran from the wound on its shoulder where the stick cut deep.*

*I shouted at the man to stop. I screamed at him. He called me names. I ran indoors, trying to get the scene out of my head. I unpacked the shopping; the bag that held the tomatoes disintegrated as I lifted it. They were overripe, mushy and completely inedible. I pulled handfuls from the bag and threw them against the wall; the pulp slid down in rivulets. I dropped to the floor and lay curled in a ball sobbing.*

*That's how your dad found me. I was shivering, gulping for air. Tomato pulp squeezed out from my closed fist as he tried to prise my fingers open. 'I want to go home.' My wail brought the landlord, who knocked at the door but went away when no one heeded him.*

*That was the worst day, Maha, the lowest point. Later, we sat on the balcony and talked into the early hours of the morning. So much to say to each other. For the first time I noticed the multitude of stars, the perfume and the sounds of the night. He said he would arrange for us to go home but as he said it I knew it wasn't what I wanted to do. I knew I had to try.*

*After that long, long night I told your dad I didn't want to go home. I made him laugh when I said anyway I couldn't go back yet – I hadn't even seen the Pyramids.*

*What if we had come home when he suggested? We would never have found you. He was trying to do the right thing, to get me help, make me happy. It would have been easy to have left. I'm so glad we stayed.*

*Maha, I've just looked up from the computer and I'm surprised to find it's now dusk. Surprised, if I'm honest, to find myself here at home. The sights, the sounds, the emotions have all seemed so real.*

*I have opened the French windows to get some fresh air. There is a harvester working in the field cutting row after row, so orderly and precise. The monotonous hum of the engine is soothing. I am too exhausted to continue for now. I will leave it a while and see if I can write more later.*

*You will just be wakening. Last evening, Maha, I watched some pointless television programme, then the 10 o'clock news. For once there wasn't much about the Arab Spring and I was glad. I was tired but of course sleep wouldn't come. I kept hearing my own mother's voice. 'If you start something, you finish it,' she always used to say. Unconsciously it's the dictum I have lived by. It helped me, I remember, that night in Cairo when I wasn't able to get the phrase out of my head.*

*Except of course there was the other thing I started, the one I didn't go through with. Forty-odd years later, Maha, and it still hurts.*

# Chapter 19

A woman was looking up at her from the street. Dressed in black, hunched and old, she looked like a beggar.

Maha was writing her postcards. She'd taken her glass of wine onto the balcony, refusing to be intimidated by the stone-throwing incident. She looked into the street through a lattice of shadow and light; her thoughts drifted to Kamillah, then to the little girls who had been playing amongst the tombs. What would be their future?

The sound of crying filtered through the branches of the tree. The cries became wails; the old woman's arms were raised in a pleading gesture. Mohammed appeared, he shouted and remonstrated with her, but the woman pushed past him into the building and Maha realised she was trying to reach her. She heard Mohammed's voice get louder as they came up the stairs, so she opened the apartment door to see what was happening. Mohammed was pulling at the woman's arm and her cries reverberated around the stairwell. Maha tried to calm the situation, told him it was all right, and indicated the woman should come in.

In Arabic, she asked her what was wrong and what she wanted, but the woman wasn't listening. She was stumbling around the apartment, touching the walls and the furniture, stroking it with her hands. She rattled the locked door and turned to Maha, her face crumpled and her crying became louder.

She took the old lady's elbow and led her into the sitting room, pushing her gently into a seat while she fetched a glass of water. When she returned, the woman was slumped sideways, her head against the gilded arm of the chair. Her thin arm with its wrinkled skin reached out for the glass of water and she looked up. Her face was blotched and one eye was a milky white. At the sight of Maha, her sobs became deeper, her frail shoulders heaved. She pushed herself up and resumed her pacing of the room. She rubbed her hand along the door jamb and the marble-topped sideboard, then with a gasp she grabbed the photograph Maha had found previously. She lifted it close to her eyes, emitted a piercing wail and hugged the photograph to her chest.

'Yaa -bunayya, Yaa -bunayya.' The woman slipped to the floor still clutching the picture.

It was difficult for Maha to make out the muffled words but she knew the woman was saying something about her son; my dear son was what she thought she had said.

'Is it your son?' Maha asked. 'Aiwa, aiwa.' She pointed to the young man who stood smiling between two people who Maha presumed were his parents. The father stood proudly looking at the camera; the woman had her head turned away but she was holding her son's arm. Maha could see it was the same woman but whereas she was at ease and happy in the photograph, now she was curled in despair on Maha's floor.

She wasn't sure what to do so she too sat on the floor and stroked the old lady's arm. 'Where is your son? Did he used to live here?' Maha spoke slowly in Arabic, hoping she would be understood.

The woman made the slightest movement of her head, then sighed. She turned to Maha, spread her hand in front of her face and let loose a strangled scream.

He's dead, was Maha's first thought, then as she looked at the red-rimmed eyes through the bars of the woman's fingers the realisation dawned. 'He's in prison. Is that what you mean, your son's in prison?'

The old lady struggled to her feet; she kissed the photograph and set it back where it had been. She seemed even more shrunken, more bent.

Maha lifted the photograph and placed it in the old woman's hand. She put her arm around the thin shoulders and leant towards her so the top of their heads touched. Maha edged her towards the door. The woman stopped to try the handle of the locked door again, then putting her thumb and fingers together in a gesture Maha knew meant 'wait a minute' she went into the kitchen and fumbled through the drawers, moving around the cutlery. She found a key and, holding it up, went and opened the door.

As they both looked in the woman began to make low moaning sounds. Stuff was piled on an upturned bed, filling had spewed from a slashed mattress thrown on top. Chairs with legs snapped were strewn across a gouged table. A mirror lay in pieces, shards of glass like stalagmites littered the floor; clothes, crumpled in heaps, lay everywhere. There was a ripped box from which books spilled, their spines broken. Some of the torn-out pages, caught by the draught from the door, skittered across the floor and the two women drew back in fright.

Maha closed the bedroom door and gave the woman a hug, whispering, 'I'm sorry.'

Mohammed was shouting to them from outside. The old woman wanted to leave. He gestured angrily to her as she hobbled away still clutching the photograph.

Maha wandered around the apartment after she had gone. She tried to recall the face of the man in the photograph but couldn't. In the kitchen she closed the cutlery drawer and found herself wondering which was his favourite cup and had he cooked meals in this oven or did he have a maid. Perhaps he had been married even – but then where was his wife now? It didn't feel like a place where a woman had lived.

She didn't know anything about him. Not even his name. She picked up her glass of wine but it was no longer chilled and a fly had drowned in the pale liquid.

She wanted to talk to James, to have contact with someone, but found the internet was down. 'To interrupt the web is the sign of an insecure government,' she shouted at her laptop. 'You get people on board through respect, not intimidation and control.'

The key, she noticed, was still in the locked door so she took it out and was returning it to the drawer when she hesitated. It lay in the palm of her hand. She argued, if Masud had given her a bit more information about who had been living in the apartment and where he was now, then she wouldn't be so curious. A goat bleated somewhere outside.

She unlocked the door again and slowly opened it. The daylight was gone and only shadows from the window danced, in shades of grey. She put on the light, a bare bulb hung from the ceiling with the torn remnants of a lampshade dangling from it. She brushed dust off a cushion, put it on the floor and sat on it. A vase lay broken on its side and she picked up the turquoise pieces trying to fit them into the jagged space in a useless attempt to make it whole again. There was a chair with the same decorative design as those in the sitting room but an arm had been smashed off, its gilded circular motif resembling a discarded ammonite.

With no real intent other than to make a semblance of order she began to sort out the mess. With a dustpan and brush she swept up the broken china and the glass from the mirror, cursing as minute pieces pierced her bare feet. She found one green flip-flop on top of a pile of clothes and another squashed between the pages of a book like some bizarre bookmark. She put them on to protect her feet. They were too big and the sole was moulded to the shape of a different foot with rounded imprints of toes. She took them off again and stuffed them into an open suitcase along with shirts and trousers. She picked up a pair of bright blue swimming shorts gaily patterned with palm trees and beach balls and threw them into the suitcase with the rest. A musty smell crept into her nostrils and settled on her clothes; she pushed her hair behind her ears away from her face.

She began to close the books and to stack them into piles against the wall. There were tomes written in Arabic that looked like text-books – books in English and a John le Carré novel, the name written in red capitals on the front cover. She ran her hand down the spines, remembering all the books there had been in her parents' house and how she had loved to rearrange them in the bookcases, sometimes in size order, sometimes in colour. It must have driven her dad mad but he never complained and so she had grown up loving books.

Did this guy love books too? He certainly had a few. A photograph album lay open; she could see the pictures were mainly of Cairo but some were taken by the sea and others of huge tankers passing through a canal, probably the Suez she thought. They look so strange, ships, sailing through the desert.

Loose photographs had spilt out of a brown envelope and she turned them over. They were large and glossy. Masud's face looked up at her. He was smiling with his arm across the shoulder of the man whose features she now recognised from the photograph she had given to the old woman. 'You were friends, of course,' she said to them both. 'What has happened to you?' She studied the face of the younger man; he too was smiling and they both looked comfortable and relaxed.

There were several more photographs of groups of men, then one of Masud, formally dressed in a suit and tie. He was embracing another man, a man who was bald but for the short grey hair above his ears and who sported a moustache clipped across his top lip. There were lots more of the two men together, some with other people present and one where the same man was standing behind a long table speaking into a microphone. Masud was sitting alongside him.

Mohamed ElBaradei, the leader of the NAC, the National Association for Change was what they called themselves. She stared at the photograph of the man; many were calling for him to be the next president of Egypt. She knew him from television, the newspapers and the internet. His face was everywhere. Other pictures showed him dressed casually in a jumper and open-necked shirt, with a megaphone to his mouth, his rimless gold glasses across his nose. He was addressing a crowd, supporters or demonstrators, she couldn't tell. Masud was standing behind him.

She flicked through the remaining pictures. 'So, Masud, you are wrapped up in the politics of it all; and someone of importance by the look of the company you keep. Who exactly are you?' she said to herself.

*Maha is our British journalist with the Egyptian name. Maybe our very useful journalist.* The words banged into her head. It was how Masud had introduced her to his friends. The words grew louder and brought with them the hot feeling of discomfort she had experienced at the time.

So what – he's an influential guy involved in politics. Not a crime, not even a story. But she had felt the undercurrent; somehow all this was proof, she hadn't imagined it. The whole set-up had been odd and then there was that other man, why was he so shocked when she'd appeared?

A thought came slowly at first, then began to race. There was something they wanted from her, they thought she would be useful to them; she closed her eyes and saw only the retained image of a bare light bulb.

This apartment, the scarf, he was grooming her. Does he think these acts give him rights? Maha climbed across the broken furniture to the window and threw it open, breathing in the still warm air. A plane circled overhead awaiting its turn to land, its lights flashed monotonously.

As a journalist she should turn this on its head, use the opportunity. Get close to the centre of things, wheedle her way to where the power was. Use Masud, use his influence. She mused into the darkness before she slammed the window shut. She wasn't going to be his pawn. Turning, she tripped over a tripod, kicking the pieces of a broken camera across the floor. Maha stooped to pick up a powerful lens, clearly an expensive piece of equipment, but it was smashed into shards. She looked at it in her hands then threw it against the wall and walked out of the room. What she wanted most, she decided, was a shower.

The shower was old and spluttered noisily but she let the tepid water fall over her head and down her face until the flow dwindled. She forced herself to reflect only on the nice part of the day as she remembered what fun it had been having a picnic with Chavi, Kamillah and Hosni.

Hosni, her hand flew to her mouth, no, surely not him as well. He had been the one to ring Masud. Was he part of it all? Had finding an apartment been all too easy? No, she told herself. Stop it, she was becoming paranoid. He's a taxi driver and a kind one.

The internet was still down, but she needed to talk to someone so she rang Wahida. The phone rang for a long time before it was answered.

'Sorry to ring you so late, I just needed to hear a friendly voice.'

'Why, what's the matter, are you OK?' Wahida's accent was more pronounced on the phone.

'No, I'm not. Intimidation, violence, secrecy – which would you like first? You've brought down a president, now what? How can a new government begin to tackle the range of problems here? Right now I feel so angry. Masud, the guy who showed me this apartment, turns out to...

'Maha, stop, be quiet. This is not your revolution. In Egypt at the moment, everything is confused. Situations are not always what they seem. Phones – it is good to be careful. Sometimes...you know.'

She looked at the familiar mobile in her hand. 'Wahida, things have been happening. I have had both the best day and then the worst. There is so much I want to tell you. I'm fed up with not understanding, angry at the complexity of it all. Religion. Politics. Wahida, are you still there, can you hear me?'

'As we are fed up with Western governments. Their talk is of democracy. Many words, but where is their action?' Wahida's voice was faint and trembled as she spoke. 'We try all ways to make our lives better.'

Silence hummed down the line. Maha sat on the floor, her back against the wall, her face burning.

'You're right, and I am being ridiculous. What's happened to me is as nothing when I remember what you are fighting for and what Salma has been through. You must think I'm pathetic.'

'No, Maha, you are my friend.' Wahida's words were softly spoken. 'There will be many things you cannot know and I am sorry.'

'I know, Wahida, but I forget. Sometimes I feel almost Egyptian, then something happens and I know I'm not. Then I feel English but I know I'm not quite that either. It's me who should say sorry.' She twisted her wet hair around her finger.

'Can we meet up tomorrow?' Wahida said. 'It would be nice. I will come for you and we will go into Cairo together.'

'Thank you, Wahida, I would like to. *Tesbahi ala khiir.*'

'*Tesbahi ala khiir*, Maha.'

# Chapter 20

'I'm sorry I was so angry last night,' Maha said, stopping to touch Wahida's arm, 'and so naive. I have much to learn.'

They had greeted each other cautiously, Maha was ashamed of her panic and emotional outburst of the previous night. Wahida asked her gently how she was but in a way that suggested it wasn't what she wanted to say.

The two women walked in silence and their hands brushed lightly, bridging the space between them. Buildings rose above their heads; deep shade drew rigid stripes across the road.

Wahida's face formed into a frown, two small lines pulled at her mouth. She adjusted Maha's scarf so that it framed her face, so the folds settled in waves around her neck.

'Maha, first I want you to know I am your friend. Will you remember always? Do you promise?'

'Oh, Wahida, I know. It's why I rang you last night; I needed to talk to you. I wasn't angry with you, just about other events and other people. Masud, for example, the man...'

Wahida put her finger to her lips. 'Tell me later, but first you must promise.'

Maha looked at her new friend who stood awkwardly in front of her. 'OK, OK, I promise. Cross my heart and hope to die,' Maha said solemnly. They looked at each other, began to smile, then to laugh, making a street cleaner pause from his sweeping to watch them.

'Don't go that far,' Wahida whispered to Maha, 'I want you always to be around.' They laughed out loud again; the street cleaner shook his head, bent over and squeezed his nose, blowing snot across the pavement.

Wahida linked her arm through Maha's and hurried her away. 'I want to show you places today, talk to some people. Perhaps they will help you to understand just a little. Come, just down here, there's someone I want you to meet.'

She stopped beside a kiosk that commanded a position on the crossroads. Cars came inches away from its flimsy structure and cyclists used it like a roundabout, furiously ringing their bells to force pedestrians aside. 'Abdul.' She called the name and a man's head and shoulders appeared as if performing in a puppet show. The man was so large he filled the space. The skin around his eyes puckered into creases, his nose flat like a boxer's, his mouth curved upwards so all his face smiled. Sweat beaded his forehead and a shadow of dark hair protruded from his shirt where it was open at the neck.

'You are welcome.' He threw out his arms towards Maha, who was unsure how to respond. 'But you are all so thin. Wahida, you know I like my mamas big.' He drew a curvaceous outline in the air. 'Something to get hold of.' The sound of his voice bubbled like the lemonade in the bottle he was shaking. He flicked off the top with his teeth and passed it to Maha. The froth cascaded over the lip and down the side onto her arm.

The kiosk was packed with sweets and cigarettes and rows of chewing-gum. Baubles made from dyed feathers hung on either side of the opening. They fluttered like trapped birds. Behind Abdul a banner in pink and blue glitter proclaimed Happy Christmas and crates of Coca-Cola and lemonade were kept cold by the block of ice that dripped into the gutter.

'Maha is from England.' Wahida tapped Abdul's chest with her finger.

'She is wanting me to behave, but how can I behave when two beautiful girls, they come to my kiosk?' He winked at Maha and a flush of warmth crept up her neck.

'Abdul demonstrated with us in January, night and day, day and night we were there.' Wahida's foot tapped against the kiosk as the memory stirred her.

'Yes, and I have the medal to prove it.' Abdul pulled up his shirtsleeve and Maha saw the angry scar curved in a letter C from elbow to wrist. He winked again and pulled his sleeve down.

'Now out of my way unless you are going to buy up my entire stock so then I can retire to Eskendereyyah.' His guffaw flew into the air and was smothered by smoke that spluttered from a car exhaust.

'*Ma'a al salama*, Abdul.' Maha turned to wave and caught him rubbing his arm. He inclined his head, acknowledging the moment shared.

She started to ask a question but Wahida interrupted, 'Wait, I need to take you somewhere else first.'

They walked further along the road, weaving between the oncoming people. Was it just like this when her mum and dad were here? Where was everyone going? Cairo, a city of perpetual motion, a restless sea stirred by an unseen wind. She looked at the man who cleaned the street, the stallholder, the suited man with his briefcase and she thought about her birth parents, their place in this tableau. Who was she, was the question in her sigh. She would never know.

She dawdled, she wanted to store all these images to recount to James later. The whiff of fresh oranges piled onto a cart, the green-ness of herbs in the lap of a woman's black robe. How could she describe the fragrance wafting from florist's shops, the exquisite blooms kept fresh by the water streaming down the windows? The spices, the pressed oils for making perfumes, men lifting their clothes to defecate on the railway line, the stench of rotting food and fresh dung from the donkeys. The million faces of Cairo. She longed to share it all with James.

They had turned off the busy road now into a wide street. Trees lined the pavement, their roots had prised up the paving stones; sand had collected in small piles. Wahida stopped in front of a pair of ornate iron gates behind which Maha could see an imposing villa. A tiled path curved towards the front door across grass being watered by a barefoot man, his robe pulled up between his legs.

The soft-hued stone of the house was solid in front of the muted ochre of a polluted sky.

Wahida took out her phone and sent a short text. A face appeared at an upstairs window. Wahida waved and received a small wave back.

Then another face appeared and the shutters were banged shut.

'This is where Salma lives.' Wahida gestured to the house. 'Her father is rich; he is a surgeon. His word is much respected but now his daughter is like a prisoner. All the family, they demonstrated too when the revolution began. On the Day of Rage, we were all there. Salma, her father, her brother and Abdul from the kiosk, arm-in-arm, united in hope. Abdul is poor; he lives in a poor place, not like this.' Wahida held onto the gates and peered through them. 'Salma's father is part of the NAC. Abdul, he belongs to the Muslim Brotherhood but now he despairs. He is frightened by what the extremists want. It is not what he believes, not what most of us Muslims stand for, but the militants, they are taking charge. At the start of the revolution we were all as one, there were intellectuals, professionals, workers, Copts and Muslims.' Wahida looked at her friend, searching her face. 'There were maids there too.' Maha wondered why that should be of particular significance. She only hoped the Arab Spring would bring about the more equal society Wahida sought for women and the opportunities Hosni longed for.

'Wahida, I have some news. Please tell Salma I think her story may be published in the UK. It is to be part of a wider piece about women in Egypt since the revolution and the fall of Mubarak. I wasn't going to tell you yet, not until it had been finalised but being here, seeing where Salma lives, has made me want to tell you so she can have hope.'

'That is good. Maha, thank you.'

'Come on, I haven't finished yet; there's more you need to see.' Wahida pushed off her scarf, as she loved to do, shaking her hair loose. 'Sometimes it feels like I will suffocate here,' she said and turned her face to the warm breeze that lifted the ends of her hair. 'I wish I could go wherever it's going.' The two women stood together looking along the street as though tracking the wind with their eyes.

Wahida stepped into the road and hailed a taxi. They hadn't gone far before she leant forward to tap the taxi driver on the shoulder. 'We'll get out here,' she said. He veered immediately across the traffic and braked to a halt in the middle of the road. Horns hooted as the two girls jumped out and ran towards the river.

'This is so crazy,' Maha shouted above the noise. 'It's like dodgems at a fairground.' Wahida grinned and pulled her by the hand. They ran up the steps of a bridge and walked along a pedestrian way until they reached a bench overlooking the river.

'The Nile,' Maha whispered. A pewter swell moved languidly beneath them, each ripple like a thread in a piece of silk. The sail of a *felucca* billowed with a crack as it caught the wind; a man in a grey robe standing in the stern guided it downstream.

'This is Imbaba Bridge; over there is the district of Imbaba. It's where we're heading. I wanted you to see our river, symbol of our past and our future. Whatever happens in Tahrir Square the Nile will always flow.'

They sat and watched the *felucca* tack across the water. The voices of women washing clothes beside the bridge drifted upwards and children bathed in the shallows, squealing as they splashed each other. Chickens scratched around the stones by the water's edge.

'Sitting here, it's hard to believe the demonstrations are still going on. My anger and anxiety from last night seems, well,' Maha paused, 'just pathetic.'

'Tell me now. It's safe here.' Wahida looked around and moved closer.

'Oh, I'm probably being stupid but last night I was so angry. It seems the guy who showed me the flat, Masud his name is, turns out to be some high-ranking political activist. He's suave, drives a Mercedes car and obviously has loads of money. Two days ago someone threw a lump of stone at me while I was sitting on the balcony and it cracked the window. Then last night an old woman, mad with grief, came to the flat and told me her son, who used to live there, is in prison. She showed me a room of wrecked furniture and his ruined belongings. The last straw was the internet was down and...' Maha could hear Wahida making small sounds.

'Maha, slow down, my English is not that quick.'

'It had been the most wonderful day.' She told Wahida about her time with Hosni and his family at the Pyramids. 'Hosni is a really nice man; he talks to me like a big brother. I think he has made it his mission to look after me. His wife and little girl are lovely and very pretty. He is funny but also serious; he has told me a lot. He also wants me to see how it is. Later I was just enjoying the early evening, the coolness – a magical time – I love it, when I heard this woman wailing and wanting to come into the apartment. It turns out to have been her son's place and she showed me this locked room. It looked like a madman with a machete had been there.

'When she went my curiosity got the better of me. I went back into the room just to look. I found these photographs of Masud with Mohamed ElBaradei, the leader of the NAC.'

Wahida sat up sharply and stared ahead at the river.

'Of course, sorry, you know who ElBaradei is. Masud and he obviously know each other well. Then I remembered what Masud once said about me being an English journalist. It wasn't so much what he said but how he said it; renting me the apartment, the gift of a scarf, I'm sure he wants a favour in return. I thought these people were genuine, now I don't know who I can trust. Even Hosni – I don't know anymore. I want to confront Masud with the photographs but I feel guilty about having snooped in someone else's possessions.' She looked at Wahida who was swinging her feet, scuffing at the walkway.

'There are many people who aim to do the right thing. The NAC, they are liberals. They want an elected government that works for all Egyptians. Must it only be a dream?'

'Probably. Because bloody religion will always get in the way,' Maha scoffed.

'You have no faith? Then your life is empty. Perhaps, Maha, you cannot talk of what you know so little about.' Wahida wiped her face with her scarf and Maha's retort withered in her throat. She wanted to say more; she'd wanted an opinion on her worries. She hesitated, Wahida's rebuke settling like a blotch on her skin.

'Do you know?' Wahida said. 'There is a saying the tourists use: "To see the Nile is to come back one day and to taste the Nile is..." Well, you can guess the rest. Come on.' She shook her head, laughed and jumped up from the bench and began to walk to the far end of the bridge. Just for a moment Maha watched her friend walk away, then she ran to catch her up and together they entered the narrow streets of Imbaba.

It was a labyrinth. The daylight, squeezed between dirt alleyways, became a twilight of shadows. Maha covered her nose against the potent mixture of damp and sewage. They walked in single file and kept each other in sight. In places the distance between the buildings was no more than a few feet and she could stretch out her arms and touch the cold walls with her hands.

They emerged into a wider square and Wahida stopped in front of a blackened structure, a gaunt skeleton, thrust into the sky. There was no roof, only walls huddled together straining to reach each other. Arrows of light kept them apart. On one wall a cross was carved into the fabric. Reflected rays of light tinted it white against the black.

'They burned it in May.' Wahida's voice sounded damaged like the building. 'It was the second Coptic church they burned. Extremists left and right are moving in. Many people died. An old man, the caretaker, there was nothing left of him, just ashes. This is not what we are fighting for.'

Five months on, and the smell of charred wood still lingered amidst mini-whirlwinds of ash whipped up by the breeze.

'They burned it at night.'

Maha looked now at the blue-grey backdrop but could imagine flames, brilliant streaks of red and orange woven together, licking at the sky, bright as a piece of modern art.

'Who was responsible?'

Wahida pulled Maha's head towards her. 'They say it was Salafi Muslims, fundamentalists who want to impose sharia law. They use the political chaos to show their strength and to persecute the Coptic Christians. They are well organised. It is not what most Muslims want and it is what the NAC is against.

'Come away now.' She beckoned Maha to follow her. 'We will go and see Gerges.'

Gerges wasn't in but his wife Lucra made them welcome. She embraced Wahida and nodded shyly to Maha, indicating she should sit down. The room was simple, bare of furniture except for two chairs with cushions that didn't match and a willow-patterned chamber pot that looked like a relic from Victorian England. Lucra mumbled something and draped it with a cloth. The only adornment on the wall was a plain wooden cross.

'Lucra doesn't speak any English,' Wahida said from behind her hand. 'So now it is your turn to practise your Arabic.'

Maha thanked Lucra for her hospitality and her face brightened at her visitor's words. Clicking with her tongue she turned to Wahida and clapped her hands. Maha guessed she had been accepted. Lucra fussed about, boiled some water on a Primus stove in the corner, while Wahida explained that Lucra and Gerges were Coptic Christians; they had also taken part in the revolution.

'You see again, we are male and female, rich and poor, all religions and classes. This is what I am trying to show you.' Lucra nodded her head at Wahida's words.

'*Aiwa, aiwa.*' Lucra was pointing at herself, then at Wahida, and she linked arms with her so the two of them marched across the small room.

Smiling at their antics, Maha whispered to Wahida, 'This lady is lovely.' Lucra made the *chai*; first she put in six teaspoons of sugar before handing her the steaming glass. It was the sweetest drink she had ever tasted and she sipped it slowly while Lucra watched. She must be about sixty, Maha guessed, but her lined face and bent back suggested she could be older. She wore silver bangles which jangled on her wrist in the quiet of the room.

'They have lived here, in this district, all their lives,' Wahida said. 'Muslims and Copts together. Now it is all becoming fractured. She is afraid to go out since the attacks on the churches.'

Lucra spoke rapidly, her voice rose and fell in unison with her hands.

'She says the state television fans the flames of anti-Christian feeling. Now there are gangs and the security forces turn their backs.' In English Wahida added, 'It is what many people say.'

The door opened and a man came in, locking it behind him. His was breathing rapidly; he sat down in the empty chair, wheezing noisily through blue lips. Lucra poured tea for him and stroked his head as he held the glass in both hands.

'Gerges, this is my friend Maha.' The man looked up and Maha could see one eye was bloodshot and a dark bruise covered his cheek. She put her hand to her own cheek remembering her recent attack and how painful it had been to move her jaw.

Gerges sat with his head in his hands. 'Wahida, you shouldn't have come but it is nice to see you. Go soon while it is still day. Tell your father it is worse here, maybe more churches will be burned. Then what shall we do?' He closed his eyes and let his head rest on the chair; soon he was asleep, his hand, contorted by arthritis, twitched as he slept.

They said quiet goodbyes to Lucra and felt their way down the dark steps into the alleyway. A soft white cloud hung in the narrow strip of sky above them but Maha could feel her heart thumping and fear, like vomit, rose in her throat. Wahida walked ahead ignoring everyone who passed by. Soon they were back on the bridge; the claustrophobia that had threatened to become panic receded.

They paused at the bench where they had sat previously, leaning on the rails of the bridge, gazing into the water. A seagull bobbed about, a dog was barking at it, jumping back from the wavelets that broke on the bank.

'I was brought up in the countryside,' Maha said, 'where there is so much space and air. At home it will be autumn now. The light will be low and clear; it will turn the hills a hazy blue. My mother will be picking the last of the blooms in the garden to bring indoors. I promised her I would be home for her birthday at the end of this month.'

The dog had stopped barking and was lying down with his head on his paws.

'Wahida, remember I told you I was adopted. Well, when he can, Hosni is going to take me to the street where we think the orphanage may have been. Where my parents found me. I don't know whether it's there or not but I need to see. Then I will make plans to go home.' She sensed Wahida's breath caress her arm and felt a hand placed on top of her own.

'Thank you for what you have shown me today,' Maha said softly. 'Men like Masud and the NAC, the voices of reason, will they be heard?'

Wahida shrugged. 'He is a good man.' The words were a sigh that fell on Maha.

'Do you know him, Wahida? Are you part of the NAC too?'

'I suppose I am. We are many but maybe still too few. Like you I am confused. I'm not sure who I am anymore.' Wahida spread Maha's fingers and touched the soft skin in-between.

*

Clouds hid the stars that night, the moon a hazy, reclining crescent. Maha tried to phone her mother but the networks were intermittent.

She wanted her to know she was going to look for the orphanage either tomorrow or the next day. She wanted her to be thinking of her when she was walking along the street. She settled on emailing James and hoped it would send eventually.

*Dear James,*

*I have a friend in Cairo, Wahida, one of the young women I told you of before. I think you would like her. Today she took me to meet some friends of hers. She wanted me to see for myself the impact the Arab Spring is having on ordinary people. Yesterday I watched little girls playing in the City of the Dead amongst the tombs where they live.*

*Enough to eat, shelter and sanitation is still what they need. It's said we're all born equal but it's not true and it's not fair. It was incredibly humbling.*

*Tomorrow, I will search for the orphanage where I lived. I didn't think it was important but now it feels like it is. I hope the building's still there, that it hasn't become a car park or a block of flats. Think of me and wish me luck!*

*I've also decided it's time to make arrangements to come home. My plan is to be there about the middle of the month, in time for my mum's birthday as I promised her. One day I want to come back to Cairo. Do you think you...*

Maha paused and read over what she had typed. Would James be excited to see her again? Could what seemed to be growing between them online survive the face-to-face? Or was it all in her imagination?

'Can love begin like this?' she whispered to the screen.

*would like to come too? There is so much I want to show you.*
*With love*
*Maha xx*

Suddenly she was afraid to think – of tomorrow, going home, everything.

# Chapter 21

'Mum, I'm going to try and find the orphanage tomorrow.' There was interference on the phone line and Maha had to shout to be heard. 'I don't have high hopes but just to be in the street where it was will be enough. I wonder if I'll feel anything at all, probably not.' Troubled by her mother's sudden quietness she tried to joke, 'I'll screw my eyes up and try to remember, shall I?'

'Maha, I have been writing you a letter. It has been so hard. I began when you went to Cairo. It's like your journey is mine all over again. I start to write, then the memories catch me out as if the events have just taken place. My tears are always close. I must finish it – I know I still have the hardest part to write. I will post it soon, maybe today or tomorrow. My silence has been too loud for too long and since you went to Egypt it's become deafening. I want you to have my letter before you come home.'

'What do you mean, Mum? Don't talk like that. It makes me feel scared.'

'Darling, I hope tomorrow goes well. I hope you find what you are looking for. I'll think of you every minute of the day and walk down the street with you. Oh, I think I hear the doorbell, I must go.' Maha had been left holding the phone. She knew the doorbell had been an excuse. All last evening she had tried to ring back but the phone lines had gone down. Maha now sat in her favourite chair on the balcony, her arms bound tightly around her knees. Early morning was erupting like a Roman candle, pushing away the night clouds. A window, caught by the sun, shone as though on fire.

She was going to miss this, she thought, enjoying the freshness of the day. A thin plume of smoke rose from below and she could hear Mohammed's wife singing.

She remembered how good it had felt last night to talk to her mother on the phone. The line had been poor but just to hear her voice had been wonderful. Her mother had talked about ordinary events like having coffee with a friend and noticing the lime tree beginning to turn. When Maha had said, 'The twelfth of October, I will be home on the twelfth,' her mother's response was lost in a sob.

What had Mum meant, 'too loud a silence'? Maha wondered, as she watched the *ful* seller ladle out hot food from the metal drum on the back of his bike. The conversation seemed a little less scary today but what was the letter all about?

'Wait and see, wait and see.' She could hear Dad's voice. He used to tease her with surprises and laugh when she pestered him to tell her what they were. She did miss him. She wished he too could know what she was going to be doing today.

Wahida had rung and offered to come with her. Perhaps she should have accepted her offer but she knew her friend had planned to go to Tahrir Square to demonstrate, angry at the burning of another church in Aswan province.

To find the street and maybe the place itself was also something she wanted to do on her own if she was truthful. She wanted to indulge in imaginings, to weave a story, to see herself brought there as a tiny baby. She had accepted being adopted means never to have a single clear identity. Always at the back of her mind was the knowledge she was once someone else – someone who had a different name, a different life map.

Here in Cairo her sense of that was stronger. She couldn't help but look and wonder. She had gained so much but she'd lost a family, a culture and a country. She was searching for her identity, she felt sure.

Come on, she told herself. She'd been looking forward to today and she wasn't going to spoil it with melancholy thoughts.

Hosni thought he knew where the orphanage had been located. He was sure he knew which street it was and he would take her there.

114

But there was something she needed to do first, something she wanted to clear up with Masud.

The sound of a coffee grinder assailed her as she entered Le Cafe but the smell of the roasted beans was warm and enticing. The proprietor recognised her, flicked his eyes towards the back and she went through to the shaded courtyard where five men sat at a table; a waiter replenished their coffee cups and wiped the spills with a cloth. They all looked up at her approach, focusing their eyes on her person.

'I'm looking for Masud,' she said. No one answered but they continued to stare. She repeated it in Arabic. The man closest to her lifted his cup, swirled the coffee around and put it to his lips, blowing across the surface. She felt his breath on her arm.

One of the men stood up. 'Ah, it's our little British reporter.' He leant towards her across the table. 'You've missed him, he's just left.' His English was impeccable.

'I am not your British reporter.' His insolence lent force to Maha's voice. 'Where is he? I have this for him.' A bird hopped around the floor in search of crumbs. A foot kicked out in its direction; it flew to another table and began to peck at the sugar. The men continued to stare. Adrenalin made her brave. 'Who are you anyway?' She was aware her voice sounded strangled. She placed her knuckles on the table and leant towards the speaker. 'Who exactly are you?'

'We know who we are and we know who you are.' The sneer came from near her elbow and she turned towards it. A young man, thin-faced with a bead of sweat on his sparse moustache, pointed his finger at her. She couldn't catch the words that were hurled at him but their effect made him push back his chair and walk out. The bird, frightened by the noise, flew into a creeper, its alarm call piercing the renewed quiet.

'My apologies. He is young.' The older man, still standing, nodded to Maha.

'And that's an excuse? Maybe this country deserves the mess it's in. Give this to Masud when you see him.' She threw the brown envelope of photographs onto the table and turned to leave.

'Maha.' Her name was strange coming from his mouth. 'We try. It is sufficient to say we are many, we pray we will be enough.'

She turned again, meeting his eye. 'Do not use my name. We don't know each other.'

She was shaking when she came out into the sunlight, her chest tight, her pulse racing; she stood awhile before the normality of the street scene began to calm her. The young man was leaning against the wall smoking. He ground out his cigarette with the heel of his shoe and pushed past her into the cafe's dark interior. Something had happened in there. She didn't know what. She walked to where she had agreed to meet Hosni, passed Abdul in his kiosk along the way. He called and waved, then shook his head whilst, like before, he made the outline of a curvaceous woman with his hands. He winked at her and made her laugh. Her fear suddenly felt foolish.

'Maybe I will come with you today.' Hosni said as Maha got into his taxi. The sticky seats, the good-luck charms bobbing from the mirror, were all so familiar and reassuring; Maha laid her head back against the rest and closed her eyes while he drove.

'Thank you, Hosni, for the offer. I'll be fine. Now you've shown me where to go I will take my time and walk slowly down the street. I recognise this junction; I know where I am. I can get home OK, it's not far. Please drop me at the end of the road. I need to do this on my own.'

He looked anxious as she stepped out. She pushed some money through the window onto his lap and shooed him away with her hands, grinning at him so he would know she was all right. He moved off slowly; she saw him stop at the corner and look back at her.

She *had* found the best taxi driver in Cairo, she thought.

*188 El-Horeya, 188 El-Horeya.* Maha let the address repeat itself in her head like a stuck record. There was nothing to distinguish this street from any other. The cobbles on the pavement were broken where tree roots had pushed through. Parked cars, filmed with dust, blocked her way and forced her into the road. A small boy was sitting in the dust piling stones into a pyramid; when they collapsed he tired of the game and began to throw them at a tin can, then at a motorbike propped up on ramps, its back wheel missing. She shook her head at him and waved her finger. He wiped his nose across his arm, ignored her and carried on. With each hit he cheered and raised his hands like a footballer scoring a goal.

She stooped to pick up a large seed pod that had fallen from a tree. It was smooth and brown. She ran her finger along its length over the round seeds, regular protuberances under the hard exterior.

She wondered if this tree had been here when she was. She looked up into its branches, its leaves filigreed like an ornament in the souk, a parasol of blue sky washed in as background. 'Have you seen me before?' she asked the tree. 'Except you wouldn't recognise me anyway because now I'm all grown up. At least I should be,' she added under her breath. She looked back at the way she'd come. The little boy was still throwing stones. She pushed her hair behind her ears and took a deep breath, then began to walk on again.

The buildings were mixed in style. Some, the colour of sand, looked like dwellings that had known a more fashionable past. Now the window frames were bare of paint and broken roof tiles lay on the ground. Stunted shrubs, their leaves covered in dust, were the only greenery in what once would have been cool and shady gardens.

She clenched her fists and scrunched up her eyes. She didn't feel anything. This street was nothing to her. Perhaps she was in the wrong place. Her head began to ache and her chest hurt. She slumped onto a wall and drank from her bottle of water, pouring some into her hand and splashing it onto her face, letting it run down her cheeks. It dripped onto her blouse and left dark stains which soon disappeared as they dried in the sun.

OK. She would walk to the end then find a cafe and treat herself to a nice cool milkshake before she went home. She'd wanted to come. She'd been. It was enough. Having a plan made her feel better as she walked on.

Yes. Shabby, with flaking paint but the gates were green and there was a tree – just like her mother said. Above the solid gates only the upper windows of the villa were visible, closed and black. Could it be? Maha crossed the road, her peripheral vision blurring. She ran her hand down the paintwork, a flake catching under her nail.

She felt like she was in a tunnel – everything had stopped, no one about. She could hear the rhythmic thud of her heart; there was stillness, black shapes before her eyes. Then an open truck trundled down the road, its crates of caged chickens rattled and bounced. The loudspeaker on a mosque began to blare out its call to prayer; a woman appeared and threw a bucket of water into the gutter. The street pulsed around her. The building came back into focus.

She put her eye against the crack between the gates. A small child was sitting on the steps in front of more green doors. Not playing, not moving, just sitting. She couldn't tell if it was a boy or a girl, she could only make out a head of black hair tilted towards the ground.

'Salama,' she called. 'Hi.' She didn't want to frighten the child. There was no response. She tried the gate; it was securely fastened, so she knocked. Still the figure didn't move. She stepped back and looked around. On the gate pillar there was a push-button bell, rusted and stuck. Beneath it were some faded, painted numbers. She rubbed at the sandy stone. The numbers were worn but she traced the lines with her finger and was sure they formed 188.

'Wow,' she said. 'Wow, wow, wow.' Not very profound words, she thought, to mark such an occasion, but appropriate, and she jumped up and down repeating them loudly. She sent off a text to James. Exhilarated and happy, she wanted to share this moment with him.

*James, I think I've found it. I'm standing in front of the orphanage. It's so exciting. Tell you more later. xx*

She wouldn't text her mum. Not yet. She'd ring and speak to her tonight.

She heard a bolt being drawn back on the gate; a man's face thrust out. His skin was pockmarked, thin wisps of hair straggled across his head. Black smudges hung beneath his eyes, his lips sunk into a mouth empty of teeth.

'Oh, sorry to disturb you, it's just I think I used to live here.' His look was blank; a blue-veined hand began to push the gate shut again.

'No, don't go, please don't go. Of course, you don't speak English. *Sabah al-khair*,' Maha babbled. She took a deep breath, struggling in the moment to formulate the Arabic words.

'Please may I come in? Did this used to be an orphanage? Because if so I think I was brought here as a baby.' She was calmer now and the man was listening to her. He looked at her for a long time, then dropped his eyes to her red deck shoes. He beckoned her to follow him and opened the gate just wide enough for her to squeeze through.

She was in a bare space devoid of anything except a tree. Its canopy cast broken shade that flitted like strobe lighting. High walls trapped the whirling dust, a single door interrupted their monochrome monotony. The man walked towards the steps, his leathery feet scuffed the ground. He put his hand on the child's head and when he looked up she saw it was a boy. The child didn't speak but came and stood behind her. In a line the three of them climbed the steps to the entrance. More doors, tall, stretching above her head to a curved portico from where a face, carved in stone, looked down. The man indicated she should go in, then limped back down the steps. The little boy stuck close to her side, holding onto her trouser leg.

She was temporarily blinded by the darkness, the only light came from a grubby window at the top of what must have once been an imposing stairway. The air was still and cool. It smelt of boiled cabbage and disinfectant. She stopped in the middle of the hallway; a warm hand touched hers and small fingers curled around her thumb.

'Hi,' she said softly, crouching down to the child's level. 'What's your name?' He didn't speak but still held her hand; his dark eyes dwarfed his face.

Where to now? She wondered, turning slowly round. Bottle green walls, broken by closed doors, formed a square hall, and the stairway loomed empty in front of her. The small hand tugged at hers and pulled her forward. The boy knocked on one of the doors, then stood rigid. He pushed down the handle and opened the door wide, framing them both in the doorway.

A man rose from behind a desk. '*Itfaddal*,' he said in a low voice.

The desk, dark and solid, dominated the room. Across it lay papers secured by an alabaster paperweight in the shape of a pyramid. There was a white plastic chair in front of the desk and fan blades rotated in the corner, but still the room was stifling. The only other adornment was a clock on the wall which ticked loudly in time with her heartbeat.

'*Sabah al-khair*,' she said stepping forward. 'My name is Maha Rhodes. I hope I am not disturbing you. I should have made an appointment but I never expected to find this place at all. Now that I have I don't know what to say.'

The man walked from behind his desk and extended his hand. 'I am Mr Nessim. Would you like to sit down and tell me what brought you here, and then perhaps everything will be clearer to us both? First I will arrange for some tea.' He went to the door and called for some *chai*.

The small boy who had accompanied Maha sat cross-legged at her feet. She passed her hand across his hair and he looked up at her.

'Don't worry about Maurice; he won't hear what we say. He is totally deaf.'

She bit her lip and for a moment closed her eyes. She felt Maurice's hand creep into her lap and twist the ring on her finger.

'I am sorry,' she said, and her eyes welled with tears. 'I never imagined being here would feel so emotional and the little boy, Maurice, it's so sad. Can anything be done for him?'

He shrugged and rearranged the papers on his desk.

'I think something is upsetting you,' the man said in English. 'Can I help? You will see my English is not good but I try. I like to use it.'

'Mr Nessim, I have lived in England for almost all my life but I was born in Egypt. I was adopted by an English couple in 1981. I think I may have been here as a baby, when it was an orphanage. I wanted to come to Cairo and to look for the place, just so I could have some pictures in my head. To trace my roots, I suppose.' She finished with a grimace.

He took the tray from the young girl who had brought in the *chai*. Tea leaves swirled in the amber liquid and Maurice jumped up and passed Maha a glass before perching on the corner of her chair. She put an arm round him but he fidgeted and pulled at his T-shirt. A brief smile touched his face before he slid off the chair and went and sat under the desk.

'It is still an orphanage,' Mr Nessim said quietly. 'It has been here since 1962. There will always be children who need a home. In Cairo there are many. For some the street is all they have. Perhaps you were one of the fortunate ones, Miss Rhodes.'

'Yes. I know I am.'

She sipped her tea. The simplicity of the room pressed in on her, emptying her mind. She breathed slowly like she was bathing in a perfumed bath, suffused by warmth. A shaft of sunlight angled through the window and lit up the dust; the tick of the clock beat out a rhythm.

'I wonder if there are any records. Would my name be written down anywhere?' She realised she had spoken out loud when Mr Nessim came and stood beside her.

'Of course,' he said. 'Now they are computerised but then there would have been a register. Often there is little information, especially in the case of the babies. Mostly they have been...' His voice tailed away.

'Abandoned.' She dropped the word into the silence. The clock gave a low chime as it marked the hour. 'I was abandoned. That's what my adoptive parents told me. I was found on a...' but the end of the sentence stuck in her throat.

'Could I see the register? Would it be possible? It would be a kind of proof I existed.' She looked up at him. 'I wonder if you can understand.' She walked across to the window. 'I was given my first name by the orphanage, my mother told me. So she kept it. That's all I know. It's not much, is it?'

He joined her and they looked out onto the shabby wall of another building.

'I can't show you today. I have to find the right register. All the records are stored in the basement. Perhaps if you could come back tomorrow I will have it for you. Shall we say at twelve o'clock?'

'Thank you,' she said. 'I appreciate your help.'

'The older children are at school but if you would you like to see the babies' room? It has always been in the same place.' He gestured the rocking of a baby to Maurice and indicated he should take Maha up.

She had almost forgotten the little boy after he had crawled beneath the desk but now he scrambled out and took hold of her hand once more. They went into the hall where the smell of cabbage was strongest. A pile of sheets had been left at the bottom of the stair; a tabby cat was curled in the folds.

The stairway was broad and sweeping. Through an open door on the first landing she could see rows of beds, some made and others stripped of their sheets. A row of potties stood outside. Further up, the stairs became narrower and a worn handrail hung rakishly from the wall. The windows were small and dirty. Maurice pushed open a door. A smell of urine permeated the gloom. She followed him; the near blackness of the room caught her unawares. She could just make out six cots in a row against the wall. A woman lay asleep on a mattress on the floor. She snored loudly as she heaved herself over, burdening the air with her smell.

Maurice walked carefully around the woman and lifted the corner of the curtain. Sunlight streaked like a dart across the row of cots and illuminated the babies. Only four cots were occupied and all but one child was asleep. Two babies lay together in a wooden cot, facing each other, the arm of one slung across the other. In another a baby lay crossways, a foot wedged between the rails. A bottle with milk lay out of reach.

She was drawn to the baby who was sitting up in her cot. The little girl wore a pink dress, the nylon material sticking to her legs. Brown eyes magnified by a shorn head watched her without blinking. A fly played around the baby's mouth; it crawled over her lips and chin.

Maha heard footsteps on the stair and Mr Nessim came in. He crossed the floor to where the woman lay and poked her hard with his foot. She grunted. He pulled back the curtains and tried in vain to open the window. He thumped his fist against the wall. The woman awoke confused by the light and noise. She saw Mr Nessim and rolled onto her knees to push herself up. He shouted at her as she hawked up phlegm into an ashtray. He stormed out of the room, slamming the door behind him. Maurice flew off too, his crying grew fainter as he ran down the stairs.

The watching baby began to whimper, small bleating noises like a lamb. The fly flew off her face only to settle again as she quieted. Maha picked her up; the baby's nappy was heavy and the acrid smell of ammonia stung her eyes. She took her to the window, the baby stretched out her hand, wanting to play with her earring. The kind of pain she had experienced once before raced through her and she pulled the baby close so the little girl's warmth was like a poultice pressed onto an open wound. Music was playing in her head.

*It is Elgar's Nimrod; the curtains are sliding silently around the coffin. I want to pull them back, to stop them from swallowing my dad. I cling to Mum; the crematorium becomes a room with no light, an empty space where grief sits on a throne touching those who walk near it.*

Maha shook her head to put a stop to the funereal music. 'Oh, Dad,' she whispered, kissing the baby's head where the soft fuzz of new hair was like a pillow made of down. She went on hugging the child, feeling her own pain surrender to the damp warm form.

Why Dad? Why here? Why now? The dad she had loved so much – why had he come to her, in this room? A moth, its wings tinged with colour, was dead on the windowsill, its still, small frame making Maha cry.

This is the end of my journey, she thought. Was this where it began? Her tears fell unchecked, for all of these babies as well as for herself. She put the little girl back into her cot, then banged at the window until it opened and she could lean out gulping at the air. The baby watched her move towards the door. Maha stopped and grabbed at the door frame, fighting the pain in her chest. She turned, then ran back across the room and crouched beside the cot. She gave the little girl the dummy that was pinned to the sheet; the baby sucked at it and went on staring as Maha fled the room. The woman was settling down again, her face turned to the wall.

Mr Nessim was not around so she let herself out. In the courtyard a few small children, those too young to go to school, were in a group, playing in the dirt with a stick. A boy kicked a deflated ball against the wall. They saw her and ran over, touching her jeans and fingering her bracelet. Their excited chatter took no heed of her tear-stained face.

'Baksheesh?' a small boy asked with a cheeky grin on his face. 'Sweets?' he added hopefully.

'No, I haven't any sweets. Sorry.' Maha smiled. 'Bukra inshallah. I will bring you sweets tomorrow.' She disentangled herself and whispered, 'M'as salama.' A bent old woman, all in black, watched from the shade of the tree and the man opened the gates to let her out. She heard the bolt slide into place behind her.

She leant against the wall to rest, completely drained. She didn't want her thoughts to take shape, scared that longing and loneliness would overwhelm her again. The smell of cabbage and urine clung to her nostrils. Then there was Maurice and the babies. She made herself dwell on the happy faces of the children in the courtyard and their noisily shouted goodbyes.

Tomorrow. She only had to wait until tomorrow, then she could come back. A shiver ran through her. She would come armed with a big bag of sweets and coloured crayons and maybe some Turkish delight.

She had just begun to walk down the street when Hosni's taxi drew alongside her.

'I just happened to be coming along this street and there you were. How do you say it? Good timing.' Hosni's voice broke into her thoughts. She looked at him through his open window.

'Hosni, I don't believe you. Have you been waiting for me?'

'No, just happened to be passing.' His grin faded as he saw her face. 'Oh, was it bad? Are you going to tell me?'

She climbed into the back seat. 'It was...' she said, and tears began to fall again. 'I never guessed I would feel like this. I can't stop crying. I have to go back again tomorrow.'

Hosni turned to look at her, his face screwed up in concern. 'Family,' he said. 'They bring us so much joy and so much pain. I was scared for you today. What did they tell you?' He pulled out a box of tissues from the glove compartment and passed them to her.

He hadn't gone any distance before he stopped the car, jumped out and opened Maha's door. 'The English, don't they think a cup of tea is always the solution? Hosni will buy you tea.'

A man squatted near the wall of the coffee house smoking. The long pipe from his hookah nestled between his open knees. From further down the road she could hear loud voices and see the stalls of a street market.

'Hosni, you knew the orphanage was still there, didn't you? Were you waiting for me? Why?' Hosni fiddled with the dirty ashtray on the table, pushing the cigarette stubs around with a spent match.

'Why do you have to go back tomorrow?' he asked, still not looking at her. 'You've been there, now maybe you just leave it.'

'No, Hosni. I can't. Mr Nessim, the man in charge, is going to show me the register where my entry to the orphanage is recorded. He says it will have been stored in the basement.' Hosni shook his head and muttered; the ashtray tipped, spilling fine ash across the table. 'Then I will leave it,' she said, puzzled at Hosni's strength of feeling.

'That will be enough.' Or would it, she wondered, as her thoughts strayed to the baby she had lifted from her cot and to Maurice in his silent world.

'The children who were there, they felt like family,' she said. 'Of course they're not but it was as though we shared a connection, a link. I can't expect you to know what I mean but it was what you said, a sense of family.'

A cloud momentarily blotted out the sun; she watched it move slowly across the sky. Smaller grey clouds were gathering, drifting into each other to form a larger mass. A breeze blew along the street, stirred the dried leaves; the man with the hookah stood up and wandered away, his arms outstretched as though sleepwalking.

Hosni pulled a creased photograph out of the pocket of his trousers and pushed it across the table to Maha. A corner was bent down and she smoothed it with her hand. She was looking at a young man in the uniform of the security forces. His expression was grim, and one hand rested on the body of an armoured vehicle.

'Nothing for two years, then he sends me this. He says now he is a tank driver. What does he want me to do?' He took back the photograph and crumpled it into a ball. 'They are thugs.'

'This is your brother, Hosni?' She asked the question but she already knew the answer.

He turned his face away and kicked at the table with his foot.

'See what I mean. Family. Sometimes it is better you not know. Then you can't be hurt.'

'Perhaps he wants to make you proud, Hosni. He will know what a good brother you were to him. Maybe this is his way.' She wished she could ease Hosni's anguish but she could only sit beside him, her hand on his arm.

'They are thugs. Their uniform is their excuse for violence. I am not proud of him. He wants something. I know it.'

# Chapter 22

*28th September*

*Two events occurred after that awful day, Maha. Happenings that made life better. Isn't it funny how so often something small and inconsequential helps you to set off on a new path.*

*First, tomatoes, those cursed tomatoes. The next time I went to the market one of the stallholders, a lady in a print dress with a scarf tied around her head, beckoned me. 'Madam, round here,' she said. 'Look, see, I kept good ones for you.' She let me feel the firm tomatoes with their bright red skin. 'The best.' Her English was accented but I understood and she smiled and patted my hand.*

*Do you know, Maha, afterwards I always bought my fruit and vegetables from her; we were friends. A lasting regret is when I left Egypt I never had a chance to say goodbye. I have often wondered what she thought.*

*The other incident happened as I walked home past a scrubby area near the army barracks. One day it was just a waste area across which rubbish gusted and grey-green grass struggled to survive. The next day a whole 'village' had appeared. Huge cable drums, left by road workers, had been laid on their side, holes cut in their core and people were living in them. Families, mothers with babies strapped to their backs. I stared in amazement. There was washing laid out on the grass to dry; fires were being poked as food was cooking in large metal pots.*

*A little girl dragged her small brother by the hand and ran to me, their bare feet brown with dust. She looked up at me, her dark eyes framed by matted curls. She opened her hand and showed me a bright yellow bead. She wanted me to take it so I picked it up, admired it, then gave it her back. 'La, la,' she said, pointing at me then running off. The two children stopped outside their cable drum home and waved. I still have that bead.*

*Maha, why have I never told you all this before? I know why, because we, your dad and I, were afraid. Afraid you would ask too many questions. That one day we might have to tell you the truth.*

*You were such a thin little girl when we brought you back to England. Almost one but only beginning to sit up. What scared me most was your silence. It was as though you had learned not to cry, learned it brought no response. You would watch us constantly; your big dark eyes followed our every movement, your thumb in your mouth and always clinging to 'floppy rabbit'. Bedtime was the worst. In your cot you would roll around, arms flailing until, exhausted, you would eventually fall asleep. We knew the reason why. I used to sit by you at night so I could hold your hand and stroke your sleeping face. Try to make up for it all. We gave you a history but one that only began when you were eleven months old.*

*Back to the story. After those two events I began to get better. Slowly at first. It was like the weight I carried around could occasionally be put down. I began to be warmed by the sun, marvel at the night which fell with such suddenness and most important of all, to notice the friendliness, the openness of the Egyptian people. They smiled, they said welcome and I felt safe.*

*I remember your dad asked me if I would like to go to Crocodilopolis one weekend with some other families. I laughed at the name and said, 'Yes, let's, it sounds like a fun place.' He hugged me, Maha, hugged me until I thought my ribs would break and I knew then what pain he too had been through.*

# Chapter 23

'James. You are there.'

'Of course, I sit waiting for the phone to ring,' he teased her. He listened while she told him about the orphanage, slipping in questions, taking her back to the green walls and Mr Nessim. 'There is a little boy who's deaf and a baby in a pink dress.' She described it all, the babies' room and how emotional she had felt.

'I can't imagine what it must have been like for you, to be back in the same room.' The catch in his voice became a pause.

The antics of the cheeky little boy who asked for sweets made him laugh again. 'James, I've booked my ticket home. I'll be home in eight days.' His whoop of delight made her take the phone from her ear.

'I'll be at the airport to meet you. Nothing will stop me. I'll be the man holding the biggest bunch of red roses in the world.'

'You'll have to fight Mum because there is no way she isn't going to be there too.'

'I have no intention of fighting your mum as long as she lets me see you first. I will love her too – just like I love you.' The words, released thousands of miles away, streamed through the open window and wrote themselves on the wall, wove themselves into the cushions and were trapped by her hand as it covered her face.

'Am I allowed to say that? I wanted to tell you at the end of our first train journey but I thought you might not take me seriously. Now you know how I feel and the next few days are going to pass, oh, so slowly. When you come back we'll...' Then the phone line had clicked loudly and gone dead.

Later, embraced by the softness of the night, she had whispered into the sky, 'Me too, James,' and she had blown her words towards a British Airways plane climbing into the sky from Cairo airport, willing it to be her courier.

*

'Always more to tell you. How blue the sky is. How, when the sun rises, it bursts into the room and lights up the painted frames of the chairs, making them shine like gold leaf.' Maha spoke into the air as she sat in the high-backed chair with its faded brocade fabric, trying to imprint the scene on her memory.

James. She didn't want it all to be too soon – after Robin – too soon for them to have met. She recognised her need to always have someone close. Someone who felt like hers. As a child it had been her parents or best friend. Later relationships had filled a void. If those ended and she found herself on her own the space around her felt like a gaping hole. This powerful need for another person's presence was inexplicable but painful all the same. She wanted it to be different with James, to love him not to need him.

Happiness resurfaced, and she jumped up and skipped down the dark inner hall, singing to herself; she'd be sensible, take things slowly. The feeling was like a smile spreading through her.

She stopped at the door of the locked room. The feel of the cold handle made her remember the young man who had lived here and was now in prison. 'What has happened to you?' she asked him through the closed door. 'Do you try and picture the colour of the sky too and how your furniture looks when the sun shines?' The weeping of his mother seeped from the walls and reinhabited the apartment. Maha contemplated fetching the key for the room again. No, not today. The wanton destruction would upset her; she would be angry at Masud again. This was her day, and she wasn't about to spoil it.

The morning was endless. She wanted to get ready but couldn't decide whether to wear a skirt or trousers. She chose the latter, then twice changed her top, studying the look in the mirror. 'You're not going for an interview – just to read your name in a register.'

Even as she said it to herself she felt a squirm of pleasure; she sat on her bed cross-legged amidst the discarded clothes. They became as gaudy as bunting as she remembered the starkness of the orphanage.

Would this morning never pass? Twelve o'clock seemed hours away. She decided she would go to the souk before going on to the orphanage. She'd buy some presents to take home: for her mum and her granny and something for James.

Mohammed's wife came across to her as she left the apartment. She stroked the scarf Maha carried, lifting it to her own cheek, her bitten nails ugly against the fine material. Garlic escaped on her breath as she smiled through her brown, uneven teeth. Mohammed sat at the foot of the stairs and watched. Maha called a greeting to him. He received it with an almost imperceptible flick of his hand, but his sullen stare remained. 'What *is* the matter with that man?' Maha's English words were meaningless to Mohammed's wife but she shrugged and smiled anyway.

On impulse Maha joined the melee of people who waited to board the bus into Cairo. She jostled her way on and found a seat towards the back. Her fellow passengers glanced in her direction but otherwise ignored her. A woman with a basketful of fruit sat opposite. She was scrubbing at the grimy window leaving greasy streaks. A man who held a squawking chicken by its legs sat further down the bus; its screeches filled the interior. The bus wove from one side of the road to the other, occupying any vacant space in the choked streets. Some passengers rocked in time with the swinging vehicle; Maha hung onto the seat in front.

The traffic snarled and the horns became louder and more persistent. A policeman stood on a box in the middle of the junction, his white uniform and shiny black boots in contrast to the dirty exhaust fumes that billowed around him. He waved his hands and blew his whistle; the traffic nudged forward jamming into even tighter spaces. Maha was beginning to feel sick, the air in the bus hot and oppressive. Worries she'd been trying to suppress crowded in as the aisle filled and bodies squashed against her.

She had wanted to tell her mum that she'd found the orphanage, to tell her she was going back there today. Twice last night she'd tried to phone her. Maha also wanted to know that she was all right. The phone had gone unanswered; she imagined it ringing bleakly in her mother's empty hall.

In her head it rang like an alarm.

She had tried again before she went to bed. The phone lines were back up but there was still no answer. 'I need to hear your voice, Mum.' A trickle of fear had wheedled its way into her head, its origins all too familiar.

*My dad has woken me, drowsy and warm from sleep. He scoops me into his arms. 'Do you want to go on an adventure? To go to Granny's house in the middle of the night?' I love going to stay with Granny and there is Granny, waiting at the bottom of the stairs with a big tartan rug to wrap around me.*

*I am bundled into Grandad's car. As we leave I beg him to wait a minute, to let me watch an ambulance race down the road with its blue lights flashing. It stops outside my house. Grandad drives off quickly. Granny is sitting in the back of the car cuddling me tightly. 'I want Mummy?' I cry.*

*I stay with them for nearly a week, even getting to miss school. When I go home Mum is there. She hugs me in a way which stops me asking questions.*

Many years later, she had made sense, her own sense, of that night, its effect clung to her still. Words like overdose or attempted suicide remained unspoken. Even as a child, before she had understood, the impact was there. Present in the turn of a handle, the finding of an empty room, no cheerful hello on returning home from school. She had become protective, watchful and sensitive to the signs. The legacy remains. Like last night when the telephone wasn't answered. There could be a hundred explanations but panic is a cymbal. She didn't want to hear its clang.

A woman screamed as a brick hit the window of the bus. It was surrounded by a mob that spread through the traffic like spilt water. Fists hammered against the sides, drowning out the cries of the chicken. Faces jumped at the window only to fall back immediately. These were not demonstrators; these were bullies, criminals on the rampage, moving in gangs, breeding terror. Maha pulled her scarf across her face and turned away but through the other side she could see a car being rocked by a crowd of males. No sooner had they come than they passed, spilling down the side streets. The shrill whistle of the policeman sounded again and the bus edged slowly on its journey. More people squeezed on as it neared the city centre and people blocked the aisle. A young man in army fatigues sat alone, a rifle across his knee. People looked but no one took up the empty seat beside him.

She hoped she was in the right place as she pushed her way along the bus and stepped off. For a moment, relieved to escape from the smell of clammy bodies, she stood in the doorway of a building, Deep cuts, recent and naked, had been slashed into the wood, crude words the vent for someone's hatred.

She melted into the narrow streets of the Khan el Khalili where the tall buildings blanked out the sun and cast blocks of shadow over the shop fronts, packed together like different-sized cubbyholes. She shut her eyes and breathed in the air. The smell of spices, thick and cloying, wafted around her; she could have been back in her mum's kitchen, standing on a chair, sifting icing sugar onto a warm, spiced, orange cake, just out of the oven.

Some spices were packed into sacks, others in dark, gnarled barrels. Like rows of powder paint, the peaks of green, red, orange and saffron yellow lit up the sunless alley, and she had an urge to plunge her hands into their powdery depths. A young woman, her dress the colour of the spices, held out a small glass in which there was a dark-red liquid. 'Karkade,' she said, inviting her to taste it. She took Maha's hand and dropped some dried purple leaves into her palm telling her they came from the hibiscus plant. She pointed to

133

where a pan bubbled away on a small Primus stove at the back of the shop. Now the liquid in the glass was ice-cold and sweet.

Around her, local people sniffed the herbs and bartered with the stallholders. It has been like this for hundreds of years, she thought, allowing the music of their voices to lull her. She listened to them and loved the fact she could understand most of what was being said.

The rows of herbs and spices gave way to more pinched alleyways and shops crammed with copperware. Plates etched in gold, silver and bronze depicted scenes from ancient Egypt and lay alongside decorative boxes inlaid with mother-of-pearl. She chose a small box, haggling over the price as both she and the stallholder enjoyed the game and joked together.

There were several shops selling gold. Pieces were weighed on tiny scales and buyer and seller, their heads close together, conversed in hushed tones. A man selling carpets beckoned her into his shop, promised her that his were the best. She shook her head and when, in Arabic, she told him she lived in Cairo, he realised she wasn't a tourist and didn't try to persuade her further.

She knew it must be hard to make a living now the tourists weren't coming. It would be a while until they come back. She thought of the angry crowds today and their frenetic chanting. Last night Wahida had said the mood was bad but hadn't wanted to elaborate over the phone. She guessed this is what she'd meant.

She found a stall of leather goods and picked up a wallet, lifting it to her nose to smell the rich scent. It was soft as she rubbed it against her cheek and she knew it was right for James. The lady who served her was tiny; she only reached Maha's chest. Her forearm was wreathed in bangles; she had rings on each finger, a turquoise scarab hung from a chain around her neck. The woman stroked the wallet. 'Gazelle,' she said, and named a price. An old man lay on a blanket inside the shop. His arm lay awkwardly at his side; his hand curled inwards.

'My father,' the woman said, and wiped the drool where it dribbled from his mouth.

Maha gave her the money, not wanting to barter. As she took the wallet wrapped in its tissue paper a turquoise scarab was pressed into her hand.

'For luck.'

She stopped to gaze at the great archways and vaulted ceilings that framed the streets near a mosque. Beneath them, for sale, were a host of lights hanging from the roof, their royal blue, gold and red lampshades turned the alleyway into a sultan's palace. Leather camels, scarves, jewellery and busts of Tutankhamen and Queen Nefertiti all vied for space.

She turned into a quieter side street away from the tourist trail and paused at a stall where a man sat smoking, watching her. She picked up a brass and onyx goblet to feel the cold surface with its swirl of greens and browns. She would love a set of these, to remind her forever of Cairo. She would come back for them before she left, she promised herself.

Her final purchases were crayons and pens and some sheets of sticky coloured paper, items she thought the children in the orphanage would enjoy. She also filled a bag with sweets and bought some Turkish delight, gooey, filled with nuts, the icing sugar, sprinkled like snow, on the top. It was placed carefully in a white cake box and tied with ribbon.

Nearly twelve o'clock. The register...

# Chapter 24

Maha read the sign at the end of the road and looked down its length. Yesterday she had felt nothing, but today it was so familiar: the tree with its heavy seed pods hanging like Christmas decorations, the motorbike filmed in a layer of dust, still up on bricks. People walked by as though this was just some ordinary day. How could they not know?

Trying to summon her courage she turned her face towards the sun and closed her eyes, seeing streaks of colour, bright against black. She took a deep breath and opened them. The world returned to shades of sand beneath its canopy of blue. She would take some photographs later. Her mum would be thrilled – and James – humble beginnings indeed.

The green gates were shut and no sound of children's voices greeted her. She knocked and waited, rubbing at the worn numbers on the pillar. Two men, their hands linked, openly stared at her as they passed; she turned away and adjusted her scarf so her head was covered. Her knuckles made a dry sound as she knocked again. She put her eye to the crack, twisting one way then the other. She could see the yard was empty except for the old woman who had been there yesterday and who was now sitting under the tree, leaning on her stick. Maha knocked more loudly and called a greeting. The woman looked up and in a ragged voice called out something she couldn't hear. A man emerged from the shadow of the building and limped his way towards the gate.

Her heart was thumping and a tingle of excitement spiralled in her chest. He fumbled with the bolt, metal grating as he worked it loose. It was the same man who had opened the gate to her before but her *Sabah al-khair* went unacknowledged as he pushed the bolt back into place and limped away.

The villa sat in the ochre-coloured space like an abandoned cardboard box. The old woman was motionless, peering at her. A leaf separated itself from the tree and floated down in a series of arcs, turning the scene into reality. She walked towards the door and mounted the steps where Maurice had sat. She hoped she would see him today. One of the doors was ajar, the interior a black line through which trapped cooking smells were seeping. As she pushed on it a blade of light shot across the tiles.

She checked her watch. It was just after twelve. The office door banged against its latch but all was quiet. She looked around for somewhere to sit while she waited. But for a plain wooden cross that hung on a nail, the space was devoid of furniture. She wandered slowly around the hallway, touched the walls, spread her fingers on the cold surface to cool her hot palms.

She stroked the wood of the banister and saw it weaving its way up and up to where she knew the babies would be lying. She had been one of those babies once, hot and wet and watchful. What had it been like, back on the day when her adoptive mother had picked her out of her cot and carried her down these stairs? Did she have a new dress especially for the occasion? She hoped the people who worked here had missed her, just a little, as she left for a different life. She pictured her mum and dad standing proudly on the steps with their new daughter. Her dad would have been smiling his smile, the one which wrinkled his face and made his eyes sing. He would have hung his arm around her mother's shoulder, pulling the two of them gently towards him. That's how it was, always, just the three of them, a unit.

What sounded like a drawer banging shut startled her and she heard low voices from behind the door of Mr Nessim's room. No one appeared, so she walked to the door and knocked, pushing it open wide enough to put her head around before entering. There were two men, Mr Nessim and a short, obese man who stood next to him.

This man went and sat on a chair against the wall, his legs spread wide apart, his shirt stretched tight across his chest. Maha felt his stare; his eyes were locked on her.

She greeted Mr Nessim who was shuffling papers, moving them from one pile to another. She offered her hand but he flicked it with his own and turned away. She was left looking at his back, his drooping shoulders, black hair snaking down his neck.

'You cannot come here without an appointment.' Mr Nessim spoke too loudly. 'I am busy. I cannot speak to you now. We have nothing for you. You will have to leave.' He came from behind the desk. He seemed smaller, older, different.

'You should not be here. You must go.' He was looking beyond her at a point above her head.

'This does not make sense, Mr Nessim,' she said, making her voice sound stronger than she felt. 'You said 12 o'clock. When I came yesterday you agreed to show me the entry in the register that recorded my admission to the orphanage. As I told you, I was here in 1980. I have come to see the records.'

The tick of the clock was loud and she watched the second hand move past the three then the four and five and six. She stepped back as he came closer. His eyebrows were drawn together in a frown, his lips shaped sounds and droplets of moisture were visible on his moustache.

'There are no records, they are lost. It was a mistake.'

Maha held her scarf in a knot at her neck. 'Why are you saying this? I don't believe this is the truth; I would like to see the director, please. This is not the information you gave me yesterday. You clearly said...'

A long hiss emanated from the man in the chair as he began to rise.

Mr Nessim indicated the door with a noticeable nod of his head. He took hold of her arm, spun her round and pushed her into the hallway. He propelled her through the outer door.

'After today I will no longer be working here. You should not come back. Go home.' He leant close to her. 'Forget this place. I am sorry.'

The slamming door pushed her down the first step and she stumbled onto her knees, her parcels scattered around her. She looked back at the closed door, solid and faceless. Ants, disturbed by her fall, ran in frenzied circles until they reformed their path, disappearing into a hole in the ground, taking her hope with them.

She picked up the bag of gifts and the white cake box, now streaked with dust. She put them on the top step and whispered, 'For you, Maurice, to share with all my other little friends.' She hoped the ants wouldn't find them first.

As she quickly collected her other bag she noticed the old woman, black and hunched, was hobbling towards her. She didn't want to speak to anyone just now. She just wanted to get away.

Tears blurring her eyes, she fumbled with the bolt; metal screeched on metal. She pulled the heavy gate open and stepped into the street. She sagged against the pillar and slid down onto the pavement. She clutched her bag with both hands, hugging it to her chest. Her tears streamed unchecked.

'Psst, psst. Mavette. Mavette.' The reedy voice was as piercing as the cry of the first bird at dawn.

'Mavette.' That name. It swam through Maha's tears, summoning memories of another time.

*Dad's hand is cold as I sandwich it between my own, and stroke the blue-veined knuckles. The night dances in shadows through the open curtains and a curved moon inches its way across the sky. I had made Mum go to bed to try and get some sleep. 'I'll sit with him. I promise I will wake you if...' The words had hung between us – Dad's rasping breath filled the void.*

*He is barely conscious, but I talk to him through the hours, saying all the things I wish I had said before. Occasionally, a flutter of his eyes tells me he hears.*

*I tuck his arm beneath the bedclothes and walk to the window, his fitful murmurings follow me. The palest hint of light whispers above the hill but the moon still silvers the garden, making diamonds of the raindrops on the windowpane. I stretch my arms and turn my head in slow circles.*

*Dad stirs; I run back to the bedside and rub his palm with my thumb, his acetone breath lodges in my throat. He has opened his eyes and is looking at me.*

*'Mavette, you've come.' He presses my hand, a tear squeezes from his eye and runs down to the pillow. 'You're here. You're here now.' He closes his eyes, his eyelids almost transparent.*

*Then he is clutching at me and straining to sit up. I cradle him. 'I thought I was going then.' His voice is strangled with fear. 'Mavette.'*

*The name is a sigh. 'We tried for so long. We never stopped loving you.*

*Not ever.' He falls back against the pillows and I wipe the perspiration from his face and moisten his dry, cracked lips with some water.*

*'Dad, it's Maha,' I whisper. 'Dad, I love you.'*

*He opens his eyes, as blue and fragile as Dresden china. I put my face down to his and hold his hand against my cheek.*

*'Maha, oh, Maha, our little darling. You brought us such joy.' His body trembles, the lines of his face become smooth.*

*I wake Mum and we lie together – just like when I was little – when I used to creep through in the morning, to lie warm and cosy between them while they read me stories. Now it is Dad in the middle, safe and loved.*

*Dawn breaks, spreads shades of pink across the sky and bathes the garden in rosewater.*

'Mavette, are you all right?' The old woman was now leaning into her. 'Where have you been? It's been so many months.' The woman's tongue flicked against her lips and she lisped through broken teeth. Maha wanted her to go away.

'I am not Mavette, I don't know who she is.' She rose slowly to her feet so now the woman appeared even more shrunken and frail. 'My name is Maha.'

The woman's neck jerked backwards, her face creased in pain. Maha caught her as she stumbled, feeling the thin frame beneath her dress. A hand came up to Maha's face and calloused fingers traced the outline of her nose and mouth. They brushed across her cheeks and tenderly swept the hair from her forehead.

'Maha.' A breath formed the word. 'Maha.' The old woman cupped Maha's chin in her hands and peered at her with screwed-up eyes. 'Can it be? It's so long, so long ago, so long ago.' Her voice tailed into a sob.

Maha stood absolutely still, staring into the old woman's bleached eyes. She took her by the shoulders. 'Who are you? Who is Mavette?' Maha shook her gently but only whimpers came from the stuttering mouth. 'Tell me, please tell me.'

'It is you. You are so beautiful. Let me look at you. So grown-up.'

Two girls with orange school bags stopped to stare; they giggled and walked on, hurled names over their shoulders, then ran off down the street.

The old woman tapped her stick on the pavement and clutched at Maha's blouse. 'Mavette.' She waved a cupped hand up and down in the air. '*Ukht, Ukht.*' The words were a high-pitched squeak.

'*Ukht?*' Maha bent down so her face was level with the woman's. 'Sister?'

'*Aiwa.*' The old head nodded. 'Mavette. *Ukht.*'

'Mavette is my sister? *Ukhti?*' She covered her mouth and nose with her hands as a wave of heat stifled her.

'*Aiwa.*' Yes, but the woman was shaking her head; her stick clattered to the ground. Maha's hands were prised from her face.

She stepped back from the old woman's musty smell, saw her leathered skin and the pox marks that scarred her cheek. 'Yes? No? I don't understand. What do you mean?' she said, tripping over the Arabic words. 'Same, same.' The old woman made horizontal

141

movements with her hands as the English words fell into the street. She poked her finger into Maha's chest. 'Maha, Mavette, same, same.' She made two cradles with her arms and rocked back and forth. 'Same, same.' A smile spread across the woman's face, deepening the lines.

An angry shout, followed by another, came from behind the walls of the orphanage. The old woman flinched. She lifted one bent, deformed finger. 'One hour,' she wheezed. 'One hour. *Hena.*' She pointed to the ground. She grasped Maha's hands and kissed them with dry lips.

Maha picked up the fallen stick and secured the wizened hand around it. The woman hobbled back through the gates and they banged shut behind her.

The world hadn't changed, the sky was high and blue, the sun hot, the trees still cast shade, but to Maha it seemed she was now a performer in a different play.

She reached forward to grasp the invisible thread that had wrapped itself around her and which now snaked across the pavement, snagging on the flaking paint, disappearing through the cleft of the closed gates.

'Same, same.' The old woman's words shimmered like a mirage, so clear but out of reach. Maha began to walk away from the orphanage, occasionally touching the wall to feel its solidity. 'Same, same. Same, same.' The swirling words wouldn't stop.

She stopped to curve her arms in the way the woman had done. A blue plastic bag, blowing along the road, caught against her legs before it fell into the gutter, scaring off birds that pecked at a piece of bread.

'Twins.' The screamed word, sharp as gunfire. 'We were twins.' The birds flew up from the gutter again, screeching in protest, while two men in the back of an open truck whistled at her as they bounced along the road.

'I have a twin sister,' she shouted back, not caring that they couldn't hear. 'I have a twin sister.' She let the words roll along her tongue, savouring the taste and texture. 'Mavette is my twin sister. 'Mavette. Now I know who you are.'

*'Granny, who's Mavette?' Granny uses her new handkerchief to dab at her lips. Earlier I had taken it from a slim box of three; each was folded into a triangle, arranged so the lace edge formed a pattern. Granny had lots of boxes of handkerchiefs in her drawer, like old ladies' trophies. Her son's funeral has been important enough for her to open a new one.*

*'Granny, tell me. Who's Mavette? That last night, before he died, Dad kept calling me Mavette.'*

*'Mavette.' A whisper, breathed into the air. Granny has tucked her hanky into her sleeve, 'Oh, darling, at my age I forget names. Isn't this a lovely turnout? It will be a comfort to your mum. Everyone loved your dad.'*

*Granny is sitting in the shade, beneath the contorted hazel, watching friends and family observe the rituals that make such days bearable. Some of them have not known what to say to a ninety-year-old who has just buried her son.*

*'Granny, you are still as sharp as a needle. You do know, don't you?' 'You have been such a delight to us, Maha. We are so proud of you.'*

*Granny takes my hand, her skin as thin as parchment; she traces the shape of my thumbnail.*

*'What pretty nail varnish? Do you know I think I could drink another cup of tea? Will you get me one, dear?'*

*I come back with the tea but Granny's head is lowered and her eyes closed. I put the cup down beside her and kiss her gently on top of her head, guessing this is a sleep of convenience.*

*I look across to where my mother stands talking. Perhaps I will ask her one day but I know I will not.*

A group of sellers huddled where two roads met; Maha bought an orange from a woman who sat cross-legged on the pavement. It was refreshing, sweet and juicy. From here she could still see the closed green gates; she looked at her watch. Who was that other horrible man and why was Mr Nessim so changed? He said there were no records. He was clearly lying, hiding something or someone.

Someone? Mavette? Nothing made sense. Would the woman come back as she said? Who was she? Could she...be her mother? The thought flitted away, not wanting to be given substance.

Near to the orange seller a man worked at a lump of clay. She stopped to watch. Several figures lay in a box at his feet. He lifted them out for her and set them in a group. Amongst them was a man carrying a basket over his shoulder, a squatting woman sieving rice, her dress pulled up between her knees, a mullah reading from a book – images she had seen so often since she had come to Cairo. She picked up each one in turn. Rough in texture, the lines on their faces, their body language captured so perfectly. The face of the young woman sieving rice was caught in a smile, head turned as though she shared her chore with others. Maha picked out five pieces and the man's face shone with joy. He put aside his work and wrapped each piece in newspaper. They agreed on a price but then he signalled for her to wait. He disappeared into the darkness of his shop and came back with a small box. He lifted out another figure. It was the head of a woman, her face framed with a grey shawl that fell softly around a sleeping baby. Maha touched the folds of the shawl and the forehead of the child. The man was unwrapping a second piece and he put it into her hand. The same, but this time two babies lay in the mother's arms. Astonished, she looked at him, searching his face, but saw only beads of light reflected in his dark eyes. The man closed her fist around the second figure and went back to chipping at the clay.

The hour passed slowly and she waited outside the gates in the scant shade they afforded. So many thoughts raced around her mind; she let them go, their meaning too much for her to handle. A child's voice squealed and somewhere a baby was crying. No other noise disturbed the quiet. She heard the bolt being pulled back and the old woman emerged and put her finger to her lips. She took

Maha's arm; they began to walk along the street. Shouts came from within the orphanage walls; two people were arguing. The bent old woman gave a throaty gurgle and turned in the direction of the angry exchange. She emitted a glob of phlegm that landed on the pavement in a frothy smear.

'Where are we going? Who are you?' Maha asked, holding onto the thin arm with its loose folds of skin.

'So beautiful.' The woman touched Maha's cheek as she had done before. 'Tafida,' she said and pointed to herself. 'Come now, come.'

They walked round a corner, each step marked by the tap of a stick. Tafida stopped, looked up at the different villas. She retraced her steps to where a new block of flats was under construction. There were piles of sand and building materials but no workers. Wooden scaffolding made patterns against the sky.

Tafida called out a name and a *boab* came up from the half-built concrete basement. They spoke in quiet voices, the guttural dialect made it difficult for Maha to understand. She heard the name Mavette and the man was pointing along the road. When he walked away Tafida sank onto a pile of bricks out of the glare of the sun. Her lips were blue and her chest heaved. She held onto Maha to keep herself upright.

Like holding pieces of a jigsaw, Maha thought, looking down at her hands, but the pieces are devoid of pictures so she didn't know how they fitted. What was she doing here, sitting on a building site with an old lady whom she didn't even know? A yellow bucket lay on its side. Next to it was a split bag of cement, its contents spilled, caught by puffs of breeze. She had just wanted to see her name in a register, to see it written down so she knew she existed but, now, she knew herself even less than she did before. She felt the urge to abandon Tafida and leave all this behind but she stayed where she was, worried by Tafida's sonorous breathing.

The *boab* appeared with three glasses of *chai* on a brass tray. Always the ritual of tea. Tafida swallowed the sickly fluid in noisy gulps and slowly recovered, her wheezing eased but her voice was cracked.

'Mavette,' she said as she stroked Maha's hand. 'Since she was fifteen, she was a maid to the lady who lived here. There was a big house. But now,' she said, throwing her hand towards the building, 'she is dead. The *boab* just told me. I didn't know.'

'Mavette is dead?' Maha's voice was small.

'Not Mavette. The woman is dead. He says now she works for the woman's daughter.' They both looked at the man who squatted beside them and he nodded and pointed.

'Tafida, please, is Mavette...? Are we twins? Is it what you were trying to tell me?' She struggled to use the Arabic *Taw' am*. Even to think twin in her head seemed unreal.

'*Aiwa*,' Tafida gurgled her reply. 'Such pretty babies.'

'But how do you know? Are you our...' Maha knew she had to ask but the question stuck in her throat, 'mother?' It was more of a gulp than a word.

Tafida lifted her head, the bead-like eyes puckered under drooping eyelids. She pulled Maha towards her. 'Poor thing. No, you poor thing. I am not your mother. The children in that place, they have no family, they only have each other.' She was exhausted by the effort of speaking and Maha felt her wheezy breath against her shirt. The stale smell of age drifted around her.

'I remember when they brought you in. So tiny. I have been there for...' Tafida held up one hand, the fingers spread out, 'fifty years. My husband, he is the *boab*. He takes care of everything. Now he is very old.'

The two women clung to each other, each with their own thoughts. Eventually Tafida pushed herself away and said, 'Now we will go and find Mavette.' And she struggled to her feet, wincing to straighten her legs.

'How far is it, Tafida? I will go and get a taxi.' Maha eased the old woman back onto the bricks and ran out to the road. '*Tax, Tax*,' she shouted, waving her hands as a battered black and white cab pulled up beside her. Tafida sank onto the seats but beamed at Maha. 'Very nice,' she said, stroking the upholstery. 'Very nice.'

Maha realised with a jolt Tafida might never have been in a taxi before. Just when she thought she was beginning to absorb Egypt she was reminded she knew so little, that her upbringing had been so different. She rubbed at the dusty stain on the knee of her trousers from when she had stumbled at the orphanage; she only succeeded in making it worse. Was Mavette who that bully of a man was hiding? But why? What if Tafida has it all wrong? 'Tafida, what will I say to Mavette? Does she know about me? Will she want to know about me? What if she's angry – hates me?' Tafida's thin hand patted her own. Maha slumped in her seat. What about tomorrow and the rest of their lives?

*But she may be your twin sister.* The loudest voice in her head defeated the doubts.

The house they arrived at was only minutes away; for Maha, it was like she had travelled from a world she knew to another place, where a different life played out.

It was a low, two-storey villa with brown shutters on the lower windows. Grass lined the central path beyond the metal gates and a gardener was hoeing the dry soil. Water from a hosepipe flooded into the road. He opened the gate. Maha was trembling. She held onto Tafida, leaning into her for support.

Somewhere in there was her sister. The house was swaying, doors and windows blurring. 'Wait, Tafida, wait. I just need a minute.' The old woman leant on her stick and took Maha's hand to pull her gently round to the back of the house where it was shaded and cool. Tafida knocked, her knock resounding inside. Footsteps approached, hollow sounds, in the space beyond the door.

Maha could only stare, her eyes fixed on the black metal doorknob as it began to turn. Heat fled her body. Black hair framed the sallow face that looked out, dark smudges underlined the eyes. The woman's eyes flicked over the two people who stood in front of her. She wore a deep blue dress with a gold necklace and matching earrings. She was about fifty. 'Yes,' she said, 'what is it you want?' Her tone was brittle and wary.

Maha couldn't speak.

'*Sabah al-khair*, madam. We are looking for Mavette.' Tafida paused. 'This is her sister,' she said, thrusting Maha forward.

The woman's eyes were wide and the drop of her earrings swung without sound. 'Her sister?' She spoke with a clotted voice and Maha found herself looking up.

'Yes,' she said. 'I believe Mavette may be my twin sister. Until today I didn't know she existed. It is as much a shock to me as it appears to be to you. I have been living in England.'

The woman was scrutinising her, nodding; some colour had returned to her cheeks. She answered in English. 'She is my maid. Yes, I can see the likeness. It is like looking at Mavette except – for the clothes,' she finished lamely. 'But...' the woman put her hand on Maha's shoulder, releasing a light flowery perfume, 'you'd better come with me.'

They followed her to a low outhouse butted up against the back wall. It had a red door and a small window where a blue-flowered curtain kept out the sun. She reached for a key that hung on a nail, unlocked the door and pushed it open. Hot trapped air rushed out and sunshine, darting in, lit up the patterned linoleum.

Clothes lay strewn everywhere: a dress tossed on top of a cupboard, underwear beside a worn-down sandal on the floor. The mattress was sideways across the bed, the base exposed. The only chair had its back broken and one of its legs protruded from a rent in the pillow like a knife in a victim's back.

Maha crumpled onto the metal springs of the bed.

'She disappeared five days ago. She didn't turn up for work and we came to look. This is what we found. I'm sorry.'

Tafida was sobbing outside the door. '*Inshallah*,' she kept repeating, each time her wail becoming louder.

'She was a good maid. She has been with us since my mother died. We know she was demonstrating. We have searched the hospitals but she's not there. These are such bad times. Who knows where she might be? Soon I will have to employ a new maid.'

Maha could hear her talking but could only watch the sunbeams flit in crazy shapes beside the discarded shoe.

'Tafida must go back,' she said eventually, 'but she can't walk. I will get a taxi.'

The woman picked the dress off the cupboard and hung it on a hook. 'No, you stay a while, I will see to her. I will get her taken home.'

Maha went to the door and put her arms around Tafida, stilling her wails.

'Thank you – for today. I will find her, then I will come to you,' she whispered into the thin hair on Tafida's head. She lifted the old woman's scarf and arranged the black folds softly around her face. She kissed her forehead and allowed Tafida to be led away.

Maha went back into the small room. She pulled out the grotesque chair leg and let it roll across the floor. She buried her face in the pillow, wanting to find Mavette but only stale urine met her nostrils.

There was a photograph in a cracked frame. It was of a young man, his white shirt open at the neck. He was smiling into the camera. She looked at it for a long time before she set it straight on top of the cupboard. As she righted the mattress she pulled at some pink tissue paper trapped beneath it. From it fell a child's yellow cardigan; each button was a different flower. First there was a daisy, then a poppy, then a blue cornflower. Maha knew their order off by heart. It had been a favourite; she had worn hers again and again. This one had never been worn.

Tucked inside was a card; a kitten in a hat was saying happy birthday and inside, her own mother's writing.

*To dear Mavette*
*With Lots and Lots of Love*
*XXX*

'Mavette *is* my sister,' she whispered. She didn't know how long she sat there but the sun moved out of the doorway across to the window making a bright garden of the faded flowers on the curtain.

She stood up and undid the buttons of her shirt, slipping it off so it lay in a circle at her feet. She took off her white trousers, placing them on the bed beside the little cardigan. She walked barefoot across the worn floor and lifted the cotton dress off the hook. She put it over her head and let it fall to her shoulders and hips. She tied the belt in a knot around her waist. She stood, her arms hanging loosely at her sides, and looked at the photograph of the young man in its broken frame. Pirouetting, she lifted her eyes to the small mirror on the wall.

'Hello, Mavette.'

*I have been staying with Granny but I've come home for my birthday. Mum and Dad lead me upstairs and make me close my eyes as they open my bedroom door.*

*'Now,' Dad says, taking his hands off my face. Holly Hobby with her big blue bonnet is dancing over the walls, the curtains and the bedspread. A bright pink cushion, in the shape of a heart, rests in my newly painted cane chair and a Holly Hobby doll sits on my bed. Aged six, nothing to me, has ever looked so beautiful. I run and jump onto the bed, bouncing up and down as Mum and Dad stand laughing at me.*

That was the birthday she was given her yellow cardigan with the flower buttons.

Maha took off the simple cotton dress and put on her own clothes again. She hung the dress back on the nail and put the sandals together. She collected pens and pencils from the floor and put them in a pot and stacked the broken chair in a corner. 'For when you come home,' she murmured. The last thing she did was to smooth out the tissue paper and carefully wrap up the cardigan, touching each button one more time. Then she tucked it under the mattress where she had found it.

She closed the door and turned the key but as it clicked she turned it back, pushing open the door again. She took a pencil from the pot and looked around for a scrap of paper. There was only a calendar on the wall, still turned to September. A red circle marked one of the dates. It was the date she'd come to Cairo. She liked that it had been a special day for her twin too – maybe an anniversary or something. She flicked back a month and as neatly as she could she tore off a strip from the bottom of the page and wrote down the address of her apartment adding just her name. She placed it on the chest of drawers. She hesitated, then lifted from her bag the figure of the woman holding the two babies and set it on top of the piece of paper. It was the only ornament in the room.

Back in the bedlam of the street she could barely think of what to do or how to get home. The *adhan*, the call to prayer began, its ancient resonance rooting her to a past she could not remember, binding her to a future she could not perceive. The melodious sound stilled her and she pressed her hand to her chest, cradling her aching heart.

She rang Hosni. The phone rang and rang then she heard a sharp, 'Yes.'

'Hosni, are you anywhere near the orphanage? Please can you pick me up and take me home?'

'I'm not in Cairo, Maha, I will call tomorrow.' He sounded tense and she could hear the engine noise from his taxi.

'Hosni, are you OK?'

'Yes, I will call tomorrow.' The phone went dead. She looked at the mobile in her hand and wondered whether to call him back but sensed it was not a good time. She took another taxi. The driver was morose but that suited her. She didn't want to make conversation with a stranger.

Mohammed was hovering and he waved a folded piece of paper at her when she stepped out of the taxi.

'From Mister Masud for Miss.' This was the first time Maha had seen him smile and he seemed pleased at his attempt at English words. 'For Miss,' he repeated, and thrust the paper forward. 'Thank you, Mohammed.' She was too weary to say more and she didn't want to be bothered with Masud either. She waited until she was inside before she glanced at the handwritten note.

151

*I think I owe you a nice dinner.*
*My driver will pick you up at 7 p.m.*
*Masud*

'Well, I'm not going,' she shouted at his signature. 'Who do you think you are that you presume I will jump at your every command? I don't need your simpering excuses today.' She was screaming now. 'Do you hear me, Mister Masud? I don't need you.' She ran into her bedroom, kicked off her shoes and fell on the bed, burying her face.

Mr Nessim, the other hateful man, Tafida; she thumped the pillow, embracing anger, as the faces paraded before her. I have a sister, Mavette, a sister I was so close to finding. The presence of loss became more crushing than absence. It flattened her, drove the energy from her core. It pushed her into a space peopled by shapes bleached of colour.

She must have slept because she woke feeling cold in the dim amber light. She tried to hold onto the images that had peppered her dreams, of Mavette, of herself, but they slipped from her grasp as sleep receded. There was something she didn't want to think about, a realisation wheedling itself forward. Her gaze flitted across the ceiling, not wanting to let the devastating thought grow but it was there all the time, getting bigger.

They knew about Mavette; she was a secret they kept. Why Mum? Why Dad? How dare they? She was my sister, my twin sister. Why did they do that to us, split us apart? How could they have been so cruel? Maha didn't want the anger to take root but it squeezed her heart in a physical pain. They had always told her she was special, that they had been desperate for a baby. Yes, so desperate they put their own selfish needs first. Why didn't they adopt them both or some other baby altogether? Why, why, why? The thoughts swirled in circles until only silent tears eased the ache.

A knock on the door of the apartment made her sit upright. Oh God, Masud, she remembered. She wiped her wet cheeks with her sleeve and opened the door. A man in a suit was standing outside with Mohammed who loitered behind.

'I'm not ready. I mean, I'm not coming. Please tell Masud, I send my apologies.'

'He says I must wait for you whatever.' His English was good. The man gave her half a smile. 'I will be in the car.' He turned and ran down the steps, taking them two at a time. She was left looking at Mohammed, who just shrugged and followed the man down the stairs.

# Chapter 25

She didn't need to go; he would eventually get tired of waiting but her conscience pricked. Cursing good manners, she rummaged in her rucksack for a voile dress she had put in at the last minute and hadn't worn since arriving in Cairo.

Fortunately, it didn't need to be ironed but she hung it in the steamy bathroom while she had a shower. 'I'm not hurrying,' she said out loud and let the warm water cascade over her face and shoulders. Some of her tiredness washed away but her head was still full of the day as she dressed. The feel of that other dress came back to her.

Night had fallen when she left the apartment but the air was warm. She gazed across the rooftops of Cairo to the distant skyline. 'Somewhere, somewhere, Mavette, you are out there.'

Mohammed's wife was cooking; a spicy pungency drifted across the courtyard. The man in the car was asleep, but he woke instantly and leapt to open the back door for her. His head nodded and he grinned. Caution made her hesitate, her hand on the door. Mohammed's low voice came from close by, the Arabic words reaching her. 'I know this man, it is all right, miss. He is Masud's driver. He will take you to him.' She looked round at Mohammed – he indicated she should get in.

The car was negotiated onto the dual carriageway and they headed in the direction of the airport. Mavette, where are you? She wondered how different tonight might have been had she found her sister. A sister – she didn't dare to believe. She wanted to think about her but she didn't know how to, the emotion was too new, too raw. She began to shiver as the car's air conditioning blasted out cold air. Rather than initiate conversation with Masud's driver she hugged her arms and hoped there wasn't far to go.

They turned into a long drive lined by trees, lit by the soft glow of uplights. Once through the avenue brighter lights illuminated a stylish hotel. Lanterns hung from each of the arches and the Egyptian flag, flanked by those of many other countries, hung from tall flagpoles set in a round bed of flowers.

The warm fragrance of the night clothed her as she stepped from the car and entered the hotel's cool interior. A vision of gold and white made her pause. Crystal chandeliers sparkled light onto the plush sofas while exotic bird of paradise flowers, arranged in tall vases, punctuated the foyer with their brilliance.

Mavette will never have been here, nor Hosni, nor Mohammed. A quirk of fate or fortune enabled her to be. Was that right? Was she a fraud, an interloper in a world that shouldn't have been hers? Born into one culture, brought up in another; everywhere there are people like her. 'Who are we?' she said as she caught sight of herself in a gilded mirror: young and slim, her naturally olive skin tanned lightly by the Egyptian sun, her black hair and dark eyes complimented by the yellow dress.

'You look very beautiful tonight. Thank you for coming.' Masud was standing beside her, holding a single rose. He gave it to her with a small bow. 'Let us go through.' He led her into a sumptuous restaurant, his hand resting lightly beneath her elbow. Attentive staff greeted him warmly and showed them to a secluded table that looked out across the swimming pools.

She was angry with this man and suspicious of his motives, she reminded herself. She wasn't going to be lured by this show of wealth.

'You are cross with me,' Masud said quietly. She wondered if she had spoken out loud.

'May we use English, your language, tonight? I would like to,' he said. Her language, was he just emphasising a point?

'I wanted to have dinner with you, not to placate you; you are a journalist. I would not insult you in that way. But I wish to explain as best I can. In these turbulent times, sometimes it seems to be an impossible task.'

'I had almost forgotten I am a journalist.' Maha gazed out of the window to where the lights from the hotel were reflected in the opal pools. Palm trees were silhouettes against the navy sky and sunbeds, with umbrellas folded, lay in ordered rows.

'Sorry, I have had...' she didn't know how to describe it, 'an incredible day. No, much more than that, but anyway...'

'Tell me.'

Masud sat opposite; the faint scent of his aftershave drifted across the table. He was watching her intently, his eyebrows meeting where his frown pulled them together.

'No, if you don't mind, I'm not ready to share it with anyone. It's too big. I still need to get used to it all myself.' She watched a young couple who were walking beside the pool pause briefly to kiss. Her throat ached and her eyes were full.

'Perhaps later, when you are ready.' He gently touched her hand. 'I have taken the liberty of ordering for us.' She looked at him and wondered if that would ever happen in England today. She shrugged; it didn't matter, not tonight anyway.

'I have asked my daughter to join us. She will be here soon. I hope you will understand.'

She gave Masud a brief smile. She liked that he had a daughter, a family, it made him more human, and he was making an effort after all.

'Maha, the photographs you found. Yes, I am a member of the National Association for Change, the NAC. It is true that I am an influential member. I am a lawyer and I advise the leader Mr ElBaradei. I am often in his company. That is why we are together in the pictures.'

'So why could you not have been honest and told me from the start? About it all – the man who lived in the apartment – who you are. And that day in the cafe. "This is Maha, our British journalist with the Egyptian name. Perhaps our very useful journalist" were your exact words, I believe. You made me feel uncomfortable. Those men, your friends, another time, they were deliberately intimidating.'

'I have learned to be cautious, but it was thoughtless and I beg your forgiveness.' Masud lifted his glass. 'To honesty. Perhaps we can begin again as friends? But you are right. When I knew what you were, I hoped we could persuade you to write it differently. Many western journalists, they talk about the "Arab Spring" and they think we are all fighting for the same thing – democracy. We are all different countries. Tunisia, Egypt, Libya, we have different histories, cultures and ambitions. In Tunisia the protests came from neglected rural areas into the towns. In Libya it is tribal. Egypt's position is complex. Here the army has enormous influence and is deeply interwoven into the domestic economy. If the rights people yearn for are to be upheld, then the military must be curtailed.' He looked up. 'Ah, here is my daughter.' He rose to greet her and Maha looked round.

She saw a young woman in a red silk dress. The simple lines enhanced her figure. Her hair was swept back from her face, kept in place by a spray of tiny flowers.

'Wahida.' Maha jumped to her feet, knocking a plate to the floor. Other diners stopped eating and looked up.

'So is this what honesty looks like?' Maha said as she picked up her bag to leave, trying to keep her voice under control.

Wahida reached the table and took Maha's hands in her own. 'Please, Maha, wait. Don't go until I have had a chance to…'

'Explain,' Maha finished for her. 'This seems to be the night for explanations. I don't want to hear anymore.'

'Do you remember, Maha, the day that I took you to Imbaba? I made you promise that, whatever, you would always know I was your friend. This is why, because one day I knew you would find out. I couldn't tell you then – for many reasons. For me, there was one reason, more than any other. We were just two friends. I liked you and I think you liked me; you liked me as Wahida, not as my father's daughter. It meant a lot.' Masud put his arm around his daughter and kissed her on the top of her head.

A waiter came to straighten the table and asked if he could serve. Maha saw their anxious faces and she sat down again, resting her head on her hand to stop the wave of dizziness. She shut her eyes to close out the light; the voices seemed to be far away. A glass of water was put into her hand and she sipped at the ice-cold liquid.

Neither Masud nor Wahida spoke. She could feel Wahida's hand still holding her own. She was tired, so tired. For a moment the vision of a little yellow cardigan wrapped in tissue paper danced before her eyes. She lifted her head.

'It seems we have a lot to say to each other.' She grimaced, took a deep breath and let her shoulders relax.

'Yes, we have given you a big shock and I am sorry,' Masud said. 'But first we will eat and I will enjoy being in the company of two beautiful young ladies.'

The waiter brought grilled shrimp set on a bed of rice with fresh salad leaves. Maha hadn't thought she could eat but as the delicate fragrance of the food reached her nostrils she began to feel hungry.

'These are Aboukir Bay shrimps,' Masud told her, 'the best in the world. Then we will have beef fillet because I think in England you like your beef. A fusion of our cultures, is it not?'

She smiled. 'Yes, it seems easier to achieve in food than it is for me. Sometimes I feel British, at other times I touch my Egyptian roots. All I know for certain tonight is that I exist. The rest has become blurred.' The candle on the table flickered, moved by an invisible draught.

She took a breath. 'Tonight my head is filled with information I learned today. I will tell you briefly. I think I do need to say it out loud so I can believe it's true. Until now I have always thought of myself as an only child. Today I discovered I have a sister, a twin sister. She disappeared five days ago. That is my story.'

She caught the glance Masud and Wahida exchanged. Wahida placed her hand on her father's arm as he went to speak.

She said quickly, 'I too am an only child. I cannot imagine what your discovery must have felt like.'

'At the moment it is overwhelming, which is why I have to have time to think; it's too soon for me to work out all the implications but I needed to tell someone.' Maha sipped her wine to give herself space. 'Perhaps tomorrow, Wahida, I can tell you what happened when I visited the orphanage. But not tonight, it's too new.'

'We understand. When you are ready.' Father and daughter both nodded. 'We can talk of other matters.'

'Thank you.' Maha gave them half a smile. 'Before you joined us, Wahida, your father was telling me about his role and Egypt's fight for democracy.'

Wahida spoke quietly, 'It is the fight of all of us. We share the desire for a responsive government and for personal dignity.' She paused, her fork in the air. 'I am part of the NAC not because of my father but because of what it stands for.'

'Is Egypt not moving in the right direction with the promise of free elections?' Maha was trying to grasp what was being said, but her feeling of disorientation persisted and she had to force herself to concentrate.

'It's what people think,' Masud answered. 'Democracy is much more than that and unless a country has the infrastructure in place it will fail. Egypt doesn't have the building blocks yet.

'How is your beef, Maha? Is it good?'

'Thank you, it's delicious.' She looked at father and daughter. Masud, so suave, an intellectual who fought with words; Wahida, so pretty, so young and so earnest – united in a cause linking the generations, all striving for change that would take more than a lifetime to achieve.

'In the UK we have democracy but we take it all for granted, at least it feels that way. People have become disillusioned with politics, so instead of trying to make improvements through the system they have become apathetic. Many no longer bother to vote. When I hear of your struggle it makes me feel ashamed.'

Masud nodded and added in a low voice, 'I believe there is a threat we all face, one that doesn't yet have a name but that will rise out of those countries where there is even greater unrest, places like Iran and Syria. Now is the time for western governments to initiate action.

'Come,' he said, leaning back in the chair. 'Enough of politics tonight. Tell me what you like about your Cairo?'

'My Cairo.' Maha laughed. 'I like the sound of that. There is much I love and much I have yet to discover. But so little time left. I have booked a flight home next Wednesday – I don't know what to do now. Maybe I will change it, look for my sister Mavette, but she may not even want to know me. I promised my mother I would be back for her birthday.' She felt a pang of pain as she thought about her mother. What would they say to each other?

'I will come back.' She looked across to where a breeze ruffled the surface of the swimming pools, the reflections shimmering and dancing. 'I want to find my sister.' The words were almost a whisper, spoken more to herself than anyone else.

'Maha, your sister...'

'Papa.' Wahida's voice was sharp.

'We will make enquiries. That is what I was about to say.'

'You must come back soon and when you do you will stay with us.' Wahida covered Maha's hand with her own. 'And I will come to London. Remember you are going to take me to the Tate Modern and I want to see the Tower of London and Buckingham Palace.'

Masud laughed. 'You are schemers and dreamers, and why not? Now we must get you home safely. Maha, take care. There are more demonstrations planned and the mood is ugly. I tell my daughter this all the time. She thinks I don't know where she goes but I do and I worry as any father would.' His tone was sombre now as he stood up, an arm around each of them.

'Wahida, before I go, there is just one thing I need to know. The day we met. Near Tahrir Square.'

'Hosni sent me.' Wahida pulled a face. 'He said I should look after you.'

'Hosni, he too...?'

'Hosni is a valuable member of our group. He is a good man; he works hard. It was he who...' Masud hesitated, 'put you in contact with me, remember?'

'Thank you for dinner.' Unsmiling, she looked at them both. 'I feel as though I am caught in a spider's web and I'm not sure who the spider is.'

She let herself into the apartment, the alien scent of its previous occupant still present. Without putting on the lights she sought the sanctuary of her bedroom, pulled off her dress, and climbed between the sheets, their coolness as soothing as a wet flannel on a hot brow.

Her mind probed places she didn't want it to go. Thoughts paraded themselves like soldiers but she jammed her eyes shut, seeing only colours and shapes behind her closed lids. She would think about it all tomorrow.

# Chapter 26

There was a shout and Maha felt the sheets pulled tighter around her. Her arms flailed, her legs fought to free themselves from the corkscrew of material. She slipped to the floor, banged her head on the wall and jolted herself awake. There was no one there, the shout she realised had been her own. Her dream crept elusively into the dark corners of the room, its effect real but its form blurred.

She used to have nightmares as a child. Always about kings and queens. Her dad would come into her bedroom and put on the light; he had made a big game of looking under the bed and banging on the curtains. Her sobs became laughs, and the two of them would crawl around the room on all fours to search for crowns or any jewels that might have been left behind. They never found any of course but by the time Dad tucked her back into bed all her fear would have gone.

She hadn't dreamt about kings and queens this time and there was no Dad to make it better. Grief was a widow's veil draped over her. She pulled on a sweater and went out onto the balcony. She didn't sit on the chair. 'It's for you, Mavette,' she whispered as she squeezed between two ceramic pots and sat on the tiles with her back to the wall.

She pulled at the dried remains of a plant. It crumbled in her hands, and she thrust it through the railings and watched the bits float down, visible only in the light from the street lamp.

She stared at the chair and the shadow that rested on it. Why her, why was she the chosen twin? Did Mavette know about her? Where is she now? What would it be like to have so few possessions, to be a maid to someone all your life? She tried to place herself in that small room. Had she gone to school? Did she love it like me? She thought of her own high school with its smart uniform all the pupils pretended to hate; her friends, the sleepovers, giggling away the night. All of it now seemed so pointless in the face of the lie on which it was based. She had been loved, protected, encouraged, always making her parents proud while all the time they knew that they had ripped her away, ripped her...from her twin sister.

'From you.'

With a start Maha remembered her imaginary friend from child-hood. Molly was the name she had given her. She had insisted that there was a place set at the table for Molly, that she had her own toys to play with in the bath. There was the time when her mum had sat on the bed to kiss her goodnight and she had squealed and pushed her away. 'You're squashing Molly. Molly's there.' Her mum had burst into tears and Dad had come running into the room and wrapped his arms around them both. Maha had asked if Molly could have a hug as well because Molly was really sad. Her mother had given a strangled yelp and rushed from the bedroom.

Molly had come to school with her and had been there when other children were horrid. Gradually Maha had learned not to tell other people about her because they got upset or made fun of her and neither she nor Molly liked that. Even as an adult she would occasionally still find herself in conversation with Molly.

She sat with her head on her hands, tossing the names around, Molly, Mavette, Mavette, Molly. What's the effect when you share a womb for nine months, limbs entwined, skin touching skin? The transient sounds of Cairo drifted around her as her thoughts swirled; a bird flew squawking towards a break in the cloud.

She looked at the time on her phone. Quickly she sent off a text.

*I know about Mavette.*

Her mum would be going to bed, might even be there already.

Perhaps the ping will wake her and she will read the words in the shadowy darkness and the night will make her afraid.

She turned her own phone off and searched the sky for a dawn she wasn't ready for. She pushed at the chair with her foot to turn it away from her. The shadow shifted, growing in size. She leant her head on her drawn-up knees. She wanted to shut it all out. 'I want you to hurt like I am hurting.' Her voice was a whisper. Now she knew why her mother was frightened when she had told her she was coming to Cairo. Her reaction had upset her at the time. Maha had hoped she would understand why she needed to go. But of course her mother was scared, wasn't she? That she might be found out, that her secret might be exposed, laid bare. Who had she been more scared for, her daughter or herself? Why hadn't she told her?

Her mother: clapping at her school concert; standing in the freezing rain watching her play hockey; daubing her with calamine lotion when she had chickenpox; mopping up the blood when she broke her nose. She shook her head to chase away the images. Who had stayed up with her all night when her first boyfriend had dumped her and life had been over? Who had come to London, because she hadn't wanted Maha to be alone on the first anniversary of her dad's death? Her mum had always been there for her. Until now she thought they had always been close.

Her churning thoughts were interrupted by a shout from a car and an answering call from some unseen figure. A dog woken by the noise began to bark into the darkness. She felt the cold from the tiles seep into her, her limbs becoming numb as faces formed pictures in her brain, a film she couldn't stop.

As a small arc of lightening sky pushed above the skyline her mum's words of a few days ago came back to her. 'I am writing you a letter.'

She felt like she stood at a crossroads. She didn't know which way to go. She turned her phone back on and punched in her message.

*I still love you, Mum. x*

She read it, feeling calmer now and more in control.

How magnanimous, a voice was saying, so now your love is to be conditional? What did she mean – 'still love you' – despite – despite what? Either she did or she didn't.

Already a pastel sun had sailed from behind the apartments opposite, to begin its journey across the sky. Tentative rays of warmth brushed the balcony, touching Maha and the empty chair.

She deleted the 'still' and pressed the send button.

She didn't remember going back to bed and falling asleep but she must have because she woke to the sound of her name being shouted below her window.

'Maha, are you there? Maha.' It was Hosni and his voice was urgent. Maha swept the damp hair from her face, feeling stuffy and hot. Bright daylight suffused the room; the window framed a cobalt blue sky. She looked at her watch, struggling to make sense of the hands that said it was nearly two o'clock in the afternoon. She pushed open the window and saw Hosni and Mohammed staring up at her.

'I've been asleep,' she said. 'Sorry, dead to the world. What's the matter?'

'You make me scared. I've rung already three times but you don't answer. And we were knocking on the door.' Hosni was shielding his eyes with his hand and Mohammed nodded vigorously, his hand demonstrating a knocking action.

'I'm OK, honestly, I was very tired. Thank you for coming to look for me.'

'Come down and we will go for a drive together.' The words sounded thin and strained.

'Can you give me five minutes, Hosni, I need a shower,' she called, but she sensed his tension. He agreed, turned away and walked towards Mohammed's room.

These showers were punctuating her life, she thought, as she towelled herself dry. They divided up episodes. Was it only yesterday that she was at the orphanage, then taking that other quick shower before she went to meet Masud?

She found her phone on the floor of the balcony where she must have left it last night. There were three missed calls from Hosni, but still nothing from her mum. Last night she wanted her to hurt as she was hurting. Now she just wanted to talk to her. The two men were squatting in the shade when she went downstairs. Mohammed handed her a small cup of coffee. She swallowed the thick strong liquid, the sweet but bitter taste lingering in her mouth. Hosni had already begun to walk towards his taxi. 'Hosni, what has happened to you, what have you done to your face?' He turned away but she had already seen the purple bruise, his swollen nose and the cut lip.

He drove without replying, past the Blue Mosque, the Citadel, and the park where she had met with Wahida and Salma.

'I will tell you soon.' His hands gripped the steering wheel and she could see his grazed knuckles.

She sat in silence to give him space, to respect his need for quiet. The beige-coloured city had given way to a dusty desert road along which lorries travelled at frightening speed, their horns blaring. They drove for nearly an hour and she was glad when he turned onto a rutted track and headed across the sand. He stopped when the track petered out and rested his head on the steering wheel breathing deeply.

'I love this place,' he said. 'We used to come here as children before my father died. Come, I will show you.'

The heat was reflected off the sand and penetrated the thin soles of her sandals, but the air was clear and a warm breeze tugged at her hair. She followed Hosni to the edge of a high cliff and they looked down into a narrow wadi formed by a long-vanished watercourse. Boulders bleached by the sun shone white, dark shadows had drawn an outline around their base. 'When it rains water still rushes down here and then the desert turns green and flowers bloom. It is beautiful; by the next day it has all gone.' Hosni sat on the sand drawing patterns with a stick. She sat beside him absorbing the peace; another view to consign to memory.

'First it was a piece of paper put under my door.' Hosni threw a pebble into the wadi; the sound of it bouncing off the rocks echoed in the chasm. 'The four-fingered hand of the Muslim Brotherhood. It could only have come from one person. I didn't show it to Chavi, I didn't want to frighten her. Then he came, my brother. It was late in the evening, Kamillah was asleep. He was puffed up like...like a film star and he strutted around the room touching things, our things, giving low whistles. He wanted money. He said there were plans, big plans, but he wouldn't say what.' Hosni picked at a scab on his knuckle and a globule of bright red blood oozed out. He smeared it across his hand.

'I wouldn't give him any, told him he was on his own now, that I didn't agree with his politics. He got angry, smashed a pot against the wall.' Hosni shrugged his shoulders. 'Well, we fought, other possessions got broken. Eventually he left. Chavi was crying.'

Maha used a tissue to wipe the blood from Hosni's hand.

'What can I do? He will come back. Yesterday I took Kamillah and Chavi to Ismailia. Chavi has a cousin there. She can stay with her for a while.'

'Hosni, I am so sorry, and after all you have done for him.'

'It means nothing now. The Muslims, mostly they want to find a peaceful way too but he is with a bad lot. They see power; they see an opportunity to promote their extremist views. Our country will go backwards, sink into autocracy, and become an Islamic caliphate.'

The sun was now a huge red ball, sinking lower in the sky. It wrapped the cliffs in a dusky pink hue. Shadows lengthened and cast shapes across the wadi floor.

'Hosni is talking only about himself. Tell me now about you.' He looked up at her and she winced at the sight of his lip, raw where the edges had yet to begin to heal.

'Enough for now about me,' he said, sensing her reluctance to move on. 'Tell me about yesterday.'

'Firstly, I can't believe it was only yesterday, it feels like a lifetime ago.' Maha hesitated. It was difficult to form the words. 'I have a sister, Hosni, a twin sister. An old woman from the orphanage – she remembered me. Can you believe that? She took me to meet my sister but she has disappeared.' She couldn't disguise the catch in her voice and Hosni began to say something but stopped, his breath collapsing into the space.

'Hosni, I know about Masud and Wahida and how you know each other. They told me last night.'

He nodded. 'It was not for me to tell you. So many secrets, secrets and lies.' He walked to the edge of the wadi and stared down into the darkened depths.

'Yesterday,' she said as she joined him, 'I just wanted to find my sister but today everything seems confused. I want to find her, but why, I keep asking myself? Yesterday I wanted to be able to buy her some nice clothes, give her some jewellery, books, take her to England sometime in the future and show her... show her what? Where I had been brought up? Show her what she has missed out on, introduce her to the mother she didn't have? How arrogant am I to think that somehow my life has been better than hers, that possessions are so important? Hosni, I know nothing about her, I don't even know if she knows she once had a sister. How dare I waltz into her life and think she'll welcome it? Would she even want to acknowledge me? Now the hardest part is wondering what has happened to her. I keep thinking of what Wahida's friend Salma went through and it makes me so scared and so angry. Is she in prison? Worse, is she... dead?' She finished with a sob. 'All these thoughts fill up my head.'

'She will be all right, she...' Hosni was drawing shapes in the sand. 'Leave it a few days and you will know what to do. Me the same, with my brother, that is the way of things.'

'I wish I could be so certain, Hosni, but thank you anyway. I feel better just having shared it.'

'Me too, you are a good friend to Hosni. This place, I wanted to bring you here. Always it has helped me to put things right.' He tapped his head with his hand and cautiously massaged the violet bruise.

She felt the evening air begin to cool. A small brown bird hopped near to them, bobbing its tail in time with its head. The wadi was shrinking into its own space and all around the desert reached for the horizon. A transparent moon, a faint outline in the sky, had begun its ascent. She brushed Hosni's wrist lightly with her hand and for the briefest of moments he covered hers with his own.

'We will be all right. I pray to Allah my country will be too.' He walked back to the car leaving flat imprints in the sand.


Cairo's skyline was still a smudged outline when they were forced to a stop by police. One leant smoking on an oil drum while another, a youth, his face more childlike than mature, stuck his head through the window. His rifle clattered against the side of the car. He demanded to know their business in Cairo. Hosni stared straight ahead, said he was taking his passenger to Heliopolis and revved the engine. The youth backed away and stood by the roadside, in his too big uniform.

He let them pass.

More road blocks had been set up on the outskirts of the city, and vehicles driven by the army and security forces were pushing into Cairo.

Hosni's face was grim; he banged the steering wheel with his hand and muttered words that Maha could only sense the meaning of. People defiant of the curfew ran down the roads. Junctions became blocked as numbers increased. Hosni swung the car round and drove along streets where buildings leant inwards and obliterated the sky.

'Stay in tonight, stay away from the balcony. There is trouble.' He left her at the apartment. Neither Mohammed nor his wife came out of their room but the remnants of the fire glowed amongst charred wood.

# Chapter 27

There was a pink envelope wedged between the door and the door post: her mother's letter? In her hand it seemed to grow in size. She held it against her chest, afraid to let the contents escape. What had her mother written? How would she feel when she read it? She turned it over but it wasn't from her mother. The writing was none that she recognised. She trembled as she prised it open. It was a card with a picture of a cute little bear holding a bunch of flowers, and inside a beautiful pressed red rose, its petals like velvet. A musky smell; she was a little girl making perfume from fallen rose petals – the memory danced in her head.

*Sending you a hug* the words on the card said and underneath James had written *'because I want to'* and in brackets: *(a whole bunch to come – see you at the airport.)*

Only four more days in Egypt, then she would go back to London to pick up her life. The flat she had once shared with Robin; she would sort all that out. He hadn't taken all his clothes when he left. They still hung in a wardrobe. She would pack them up, return them to him. She wondered if he had moved on and if someone else's toothbrush now stood beside his. She realised, as she wiped the dust-smeared window and the muezzin began his baleful call to prayer, that she didn't care. All of it's a million miles away. Who was Maha, the journalist, anyway? Who was she now?

She picked up the rose. She felt she knew James better than she'd known any man before – but they'd never been lovers. A little voice of uncertainty persisted – what if his memory of her was exaggerated, what if he was disappointed, what if she was? Maha breathed in the flower's scent and reread the card; she felt a thrill run through her. It will be all right. We will be all right. She waltzed around the room holding the card like a dance partner. She stood the card on the sideboard and placed the rose in front of it. She flicked on the television but the screen was blank. Only mournful music came forth. Phone networks interrupted, the internet down again. Never mind, it would go later.

*Dear James, I have just opened your beautiful card with the rose. I can't tell you how happy it makes me feel. It came just at the right time.*

*James, incredibly I have a sister, a twin sister. It seems too surreal to even type the words. But she's disappeared. Her employer thinks she has been caught up in the demonstrations. She doesn't...*

She slammed the lid of her iPad shut. She wasn't going to tell James her news by email. She wanted to talk to him. She needed to tell him in person. She hugged her knowledge close. 'Communication channels sabotaged again. So much for free speech,' she shouted towards the open window.

Would she know what to do about her sister if she left it for a few days as Hosni had said? She didn't have a few days that was the problem – four: she counted them out loud. How could she go home ignorant of what had happened to her? She contemplated whether to go to the police or visit the hospitals but she knew she would be ignored, shrugged off. She didn't understand the system enough to know where to start. Worse, could her probing even place Mavette in more danger? Could she return home without trying?

The sudden rapid noise of gunfire rang out, the sound dissipating between the apartment blocks. Over, before she could be sure of what she'd heard. She moved towards the window. People were on their balconies, shouts and gestures of shock passed from one person to another. An army truck screamed down the road. The noise freaked a goat, its bleat pitiful as it ran in terror. A small boy with bare feet chased after it with a stick.

Smoke tainted the air and a plume of grey spiralled into the night like a cloud drifting across the sky. In the distance, orange flames illuminated the darkness and sirens sounded. She shuddered and closed the window, reducing the traffic noise and the familiar night sounds of Cairo. She was trapped, could only stare at her reflection in the glass. Bright stars crowded the sky, their outlines indistinct as she fought back the tears.

She wanted just to sleep, so she went to bed early. She'd gathered up the gifts she had bought and folded a few of her clothes and packed them into her rucksack. She tucked James's card under her pillow, clasped it in her fingers. She resolved to go and see Mavette's employer one more time, to check if there was any news of her. She would dredge up her rusty written Arabic and write Mavette a letter, to tell her who she was and how to make contact. Then Mavette could choose. Maha knew the wait might be endless.


The apartment door was being shaken, someone called her name.

The lock rattled, the noise of the swinging chain loud in the hushed hallway. She jumped out of bed and stood petrified before the door; the muffled voices behind it became more urgent. She opened it on the chain. Hands pushed against the door. Dark figures filled the space, backlit in the shadows of the stairwell.

A man was slumped between two others, his knees buckled, his arms limp, his body kept upright by those supporting him.

Instinct made her open the door wide. They stumbled inside and eased their companion to the floor. Blood pulsed from a wound on his head and the whites of his eyes rolled as they turned him on his side. An odour of sweat and urine rose to choke her as she looked at them, one prone and barely conscious, the other two crouched beside him.

The smaller of the two looked up, pushing off the rakish cap so it fell to the floor. Long hair spilled down over narrow shoulders. Maha stared into a familiar face, features identical to those she had seen in the mirror all her life.

'*Shukran*, Maha.' It was only a whisper, then a hand, fingers stained with blood, reached out to her and Maha took it, felt its warmth in her own. 'Hide him, don't waste time.' The Arabic words were harsh, spat out by the other person. The young man, his face grimed with dirt, was using his scarf to scrub at bloodstains on the floor. 'They will come looking, maybe here too.'

Maha grabbed the key of the spare room, unlocked it, and pushed it open. She cleared a space on the floor. Together they hauled a slashed mattress out from beneath the broken furniture and laid down the injured man.

Angry shouts nearby multiplied in the night. Maha whispered for the trio to be quiet and relocked the room where they huddled. Down in the street she could see men in uniform, maybe four or five, randomly kicking at parked cars and throwing stones at ground-floor windows. Three ran into the apartment block opposite. Two came her way. In the courtyard there was the clatter of boots, loud swearing, and thuds as people's doors were pummelled on the landing below. She heard Mohammed shouting at the men. 'English woman, English.' She knew he was trying to warn her. Fists were hammering on her apartment door, more foul oaths. Mohammed continued to protest.

She grabbed her scarf, wrapped it like a shawl over her nightdress and, willing her voice to sound calm, she shouted in English, 'Wait.'

She fumbled at the door, took her time, pretended to unfasten the chain. She opened it a fraction. Two men in the uniform of the security forces brandished guns. They forced the door wide. It seared across her toes, and she yelped with pain as she was pushed backwards. They ran through the hall into the lounge, banged their guns against the glass of the windows and overturned chairs.

She followed them. She yanked open the drawer of the sideboard and took out her British passport and her press pass, waving them wildly in the men's direction. She slapped them onto the marble top.

'I AM A BRITISH CITIZEN AND A MEMBER OF THE PRESS,' she screamed. 'WHAT THE HELL ARE YOU DOING IN MY APARTMENT? GET OUT.' She pointed to the door and screamed again. 'GET OUT. NOW.'

One of them hesitated, studied her for a moment. The other, an adrenalin-charged youth, swept her passport and pass onto the floor and sneered in her face. She ran back into the hall; the noise that erupted from her mouth gathered force, trapped by the walls. She placed herself in front of the locked door and with a further piercing yell the words tore from her.

'GET THE HELL...' The youth slammed open the door of her bedroom sweeping the butt of his rifle in an arc, probing the space beneath the bed.

'*Imshi, imshi.*' The Arabic insult came from Mohammed. He was hovering outside beside the stair rail, gesturing angrily with his arms.

An urgent yell from the street was drowned by the noise of a vehicle revving loudly. The older soldier answered the shout, he pulled at the younger man and shoved him out of the door.

'Leave the bitch.' Further insults grew faint as the two men ran down the stairs, two at a time. They pushed past Mohammed, raked his shins with their rifles and slapped his face as he buckled.

She stood in the doorway, shivering in her nightdress, clinging to the door post, too shocked to move. Mohammed's breathing was louder as the noise outside receded. He came towards her, his hand to his face but he was grinning, his thumb raised.

'Miss Maha teach me English. Yes? Get the hell...' His accent curled around the words. He prised away her hand and eased her gently inside the apartment, then closed the door, leaving her alone in her own hallway. She heard the slap of his shoes as he went back down the stairs.

They had torn a shirt into strips and were winding it around the man's bloody head when she entered the room. Both stopped as relief flooded their faces. They gestured with their hands in approval of her actions. She could see the injured person was not much more than a boy and his long, damp eyelashes lay dark against his face. His eyes fluttered open; he grimaced weakly as she leant over him. His arm was twisted at an angle by his side and rivulets of sweat or tears streaked down his cheeks. She had brought a glass of water and a flannel. She knelt down and put the glass to his lips, allowing the cold liquid to moisten his tongue. He lay back exhausted.

Maha sat on her heels and looked at the young woman who had taken off her jacket and tied her hair back.

'Mavette?' Maha let the name fall into the space between them. Mavette looked back at her and her eyes acknowledged her name.

'How did you know...where...? I don't understand,' Maha said quietly.

'I have known about you for some time now. From not long after you came to Cairo – I was told – but my mind was unsure what to do. I wanted to think, to be sure I was making the right decision. Tonight we needed a safe house. I said it would be all right, that we could trust you.'

The voice sounded like her own. Warmth suffused Maha's body as she leant forward and wrapped her arms around her sister.

She wanted to go on holding her but said, 'We need to get this boy to hospital, his arm is broken and he needs stitches in his head.'

'No. No hospital.' The other man's words pierced like bullets; his eyes raked Maha's face. With a shock she recognised him as the one who had been so insolent in the cafe. Stung by his tone she recoiled, turned away to escape his stare.

'We will sort him. I will get help,' he said.

Maha looked at Mavette who nodded.

'If he goes to hospital, they will find him. The security forces – they search the hospitals, they will take him and then... We have doctors.'

The young man took Mavette by the shoulder and twisted her round. Words Maha couldn't hear were exchanged as they hovered over their companion, whose moans whistled on his breath, loud, like a *khamsin* that blows in from the desert.

175

'Youseff will go soon. He will get transport. We will take him to a doctor. We are used to it.'

Maha looked at her sister. Their faces were so similar but their lives were a million miles apart. She cringed as Mavette strapped the man's broken arm to his side using a belt. Rags to bite on were stuffed into the boy's mouth as his cries rose. His teeth clamped, his forehead was wet with sweat glistening in a shaft of moonlight, the room's only light.

Maha heard a soft tap on the outside door. 'Psst, Maha. Mohammed.' Another soft tap. 'Psst, it's Mohammed.' She opened it slowly, peered first through a crack, then more fully as she saw Mohammed's face in the darkness. He was holding a tin tray; on it, four glasses of *chai* steamed. He pushed it towards her and winked. As he turned to go back down the stairs she heard him chuckle. 'Get the hell,' he muttered to himself. Despite everything Maha smiled.

Youseff swallowed the thick tea in a single gulp and Maha passed him the spare one that, clearly, the wounded boy could not drink. For the first time his face softened and he whispered, '*Shukran,*' his quiet thank you, a gift to her.

She fetched a bowl of warm water and fresh flannels, bathed their friend's face and neck and removed his shoes from his sockless feet. Nasser, they said his name was. He was conscious; his breathing shallow but more peaceful. Blood still oozed but more slowly now through his makeshift bandage, a red badge on his head.

Youseff and Mavette washed their own faces, wiping them with the flannels, allowing the warm water to soothe.

'I will go and be back before it is light,' Youseff said. 'The fighting will have stopped.'

'Be careful.' Mavette touched his arm lightly and then he was gone.

Left alone, Maha and Mavette were silent, avoiding eye contact. It was too difficult to find words and yet there was so much to say.

'You speak Arabic well.' Mavette was sitting on the floor, her head down and her arms around her knees.

'It was hard when I first came to Egypt but now, with practice, I am getting better. I studied it at university.' Maha stopped, her words faded, their implication dropping into the chasm that separated them.

'It's all right,' Mavette said, and reached across to her. 'Now we have found each other we must not be afraid to speak.'

Maha nodded, her throat ached so she was able only to smile. To give herself time she searched amongst her clothes and found a T-shirt and a towel. 'I'll stay with him if you want a shower and some rest,' she said, indicating her own bed.

'I would like that but only if you will rest beside me. He is quiet, there is no more we can do for now. We will leave the doors open, then we will hear him.'

Nasser whimpered, tossing his head from side to side, and Maha sponged him with a cold cloth so that his hair lay flat and black. She gave him another sip of water and lifted his cold hand into her own.

She felt the faintest response and his eyelids fluttered open, but only for a moment.

She heard the shower being turned off and waited for a few minutes before she joined Mavette in the bed. She slipped under the sheet and they lay together breathing in unison. Certain that Mavette was asleep she gently put out her hand to touch Mavette's shoulder. Her sister's head turned on the pillow to face her.

'Sorry,' she whispered. 'I needed to know you were there, to be sure you were real. Are you here, next to me? In Cairo? I can't believe it. You might have been anywhere.'

'As an orphan and then a maid – well, you don't go far, Maha.'

'No, I suppose not. I'm sorry. All the time growing up I never knew. I only found out about you two days ago. I went to where you live but couldn't find you.'

'I know. When I went back, Madame told me you had been. She said you had straightened my room; that I should go to you.' Mavette's whisper folded into the bedclothes. 'She said you were nice. She has been good to me, they all have. Wahida, Masud, his mother.'

Maha propped her head on her hand, her elbow denting the pillow.

Moonlight flicked across the walls of the bedroom.

'You know them?'

'Yes, of course. Madame, she is Masud's sister. I worked for their mother until she died. It is because of them I joined the NAC.'

'But...'

'I would not let them tell you, Maha. I begged them. I didn't know what to do. How you would see me. It was better I let you go back to England, then eventually we would both have forgotten again.'

'No.' Maha lay back on the pillow, feeling the dampness of her sister's hair. 'Never that.'

Outside on the window ledge a pigeon cooed softly, its call answered by another.

'Mavette, in your room I found a little yellow cardigan wrapped in tissue paper. I...'

'It was the one thing I ever owned that was just mine. I was about six or seven. Tafida, she helped in the orphanage, she was the *boab*'s wife, she brought it to me, I remember. I never knew where it came from but I knew if anyone found it then all the other children would get to wear it and it would be spoilt. It was the only present I've ever been given. For years I hid it behind a loose part of the wall. There was a card with it. I hid that too. I will always keep it. One day I hoped my child...' Mavette paused, the tension palpable, the silence frail.

The young man in the other room cried out and Maha went to him. He was sleeping fitfully; she eased him onto his side and propped his back with a cushion. His head wound seemed to have stopped bleeding and the stain had darkened. She stroked his arm wondering what mattered to him, where he went in his dreams.

'Your card, Mavette.' Maha's words stalled as she returned. 'My... mother sent it. It was her writing. I had a cardigan exactly the same for my sixth birthday. I can't explain it – I never knew – about you.'

178

'There was another time,' Mavette said. 'A parcel came but when I opened it, there was just paper, nothing inside.'

In the dark, Maha's hand sought her sister's.

'Did they tell you about me?'

Mavette paused, remembering; her eyes large in her face. 'I think I was about eight or nine. Tafida, she told me that once I had a twin, someone who looked just the same as me but she had been taken away by a man and a lady. I cried at first because some of the other children had sisters or brothers and I wanted one, too. But it didn't change anything. What could I do? After a few hours, what Tafida had told me slipped from my mind. They had only been words.'

In the quiet Mavette's breathing became deeper and Maha let her sleep. Questions buzzed in her head, the polluted truth of her life making her limbs restless; she watched as shadows striped the wall.

Mavette lay on her side, her feet drawn up. Maha curled around the curve of her back, skin touching skin, their legs entwined. For a moment her nose wrinkled; the smell of boiled cabbage was fleeting. They both slept.

As the ebony sky bruised to purple and night segued into day they came back for him. Youseff brought another young man and together they lifted Nasser to his feet. His cry of pain made Maha run to his side but Mavette pulled her away and shook her head. Youseff hoisted him onto his shoulder and the men fled down the stairs into a waiting car. Like smoke in the wind they were gone. The two girls, left now in the empty hall, took each other's hands. Maha's face crumpled, they hugged and their tears mingled.

'We must clear up in case,' Mavette said, breaking away.

'In case what?' Maha watched her sister fill a bowl with water.

'It is possible the security forces will return. Maybe they know something or nothing but they could come back just to frighten you. Mohammed will look out for you but...'

'Mohammed, is he too part of the group?'

179

'No, no, but he is an honest man.' Mavette stopped, scrubbing at the smeared blood on the floor and looked up at Maha. 'He was angry when Masud gave you this flat. The boy who used to live here was like a son to him. He wanted no one here, especially not a foreign woman. He wants it to be ready for when...' Mavette shrugged, 'if he comes home.'

Stung by her sister's description of her, Maha flinched in the lightening gloom. 'Will he come back?' Her question was stark.

'He was a photographer; he took many pictures. Good pictures. They smashed his camera, they smashed him, destroyed his photographs. They broke his arms. We have to go on. Hope brings optimism. Come, stop talking, we must hide this mattress, cover it with the furniture again.'

They worked hard until all looked as before.

'Youseff, I saw him first in Le Cafe in Heliopolis. He was also angry,' Maha said as they finished.

Mavette's laugh was dry. 'You gave him a shock. He told me it was like seeing me in a different body. He resented you and what you represented.' She paused to rinse out the bloody cloth. 'He says I should marry him but I can't. I can't do it.'

'The photograph by your bed, is that...?' Maha saw Mavette turn away.

'No, it is not Youseff. It is my husband.' She sat down on the floor, her hands in her lap. 'We have been married for five years. He has such plans. He is determined we will have a good life. He wants to be an engineer.'

Maha waited. She could hear the *ful* seller's shout in the street below.

'He said he would go just for two years to make some money. He wants so much for us. For me not to be a maid. He went to Qatar. At first he wrote home every month, money came. He said the work was hard, that it was hot, much hotter than Egypt. Then, after half a year, nothing.' She swiped at a fly that buzzed persistently around her head. 'I have asked his friends, anyone who was there with him, but they don't know. Their eyes are empty.'

180

She stood up and made a face as she retrieved her blood-stained clothes. 'He is the reason I demonstrate, the reason I joined the NAC. So men like him, good men, don't have to go abroad...to be exploited. Their own country, my country, should be enough.'

Her sister's sadness reached inside and became Maha's sadness too.

'I must go.'

'No, don't go so soon.' Maha's choked words were a plea.

'I have to... Madame, she will expect...'

The gulf, like a jagged line, shot between them. Maha's hands hid her face.

'Wait.' She rummaged in her rucksack, pulled out her yellow dress, the one she'd worn to dinner with Masud. 'Wear this instead.'

Mavette held the dress out in front of her, then slipped it on, wrapping her own scarf around her head and shoulders. They looked at each other and giggled, like children dressing up. The sight of themselves in the mirror made them stand still, side by side, identical faces. The fine bone structure, arched brows above dark eyes. Mavette a little thinner, shorter by an inch, her skin olive beside Maha's light tan.

'Hello, twin,' Maha whispered to the reflection. They came together then, their cheeks touching. 'Hello,' was the soft reply.

As Mavette ran down the stairs she stopped, her hand grasping the rail. She turned and looked up at Maha.

'Later today,' she said, 'can you meet me? There is a march against the burning of the Aswan churches. We'll go, not to march, not this time, just to be there. Please say you will come. First we will go to Groppi's – have some ice cream.' Mavette's face was bright above the yellow dress. 'Madame will let me have the time off, she will be so happy I've found you. Maybe Hosni will drop you – he knows Groppi's – about four o'clock.'

'Of course I'll come. Go carefully. Already I can't wait.'

# Chapter 28

Exhausted, Maha had fallen asleep; she was woken now by the glare of the sun. She pushed back the sheet to allow the air to cool her skin. Her hand stroked the side of the bed where Mavette had lain. A slight indentation in the pillow marked where her sister's head had been.

The injured boy, where was he now?

She thought about Mavette's humdrum existence and tried to reconcile Mavette the maid with the brave, feisty young woman she'd met last night. Poverty, oppression, such a different life from the one she'd experienced. If she had remained in the orphanage it might have been her who now risked her life, for change, freedom. She hoped she would have had the courage.

Fervour and excitement is just an addiction, as potent as any other.

She remembered the war correspondent whom she'd met in a bar saying that. 'A drug' was how he'd described his way of life. It enabled him to live on the edge, reminded him he was alive.

She stared at the sky, high and domed like a cathedral. How will I get used to England's skies again? Autumn skies, ever changing, pale in colour, grey washed with blue, the sun's rays piercing through storm clouds.

It was only hours since Mavette had gone, hurrying down the street in the yellow dress. Every minute was just another in the long wait until the afternoon when they would meet again.

She had tried to analyse her feelings, to work them out but did she want to? She could say she felt whole; that the shadow that's always been there now has form and a face. Words, just words, tired, worn clichés, she thought. How to describe the small glow of warmth, the frisson of excitement spreading from her head to her feet, down her arms and into the very depths of her body.

'I belong,' she whispered. We're connected by unseen genes, we were both once held in unknown arms, we share a history. We're intrinsically bound. At times her thoughts were a chaotic jumble, at others joy erupted like a bubble breaking from the surface of a pond. She wanted to reach up and touch the sky. Needing a distraction, she opened her iPad and found a new email from her mum.

*Darling Maha,*

*Mavette. It hurts just to write her name. All of this has been hidden away for so long. You said you know about her. I'm glad you do but I wonder what you know. Did they speak of her at the orphanage? I am desperate to hear but also afraid to open a door behind which there is so much pain.*

*I am taking the coward's way out sending an email but I want you to have read my letter before I speak to you. It took me so long to write, it was hard. It can only explain what happened, not why, never why. I posted it at the start of the week. They said it would take four or five days but events are so dreadful out there. I can't watch the news at night. I so want you home.*

*I wish the past had been different – I wish so many things but it doesn't help – nothing can be changed.*

*Maha, whatever else, remember Dad and I loved you both more than anything else in the world.*

*I'm not around for a few days. I'm painting in north Wales, with the art group. They 'bullied' me into going with them. 'Make the days until Maha comes home go faster' was their argument. They are kind though. I think they can see I have been a bit of a mess recently.*

*Now I'm wittering. None of this is important. Especially to you right now.*

*Maha, I'm sorry. I hope it helps.*

*Love you lots*

*Mum xx*

She knew her mother would have read what she had written a dozen times before she pressed the send button. She could imagine her as she wandered around the conservatory, plumping up the cushions, watching the leaves skitter off the trees in the wind. A feeling, a sink hole, deep and empty, made Maha's body ache.

Dad and I loved you both. She reread the words. Mavette and her bracketed together, twins in a womb. Maha closed the lid of her tablet with a bang.

She watched a money spider hanging as though suspended in mid-air, her movement making it sway on its invisible thread. 'Hey, spider, you and me both.' She knew what it was like to be suspended in nothingness. Ahead looked scary, going back not an option.

Now she was talking to spiders. The hours ahead seemed endless. In England it was still early in the day, too early to phone James. She wanted to tell him, tell him she had found Mavette or rather, to be correct, Mavette had found her. Last night was like a grainy black and white reel, spliced and edited, going round and round, the meaning hard to grasp. Still feeling too tired to make sense of it all she wanted only to remember lying beside Mavette and it feeling so right, so perfect.

# Chapter 29

Hosni will take her to the Corniche. She had told him little over the phone. We are learning to be careful, she thought. She tried to phone James but only got the annoying voice that announced 'this phone is turned off, please try later'. It was still early on a Sunday she supposed, looking at her watch and calculating the time difference. She sent him a text.

*Can't wait to speak to you later. Some very, very exciting news to tell you. Other things have been happening too but they may have to wait until I see you on Wednesday. You know – phones etc. XXX*

Hosni's taxi drew up under her balcony and he sounded his horn to summon her. She ran down the stairs and jumped in. 'You are all right?' Hosni asked without turning his head. He was staring ahead through a smeary windscreen. 'You will be angry with Hosni now – after all that has happened. I think you don't want me to take you in my taxi anymore.' His worry beads clacked as he fiddled with them; his English was stilted. 'I couldn't, you know, tell you anything. She, she wouldn't let me. I wanted to but I promised her.' Maha nodded slowly. He turned off the radio. She looked into his rear-view mirror and could see him biting at the scab on his lip – a small piece came away, leaving a pale pink streak of new skin.
'Yes, Hosni. You are right. I don't want you to be my taxi driver.' She gathered up her bag, opened the door and stepped out. It closed with a clunk. She pulled open the front door of the cab and sat down. 'You are my friend and friends sit in the front seat – but I'm still paying.'
He lifted his head until their eyes met. His bruise was a fusion of violet and green, less livid than before. He wiped at a speck of blood

with the back of his hand, then grinned. 'That is good, that is very good. It pleases me. Maha and Hosni, we are true friends.'

'And Mavette,' she said. 'Maha, Hosni and Mavette, all friends.'

Hosni jabbed on his windscreen wipers so that dust smeared in train tracks across the window.

'Now, are you going to take me to see her or not?'

'Of course. Let's go. I am happy.' He revved the engine and pulled away from the kerb. He saw Mohammed in his wing mirror wave at him, something white in his hand. 'Later, Mohammed, later,' he shouted out of the window. Mohammed watched them go. He rubbed sleep from his eyes, stretched and rewound his scarf around his head before he climbed the stairs and pushed the letter with its English stamp and bright blue airmail sticker under Maha's door.

'Hosni, there is something I want to know.' She was holding onto the roof strap as the car swung between the impatient trucks and buses. Security vehicles were everywhere. They herded the traffic along the main streets and blocked off other routes. Sitting in the front gave her a view she wasn't so sure she enjoyed. 'We have a fairground ride at home, we call it dodgem cars, it's just like this,' she shouted above the shrill whistle of a policeman who was completely ignored by the road users.

'What do you want to know?' Hosni's kept his hand on the horn and they moved forward in a series of lurches.

'How did Mavette know about me? She said she had known for a while.' Hosni wound up the window so it was easier to hear each other speak. Maha coughed as traffic fumes and heat blended like soup inside the cab.

He hesitated as he rubbed the side of his nose. 'We, that is Muslims, believe our lives are mapped out before we are born. Allah decrees our destiny. That first day at the airport, when you had just arrived, it was not by chance I picked you up. It was written.' He glanced sideways at her. Did he think she would laugh at him?

'We would call it fate,' she said. 'I've never been sure what I thought about the concept – until now.'

'It was like Mavette was in my cab,' he went on. 'So alike except you were...'

'Posh.' She supplied the word, red heat spreading up from her neck to her face.

'Yes, posh. I like that word, posh.' He laughed. 'I knew Mavette through Masud and the NAC. I remember the first day I kept looking at you in the mirror. Of course I didn't know for sure then, but when you began to talk about searching for an orphanage, then I knew. I went to Masud. I think he told Mavette about you. Your sister is strong, she is brave. She will not always be a maid.' He drummed on the steering wheel. The heat in the cab was too much and Maha opened her window a crack. Warm air rushed in.

'She came to see me. She made me promise not to tell you about her. She said soon you would go back to England. I said she should meet you but no – she is stubborn too – I expect she had her reasons. So then Hosni has a big secret and it made him feel bad. What could I do? We all had a big secret but Mavette's wishes were...'

'More important,' Maha finished. She lifted Hosni's beads from where they lay over the gear stick. They were smooth and round, different shapes and sizes. She held them in the palm of her hand. 'You were right, Hosni. I was a visitor to Cairo, here only for a short time. It was for Mavette to decide.' Even as she said it she couldn't now imagine not knowing about her twin. Already a space that had lain empty had been filled. 'I'm so glad she found me,' she whispered.

'Today, why are you coming into the centre of Cairo? It is not a good place to be. I will take you both somewhere else. Much better.'

She laughed. 'I am always such a bother, Hosni, and you look after me so well. We won't be marching. Don't worry.' She playfully poked his arm. 'Mavette wants to support the demonstrators. It means so much that she wants me to be there with her. It's to be a peaceful demonstration. She says people are protesting at the authority's failure to investigate the burning of Coptic churches.

Surely it's the right way to go about it.' Maha paused as she thought about Wahida's friends in Imbaba and the despair of the old man. 'They want the right to worship.'

'I know. I know what it is for. Yes, it is right. It is good but why do you need to go? I will take you to the park, somewhere else. Talk to Mavette.'

'Hosni, stop worrying. Mavette knows what she is about. Anyway, first we are going to Groppi's to have some ice cream. Maybe we will go no further. I have heard the pastries are yummy.' Hosni shook his head, worry bleeding into his expression.

'How are Chavi and Kamillah?' she asked to try and lighten the mood.

He smiled. 'Kamillah, she has been paddling in the water, in the Suez Canal, with her cousins. She thinks Ismailia is the best place in the world. I am glad they are not here but I miss them. I hate all this.' His fist banged on the windscreen as an army vehicle pulled out in front of them and four young men in the back waved guns above their heads. 'They think it's a carnival.' He swore under his breath.

'Hosni, on Wednesday, please will you take me to the airport. It has to be you; it's like completing a circle. But I warn you now I will probably cry.' Her laugh caught in her throat. 'You showed me Cairo, taught me to love it. I will come back. Especially now. Mavette is my special reason to return.'

He nodded. 'Women, when they have minds of their own, it is bad. Much trouble for Hosni,' he said as a whistle escaped through his teeth. Maha looked at him sharply to see a grin tugging at the corner of his mouth and soon they were both laughing.

'Will you drop me here? I want to sit beside the Nile for a bit, say goodbye. Think a little.'

'OK, but you take care. Call me if ...'

'I will. And, Hosni, thank you.'

The Corniche curved away in front of her; a wide ribbon of concrete linked the bridges. People were walking. There was a woman who pushed an empty pushchair; the small boy, hoisted onto his father's shoulders, clutched a pebble, eager to throw it into the river. A pale-skinned man in sportswear, his blond hair wet with sweat, passed Maha without a glance. Beneath a lamp post an old man was asleep, his hands behind his head.

The Nile snaked between buildings, wind funnelled in the spaces and stirred the water's surface. Music from a river boat drifted across the water and a small dinghy with a red sail tacked from side to side.

An armoured vehicle raced along the Corniche towards the 6th October Bridge, its headlights full moons in the soft light.

She sighed. A log floated in the current. On you will go, she thought. Where to? On to Alexandria, across the Mediterranean, round by Gibraltar, past Portugal, France. Home.

Her childhood home. She tried to put herself there, her old bedroom, the oak tree in the garden that she had fallen out of – she'd been taken to casualty to get stitches in her chin. She rubbed the scar, now smooth, recalling the memory.

'I want to see your Cairo. Take me there,' James had said in one of their late-night phone calls. She will do that; they will come back together. He will meet Mavette. Tomorrow she would go to the orphanage to see the children and Tafida. She will be so happy for us, for both of us. She smiled at the memory of the tiny old lady bent and worn, so determined to take her to Mavette. What stories, she wondered, might Tafida have to tell?

'Goodbye, river Nile.' She blew the words across the rippling band of light cast by a disappearing sun. She turned away and began to walk from the Corniche towards Talaat Harb Square and the famous Groppi's.

On her way she passed old tenements, rubbish and debris strewn across the pavement. Two men, their faces grim, were boarding up their shop front, the hammering of the nails incessant in the narrow street. How often of late have they done the same? Other shop fronts and doorways had been similarly protected. Barricades against what, against whom?

Mavette wasn't there when she reached the slightly shabby art deco building with its neon sign. The architecture spoke of a more affluent time. The exterior was elaborately tiled, pink, orange, white and yellow tiles making up gaudy flowers around the doorway; graffiti formed a puckered scar. Chipped pillars supported a balcony over which a shirt had been hung out to dry.

The interior was cool with more tiles. High ceilings arched like a cathedral's dome, once elegant fretwork chandeliers hung like teardrops. Light from the large windows dappled the tables. Maha breathed in the humid smell from the huge palms and glossy-leaved plants that graced the colourful pots and offered privacy to the diners. The place was quiet, nearly empty. Few people were eating the once famous ice cream sundaes. She sat where she could see the door. It was cold. In the eerie quiet, the cafe was more like a mausoleum. She tried to imagine the place in its heyday, crowded with the best of Cairo's society, fashionable men and women who wanted to be seen. Cairene politicians, dissidents, French bourgeoisie and British dukes, heated debate, decisions thrashed out, the uniformed waiters flitting from table to table.

'You are far away.' Mavette was standing by the table, her Arabic gentle. She wore Maha's yellow dress and her straight hair framed her face.

'You look so pretty.' Maha put out her hands and Mavette took them. Then they hugged and laughed, moving the chairs so they could sit side by side.

'What do you think?' Mavette's arm swept the room. 'This is the famous Groppi's. I will buy you an ice cream,' she said. 'What would you like?'

Maha began to protest. 'I'll get them.' But she read the look on Mavette's face. ('Your sister is stubborn,' she remembered Hosni's words.) 'Thank you, anything but...'

'Banana flavour,' Mavette finished. 'Me too,' and their giggles brought a waiter at a run to their table.

'The boy, Nasser, he will be all right, his arm is fixed.' Mavette spoke from behind her hand even though no one was near. 'And

Madame, when I told her about you she clapped her hands. She was very happy. I am lucky; she is good to me. It is not so for all maids.'

Maha watched as Mavette fiddled with the drooping flowers in the small vase on the table.

'What do you think they were like?' she asked. 'Who?' Mavette said, smelling the blooms. Yellow petals fell onto the tablecloth. 'Our parents, our mother.'

'Oh, it's too long ago. In Egypt, Maha, it is not so unusual. Babies get abandoned, especially girls. There is such poverty. That is why now we fight for a better world. Tell me, what is England like? I think it is cold and it rains all the time. Tell me about your growing-up.'

What could she say? Maha wondered. Everything about her childhood and her life since only emphasised the difference. She felt a stab of anger towards her mother but it was quickly followed by a wave of guilt.

Mavette was watching her. 'You must not be afraid to tell me. Once we were together, then we were not. The reason we do not know. Only others can tell us. Now we are together again but we need each other to fill in the gaps so we can go on – if you want to that is.' As she spoke Mavette's eyes scanned Maha's face in search of an answer.

'Mavette, you are generous and kind. Let's do that, fill in all the blank spaces, the good bits and the bad. You may have to help me with some words; sometimes my Arabic gets mixed up. We will always have each other now and, ridiculous though it may sound, it feels like we have never been apart.'

'I know what you mean. We fit. Do you think that's how all twins feel?'

'Well, I don't know but I still like repeating, I am a twin, I have a twin sister.' They giggled again; the waiter looked at them quizzically as he brought their ice cream.

'You first then,' Mavette said, 'and don't miss out a single part. There is one question I want to ask. Are you married too?'

Maha stretched out her hands. 'No. See, no rings. Maybe one day.'

'Someone then, someone special?'

'Yes, but we have a way to go.' She found she wasn't ready to share James with anyone yet, not even Mavette. 'I will tell you about him later, he comes at the end of my story.'

They talked, first one then the other. Snippets of their lives lay scattered on the table. The sky outside turned raspberry red then mauve. Now the chandeliers cast shadows where sunshine had rippled.

'We are sorry but we close early today.' A man in a white shirt was standing by the table. 'There are many people outside, we are afraid there may be trouble.'

They both looked up, amazed to find they were the only ones left in the cafe. Waiters were pulling tables away from the windows and stacking chairs in a corner. As the two women left, the staff left too, melting into the crowds.

The square was full of people who pushed and jostled, their shouts rising above the traffic. Mavette took Maha's arm, they edged away from the main road and forged their way down a side street. It was nearly dark but the temperature was still warm. A smell of sewage or blocked drains hung in the air. Maha pulled up her scarf. She copied Mavette and secured it around her shoulders and over her head.

'The march, it is heading for the Maspero building,' Mavette shouted to her. 'It's the State TV and radio offices on the Corniche. Not far now. We protest there, under their noses to make our point. No longer is there lethargy. We want security and the right to choose. We will see them, the demonstrators, come under the bridge soon.' Maha followed Mavette acutely aware of her sister's allegiance to the marchers. She knew if it was not for her Mavette would be with them.

They could see the building ahead with its round base and central circular tower. All its lights were ablaze. It looked like a birthday cake with a candle on top except for the barbed wire and metal, twisted into grotesque statues that destroyed the image. Suddenly they were channelled into the centre of the street. Military police stood in rows on either side. A riot shield prodded into Maha and she stumbled. A baton was raised above her head. The soldier, who made guttural noises like a wild dog, leant against her and shoved her forward.

'Mavette.' Her cry made her sister turn and she felt Mavette's hand take her own and pull her away.

The sun had set, only pale streaks of light remained in the sky. The Nile was a restless thread, empty of boats.

'Look,' Mavette said, raising her hands in the air. Hundreds, even thousands of protestors were walking towards the television building. Some carried candles and at the front was a cross. Mavette clapped her hands and stretched across to take an Egyptian flag from one of the marchers. She held it out to Maha and together they waved it as the crowd streamed past.

'See,' Mavette shouted into Maha's ear. 'Many, they carry the cross and crescent. It means Muslims and Christians united. Do you hear the chant? "Muslims and Christians are one." I am proud.'

'This is what makes it all worth it,' Maha shouted back.

They stood together, arms around each other holding their flag.

At first there were shouts; the chanting faltered. Then a swarm of batons. Maha saw the police twist and duck as stones and rocks were thrown from behind their ranks. The marchers began to run, some forwards, others back in the direction of Tahrir Square. Gunfire, rounds of it in short bursts, pierced the mayhem; a siren, loud and screeching, became deafening as it screamed closer.

They ran. A pick-up truck swerved along the road, the back filled with men who shot randomly above the crowds and at the windows of the buildings. Glass showered onto them. Panic spread as there was more gunfire and the air became filled with dust and the clawing smell of tear gas.

Maha was gulping in great mouthfuls of air, her breath wheezed in her chest. Mavette was doubled over; she clung to barbed wire wrapped around a pillar. The crack of gunshot exploded in Maha's ears as dozens of police charged amongst the protestors, beating them down. Rocks were thrown from all directions. Something hit her, pain split the side of her head, myriad red lights swam in front of her eyes. A stone, white and smooth, lay at her feet, cold, inanimate. Mavette's legs had buckled, her hand was over her head; her screams tore into the fuzz that surrounded Maha.

'Mavette.' Maha was down beside her, shielding her from the kicks thrown by running legs. She wrapped her arms around her sister's shoulders. Warm and sticky, she stared at her hand, hennaed now in bright red blood. 'Mavette, what's happened?' She turned her round. Mavette was clutching at a space below her shoulder; blood pulsing rhythmically, the stain on her dress a red corsage.

'Oh God, you've been shot.' Mavette's eyes were pools of black in her pale face, blue lips moved forming soundless words.

'Help me.' Maha tried to halt the fleeing crowd, but her cry was drowned by the wail of sirens. A man fell and tripped over Mavette. Maha could smell his breath. She grabbed his shirt, shaking him. 'Please help my sister.' Perhaps it was the English tongue that made the man bend down and pull Mavette to her feet. He ran with her, heedless of her yells. Maha took her other arm and ran too until Mavette became heavy between them and her legs dragged along the pavement. The man pushed them into a space between two buildings beneath the arch of a doorway and ran on.

Mavette crumpled against the wall, one leg protruding onto the main pavement. Maha pulled her further in and propped her up against the rough wall. She was moaning, a primitive sound that escaped from quivering lips. Her face was ashen but she gripped Maha's hand, pinching the skin between her finger and thumb. Maha tried to tear her scarf into pieces but couldn't do it, so instead made a ball of one end and pushed it into the wound, holding it there, to try and stem the flow of blood. She let Mavette slump against her shoulder and with her other hand she stroked her sister's hair.

They were in a narrow alleyway that smelt of damp and faeces. Maha could see the sky, a slit of inky black. One star brightened the gloom. The running crowds, the screams, the gunfire and the sirens were still loud but they felt distant as she closed her eyes. Her head throbbed; she fought rising nausea. A shuffling sound jerked her awake. A dog stood a few feet away, its whole body shaking, its teats red and heavy, its tongue lolling from the side of its mouth. It pawed at a small oily puddle.

So thirsty, Maha ran her tongue over her lips, and at the same time Mavette asked for water. Maha splayed open her hand. Where was the water bottle she always carried? She stared at her blood-streaked skin willing the water to materialise. All she could do was work up a glob of saliva and use it to moisten Mavette's lips with the tip of her finger. Mavette managed a weak smile, but winced as pain overtook her. Maha rocked her.

The yellow dress was grimed with blood and dirt, the voile torn. The colour of daffodils. She could see them beside the stream in her mother's garden pushing up between the bright new blades of grass, defying the wind and rain. The sun was shining, melting the frost that had turned into silver droplets of water hanging from the flowers' trumpets.

'Stay awake,' she said to Mavette. She stroked her cheek, traced the shadow around her eyes. 'I am going to get some help, find an ambulance, a stretcher. We will get you away from here.' She lifted Mavette into a more upright sitting position and used the other end of the scarf to bind Mavette's hand to her body so it pressed against her shoulder. 'I'll be quick. Wait, Mavette, wait,' she whispered, kissing the top of her sister's head and letting the skin of their cheeks touch.

Men and women were fleeing along the Corniche. An old man walked in the opposite direction, his face creased in concentration as though his daily walk had been hijacked. He was pushed from side to side until he was turned fully around and he began to walk back the way he had come.

Maha shrieked, 'Help, I need help.' She grabbed at clothing as people ran past. Sporadic shots were fired in spattering rounds, ricocheting into the crowd and chipping chunks from walls. An army personnel carrier, its headlights two circles of scathing light began to zigzag along the street pushing protesters to the side, knocking down those who couldn't get out of the way. It mounted the kerb, swept the pavement, bounced off the walls.

From the alley Mavette saw the fender of the vehicle just feet away as it careered past, thudding into the corner of the building. It came to a juddering halt. Gears screeched, metal on metal. It was slammed into reverse and sped away. A block of stone worked loose by the impact dislodged itself from the narrow balcony above. Mavette watched it fall. Time slowed. Then there was black.

# Chapter 30

Will Maha have received my letter? It is Sunday. It should have arrived yesterday or today. I remember in Egypt how quickly we had become used to the weekend being a Friday and Saturday, Gareth at work on a Sunday had felt quite normal.

All yesterday I had hoped she might phone or text me. This morning too, but the phone remains stubbornly silent. I have tried to see her reading it, to feel what she must be feeling. Everything she has ever known, thrown in the air. Who she is, who we were. Who I am. I had finished the letter, sealed the envelope, relief washing over me. It was cathartic, like unburdening myself to a counsellor.

There had been a hollow sound, as I dropped my letter into the postbox – immediately I wanted to retrieve it, would have given the world to have it back. The bright red box with its ER carved on the front had stood as a monument to my shame; my guilt streamed from its gaping mouth.

Today is a dank day, the light level low. The leaves from the vine have begun to fall; they lie in hues of purple and red stuck to the ground like torn paper from a billboard. I mooch in the garden deadheading flowers, their colour faded. I pick the allium heads to put in a vase, skeletal spheres, a fragile form of beauty.

It is the stillness I notice. Early afternoon but there are no cows lowing or tractors at work. No sound of wind in the trees, leaves hang silent unmoving, mourners at the funeral of summer. The light has turned an eerie yellow; it licks the hedgerows, has silenced the birds. It is the sort of stillness that heralds a storm, when all the energy of the earth is sucked away. I go indoors.

If only she would contact me. I need to hear her voice. I know tragedy leaves scars and can become the background upon which everything else is drawn. I have lived it. Please, Maha, don't let it be like that for you. Please ring.

There is no email either, I check again. Give her space, give her space. Take the wait as part of the punishment. I cry out against the voice in my head. A copy of my letter sits there on the computer, written a week ago, stark black letters on a white screen. How can a series of shapes, of squiggles come together to give a meaning that will wring such destruction?

*2nd October*

*My darling Maha,*

I can't read on. I sit, too cold to stir. Grey is the colour I see.

*2nd October*

*My darling Maha,*

*I keep trying to write this letter but it's hard. My continued silence would not put right a wrong that was committed and I want most of all to say I AM SORRY. I feel, as I am writing, that your dad is close and I know he would want to say the same. If I drift into excuses, disregard them for there are none.*

*This is at least my third attempt. The others were all about the background stuff. All about me. You don't need those bits; I will share them with you at a later date. This is your story. Now I think I must start at the point where you came into our lives and tell it as it happened. I hope when you come home I can fill in the gaps and answer your questions. Most of all I hope you will forgive me – us.*

*Your dad always referred to it as my 'mushroom moment'. In Cairo a group of the wives used to meet each week for keep-fit and they asked me if I would like to join them – we weren't allowed to work, so we found all sorts of ways to pass the time! This particular morning a lovely American lady, who always made us laugh, arrived so late we had already drunk our coffee. She was returning to America soon and we were going to miss her. She sat on the sofa beside me and proclaimed to the group.*

*'You'll never believe it, today of all days, the Commissary has no button mushrooms, none. We have Larry's boss coming to dinner; I must have them for my recipe.'*

198

*There was silence. Everyone else, all of us, British or Dutch, looked at her. We hadn't seen any kind of mushroom for months, never mind button mushrooms. Her eyes swivelled around the room.*

*'Oops,' she said, as we all began to laugh. 'I guess that was the wrong thing to say. I forget you guys don't have a Commissary.'*

*I can hear you saying, Maha, 'What do mushrooms have to do with me?' Well, I got talking to her, Kim, her name was. I asked her what she would miss about Cairo when she went home to the States. Without a pause she said, 'I will miss the twins.'*

*'The twins.' I must have sounded surprised; she went on to tell me how each week she visited an orphanage and just for a day took out one or sometimes two of the children. Recently she had been taking out twins, tiny scraps she said they were. They had been brought to the orphanage two months before having been found abandoned on a rubbish tip. Then they had been newly born, their cords still attached.*

*Now you know those twins were you and Mavette.*

*I heard myself say. 'Would I be allowed to take them out when you go home?'*

*Kim, I recall, grabbed my hand, and said, 'Would you, that would be really great. I worry they won't survive. I love them to bits. It would make me feel so much better. Come with me tomorrow, I'll show you what to do, introduce you. The orphanage doesn't seem to mind who takes them out, they have no idea of where I go. I suppose it's just two babies off their hands for the day.'*

*Your dad listened to my chatter that night. He was quiet. I had bought some feeding bottles and some baby milk on the way home as Kim had suggested. She said she would give me the clothes and nappies she had collected because I would need to change you when I took you back to the villa.*

*Next day, Maha, Kim took me to the orphanage. It probably looks now as it did then. I remember huge green doors and a big flame tree in the front. There was no one about, which Kim said was usual. She took me up the stairs to the top of the house. It was stifling. You were in a dark room, the sunlight kept out by closed shutters. The smell of ammonia pricked my eyes. There were several babies, all in cots, some sat staring through the bars, none of them made a sound. The two of you were in a cot together, lying curled up, touching, both asleep. Half-empty bottles of milk lay beside you. Flies crawled on the teats and around your mouths.*

*Kim nodded to a woman who lolled in the corner. We picked up the two of you and took you down to the car. It was that simple. I held you as we drove back to my villa. You were both sodden and by the time we got there so was I.*

*Kim showed me what to do. First strip you down, bathe you and dress you in the clothes she always kept at home. Wash out the clothes from the orphanage and hang them out. They would be ready then to dress you in when it was time to take you back. Then feed you.*

*Kim went back to America ten days later. I borrowed a carrycot from another of the ladies so I could transport you in the car. You used to sleep on our bed, two tiny souls. I used to put you down one on either side so that you would be cooler but somehow you always found each other, always lay touching skin against skin. I used to sit and watch you sleep. You would both whimper softly, screwing up your little faces and smiling in your sleep. I longed to know what you dreamt of.*

*You were both so hungry. You would suck and suck as though you expected the teat to fall out at any moment. I suppose you were not used to being held and allowed to finish a bottle.*

*Caring for the two of you changed everything. I loved you from the very beginning. You would lie in my arms, your eyes never leaving my face. I felt love creep in; it lodged inside me like the stone of a fruit.*

*The shadow cast by my miscarriages grew fainter. I began to rationalise an event I've never spoken about, even to your dad. It happened when I was just a teenager. When you come home, I think now, I would like to share it with you. It makes me sad to realise guilt has so long been my companion and that I allowed it to touch your father's life and your own.*

*Dad took to coming home at lunchtimes on the days you were there. He would feed one of you and me the other. I used to listen to him talking to you, telling you all sorts of tales, how the desert was beautiful, how the Nile made the fields green. He told you about England too. You both responded with such solemn stares but as you got to know us you began to give us smiles. When your dad went back to work he would pick each of you up in turn and kiss you on the forehead.*

*We grew so fond of you. We never broached the future with each other because I don't think either of us could contemplate the day when we might have to say goodbye.*

One day we were travelling home from Ismailia, a trip we sometimes took at the weekend with other expatriate families. Most of them had children but we weren't the only ones without as some of the single men would come along too.

The sun was going down over the desert. I hope you get to see that, Maha. It is so beautiful, like a huge ruby. It turns the sand deep orange.

We had an Abba tape playing in the car. They were singing the song about having a dream. You know the one I mean and I know you will be smiling as you read this. I was singing along with them.

Suddenly I knew what we had to do.

I clutched at your dad's arm. 'The twins, we have to adopt them.' I remember he stopped the car on the long desert road. Without a word he took me in his arms and kissed me. As the red sun dipped into the sand, setting the horizon on fire, the idea to make you ours was conceived.

(Now you know why that song was always a favourite. By the time you were five you could sing it too.)

The adoption process is a long story but I will try and keep it short. Your dad asked Shafik to help. He was the legal man in the office. We needed someone who knew the system, or more accurately, how to play the system. Without him we would never have succeeded. Endless forms, endless permissions to obtain, documents that required stamps from this department, another stamp from somewhere else. We kept appointments whenever we were told to, we attended conferences where we never said a word – all the conversation was in Arabic. Tea would be served, men would nod; envelopes would be handed across the table, signatures obtained. 'Making friendships' was how Shafik described it.

On the British side it seemed almost as drawn out. We were helped by the fact that about two years before we had gone through an adoption assessment and been accepted – we had not pursued it when I discovered I was pregnant but, well, as you know, the pregnancy wasn't to be.

On one of his trips back to the UK Dad contacted the agency and reactivated the process. They were brilliant. We both had to fly home for a few days and meet with specialised social workers used to dealing with foreign adoptions. Medicals, questions, more questions, probing and intrusive. I think we felt we were running a marathon with lead weights tied to our feet.

All the while the two of you grew stronger, your little arms and legs became less sticklike and your hair began to grow, dark and straight, *framing your olive faces, mirroring the colour of your eyes. I used to come and collect you each week and you would kick and gurgle, both fighting to be picked up first. The days I had to leave you in the orphanage were awful. I used to imagine you still in dirty nappies waiting to be fed. Did you wonder where I was, did you wait and wait or was survival the only instinct?*

*We had setbacks. Just when the process seemed to be going well there would be an obstacle put in our way. There were tears of despair and frustration, times when your dad and I clung together gleaning strength from each other. It was like a pregnancy I imagine, when slowly you move from being a couple to being would-be parents, a metamorphosis, fragile and precarious. Many months passed, then on October 5th, a date imprinted on my mind, your dad came home early; it was only about three o'clock in the afternoon. He rushed in, calling to me as he ran up the stairs. He tried to look serious but he couldn't. You know what he was like, Maha. His face always gave him away. His grin burst through. He had his hands behind his back.*

*'Guess what?' I tried to grab his hand but he sidestepped me and danced around the table waving two envelopes.*

*It turned out the office representative had gone home sick and your dad had been given the two company tickets for President Sadat's annual victory parade scheduled for the next day. 'Only a few rows from the president, so best bib and tuckers to be worn,' he said, mincing around the room. He pulled glasses from the cupboard and opened a bottle of wine. 'Pity there's no champagne, we need to celebrate.' Wine in the afternoon! His excitement was infectious and I was happy for him.*

*But I knew there was something else and he knew that I knew but we both played the game. It was the smile in his eyes and the way his lip curled upwards, the way he glanced at me sideways, the way when you know someone you can read the signs.*

*He took me out onto the balcony and ceremoniously poured the wine. We chinked our glasses. He said, 'Oh, I nearly forgot, this came today too.' And he handed me one of the envelopes.*

*Inside were the adoption papers, signed, stamped and delivered. At first I couldn't make sense of what it was. Pages of Arabic, then more pages of translations. 'They're ours,' your dad said. He grabbed me round the waist, wine spilt across the balcony, he whirled me through the bedroom, until dizzy with joy we fell across the bed. 'The twins are ours,' he kept repeating until we were both crying and laughing at the same time.*

*Maha, I don't remember much about the rest of the night except that I lay watching the sky lighten. A feeling of peace like a comforter had settled over me and I didn't want to close my eyes and let it go.*

*October 6th, 1981. History has recorded what happened that day – President Sadat was assassinated.*

*History has only recorded a part of it.*

*We were sitting in a vast stand overlooking the parade ground. The president, his bodyguards and important dignitaries were, as Dad had said, only rows away. The military bands played stirring music; the spectacle was colourful and impressive, full of pomp and ceremony. Soldiers and troop trucks towing artillery paraded in a continuous line. Five Mirage jets flew overhead, streaming their colours behind them. We were all looking up roused by the noise and the close proximity of the planes. I mouthed words to your dad, thrilled by it all.*

*I didn't see the dismounting soldier, only heard the exploding grenade. I choked on the acrid smoke and felt your dad pushing me to the ground. Chairs were thrown. They bounced off the crouching people. My mouth was full of grit. As I recall this, Maha, it seems like I am back there. I remember the woman who had been sitting next to me. I had material from her dress scrunched in my hand, it was green satin. I thought I was going to die and I kept whispering your names over and over.*

*There was chaos, gunfire, the sound of helicopters landing, bodies lay around us like discarded rubbish. We were led out of an exit but we had no idea where we were. There was no traffic, just people walking in silence. It was hours before we arrived home. By then my feet were bleeding; I had walked most of the way carrying my shoes with their too high heels.*

*We didn't know whether President Sadat was alive or dead. A state of emergency was declared with a complete news blackout. We collapsed, exhausted, into bed.*

*It was the sound of knocking that woke me, a persistent muffled knocking. I shook your dad awake. It was his boss. He pushed through*

203

the door as we opened it, banged it shut and leant against it while he struggled to catch his breath. He had risked his life to reach us.

It seemed a Lebanese group was being blamed for the attack on Sadat. All sorts of rumours were flying around. The president was dead. He was paralysed, a vegetable. No one knew. Dad's company and the boss were Lebanese, under suspicion. The belief was we had to get out of Cairo.

He told us we must go at first light. I think I screamed 'The twins'.

'No, with the babies, get the twins and go,' he said. 'Not by air, the airport will be closed. The company driver will come; he will take you to the Palestinian border.' He gave us a package of money. 'You will need it to get out.'

There was no more sleep that night. We decided to leave everything behind. We only took a bag with passports, made-up baby bottles, some clean baby clothes, a few photographs of the two of you and most important of all, the adoption papers.

Abdul the driver came for us as dawn broke. He was nervous. His constant thrumming on the dashboard increased my fear. There was some traffic but not like usual. Soldiers were at every junction. They stood in groups, jumpy and restless, sometimes discharging their rifles into the air.

We had to bang on the gates of the orphanage, a noise echoed by the thudding of my heart. Tafida, the boab's wife, opened them and when no one answered our knocking on the main door she pulled a key from beneath her dress and let us in there too. She put her finger across her lips. 'Big boss here now, madam. Since yesterday. Bad things have happened in Cairo.' She shook her head. 'He not like.' She touched both our faces.

We didn't know what she meant but we found the man asleep on the desk in the office. Not the usual man in charge, whom we had come to know, but someone else. He had clearly slept there all night and was bleary and slow when we shook him awake. We told him why we had come; your dad pulled out all the papers and spread them in front of him.

As I write this my palms are sweating and the words are swimming on the page.

The air was stale, it smelt of sleep. There was a big clock on the wall. The hands were stuck at six o'clock and the second hand lay at an angle where it had come loose. Every detail is etched in my mind.

*Ignoring us he barked for chai. He picked up the papers and glanced at them, then tossed them aside. I held Dad's hand, our hopes clasped tightly in our clenched fists. The man sipped his tea and tapped a pen rhythmically against his chair.*

*'You can take one. One only.' The words shot from his mouth, hitting us like missiles. 'You must go and not come back.'*

*We were in front of his desk, an old desk of faded wood, scratched and blotched with ink stains. He pushed the papers towards us. 'Sign here, then leave.'*

*'We're not signing anything. What do you mean, take one? We have all the correct documents; the adoption is in order. We are to take the twins.'*

*'You can no longer come to this place. I am in charge,' he shouted. 'I will tear up the papers and you will go.'*

*Your dad recovered first, Maha. I had sunk onto a chair.*

*'The papers. Look, read them.' I knew Dad was trying to stay calm but his voice was shaking. The man stared at us, power puffing out his chest.*

*'What do you want? Money?' your dad shrieked at him. 'Here.' He took out a bundle of notes and threw them across the desk.*

*The man's arm flew sideways, scattering the notes so they showered off the desk and floated to the floor.*

*'OK.' He made as if to tear up the documents. He had risen from his chair and stood silhouetted against the window; a malicious grin contorted his features. He wore control like an extra layer.*

*Your dad moved towards him. I held him back. It would have made it worse. I pulled him out of the room and up to the nursery.*

*Maha, I remember I was screaming, 'We can't, we can't, we can't,' but no sound left my mouth.*

*I don't know what we intended to do. Grab you both and run? It would have been impossible. He would have prevented us. Say goodbye? I don't know. I can only tell you what happened next.*

*We went into the room where you were. All the babies were asleep except you. A woman snored, her face to the wall. You were sitting up in the cot and you stretched out your little arms to us. Mavette was curled around you, sleeping making small sucking sounds on her thumb.*

*I picked you up and held your cold, wet body to me.*

*'I'll come back for Mavette, it will be all right.' Those were Dad's
words and we wanted them to be true. At that moment they were true,
Maha. Later we tried, we tried for so long.*

*We took you downstairs. We were like programmed puppets except
puppets don't feel the grief and guilt that began then and has never, ever
gone away.*

*The man was watching through the open door.*

*'Which one?' he growled.*

*'Maha.' I whispered your name and your dad began to shout and
plead with him. The man pulled the papers together and read them
slowly. The money still lay strewn on the floor. The clock remained at six
o'clock.*

*He looked straight at us, I can still see his eyes. He handed us a set of
papers, then holding our gaze he ripped up the others, letting the pieces
fall into the rubbish bin. 'Leave now. I am being generous.' Those were
his words, Maha. They made no more sense than anything else at that
moment.*

*As we left, Tafida hurried across to us. Her hand flew to her mouth
and she gently kissed the top of your head.*

*That was how it happened. Why did we not do it differently, argue
more, demand more? I have had 30 years, 10,950 days and nights to try
and answer those questions but still I can't.*

*Abdul drove us out of Cairo. We didn't cry; I held you tightly; we just
sat in numbed silence while the car ate up the miles. We couldn't have
reached the border without his help. He had long conversations, drank
chai with officials, he obtained the permissions we needed, the signatures
on the papers. We never asked what changed hands. You didn't cry
either. It was as though you knew. You fed, you slept. We crossed the Suez
Canal. Abdul took a photograph of us beside the water. It was the only
one we ever showed you from your life in Cairo. We kept it for you. I
hated it.*

*We kept travelling regardless of the clawing heat and dust. Up to El
Arish and along the coast road until eventually we reached the border
town of Rafah.*

*Abdul left us, he waved, his figure growing smaller as we walked
across the border into Gaza.*

*I can picture you as you read this letter. You will be curled up in a
chair, one leg tucked beneath you, twisting your hair and hooking it*

206

*behind your ear. The pose is so familiar; the little girl listening to stories, watching television. The teenager, sometimes cross, sometimes funny, losing yourself in the music of the moment. I ache for you as my words sink in.*

*The facts are painful to describe, the emotions even harder. Perhaps when you come home I can try and tell you a little of how we felt for months, for years afterwards. Forever.*

*You were such a joy to us, you were what made us live. We never gave up hope of bringing Mavette home. Your dad tried, he went back to Egypt so many times. The orphanage was closed to foreigners. He was always rebuffed. The company tried, they were so good but it was as though Mavette had never existed. The lies grew, the excuses proliferated. Personnel changed and hope faded.*

*We have never stopped loving her. Every year on your birthdays we sent a card and a present to the orphanage. I would buy you matching dresses or knit identical cardigans. I never heard whether the gifts ever reached her but I went on sending them anyway. It was such a small thing but we needed to do it for her and for us.*

*Maha, there is so much more I could tell you. I carry the guilt of what we did; it will only die when I do. Do I regret what we did? I can't answer that. We should never have separated you from your sister but to imagine not having the love and happiness you have brought us is also inconceivable.*

*I said I would make no excuses. I don't. One day I hope you may understand and forgive us just a little. One day maybe Mavette can do that too. Come home soon, darling. I need to give you the biggest hug in the world.*

*Mum xx*


The phone rings, reverberating around the room. Maha. My finger fumbles for the green button. 'Maha,' I sob into the pause.

# Chapter 31

It isn't quite light but I no longer want to lie in bed. My memories, my thoughts, weaving themselves into a blanket that threatens to suffocate me. Downstairs I put my coat over my dressing gown and push open the door of the conservatory. The cold air is still, a respite for the autumn leaves which fall in flurries when the wind blows.

As a child, if I was asked when my birthday was, my reply always used to be, 'When the leaves fall off the trees.' Now that time is here. 'I'll be back for your birthday' was what Maha had promised, and today she is coming home.

I think back to the weekend when she first told me she was going to Egypt. I hadn't been able to sleep that night either. Concerned, she had joined me in the garden, we talked, I remember, we drank tea as the sun rose. Today, long shadows cross the lawn and the dew is heavy. I pause beside the bench where we sat that morning, run my hand along its painted wood. I was so scared back then, so afraid of her going to Cairo, afraid she would find out, afraid of her reaction. All so pointless now. I was angry too at Gareth, for dying, for leaving me with what we had never told her, for leaving me with the decision of what to do. Why had we never told her she had a sister, told her the story? How much easier would it have been for her to have grown up with the truth?

I stand and watch a heap of soil quiver as a mole digs frantically, deep below the ground. I envy it its singleness of purpose, its activity, its blindness and the darkness in which it lives.

A smudge of white is beginning to backlight the Edge, bringing into focus the remaining black-wrapped bales of silage scattered like tombstones in the fields across the valley.

My friend has brought me to the airport but she is waiting outside. This bit I want to do alone. I hope I can. I watch a plane land, descending from banks of white clouds that chase across a grey blue sky. Watch as it taxies slowly, then connects like a leech to its walkway. Now it is out of sight. I have been shown to a room and provided with coffee. Every kindness offered. I can't settle, the four walls suffocate me. Time is interminable; my eyes search the corridor where I choose to wait. I can see people walking below, their legs and feet reflected to infinity in the glass panels. It is quiet, the air conditioning a background hum like swarming bees. 'She's back in time for my birthday. She's back in time for my birthday.' The words sing in my head.

The door is opened by a member of staff dressed in a smart blue suit, her patent high-heeled shoes shiny on the tiled floor. She holds it open to allow the two young women through. My breath checks in my throat as they walk slowly towards me. There she is, her arm still held in a sling, her walking stick tapping on the floor. The other girl steadies her by the elbow.

I can only stand and watch them come closer. All sound is hushed, time suspended. I take a hesitant step forward, and then I am running. Her familiar, unfamiliar face is misted by my tears. I grasp her thin frame, feeling her tremble; I bury my face in her black hair.

'Thank you for bringing your sister home.' I whisper the words as I let her go. Her eyes are pools of pain. 'Mavette. Mavette. It's you. You're here – at last.' I touch her cheek, feel her tears. The other girl speaks to me in English. 'Maha was my friend. We wanted to come with her. I am Wahida.'

We walk together through the pine doors into the airport's softly lit chapel. The white coffin is beautiful in its simplicity. It rests alone on the raised dais. Music plays, clothing the space, cocooning us from outside.

I place my flowers on top of the coffin, the ones I picked today from the garden, when the early morning air had been cold with a hint of frost. Bright dahlias, summer's last gift.

A bunch of red roses already lie there, tied up with twine. From the young man who had come to see me, who had cried with me, our grief connecting us. He had been so nice, so kind, and so sad. I read the card:

*For my beautiful Maha,*
*A love so new. Forever ours.*
*James x*

We are three women holding hands. I stretch out my arm to touch the coffin so Maha can hold hands too. No words, no thoughts, just silence wrapped in music. Time passes before I step forward and kiss the coffin. Mavette follows me and for a moment she rests her head on the white wood, her black hair falling across it. Red, white and black, I think, the colours of the Egyptian flag; my tears fall.

The light is bright when we leave the chapel. It floods the corridor, harsh and white.

'Please will you stay?' I search Mavette's face, my hand resting on her uninjured shoulder.

The two young women look at each other. 'No,' Wahida says. 'Thank you. We can't do that. We have seats on the return flight. My father, the airline, they have arranged it.' She takes my hand. 'Perhaps we will come back another time. Maha wanted to show me London, we were going to go to the art...' She can't finish.

'Your father has been wonderful. Arranging – everything. Without him...'

'He wanted to. He loved her, we all did.'

Mavette speaks softly in Arabic and Wahida opens her bag pulling out a letter. 'Mavette says this is yours. It was behind the door of Maha's apartment. I think it came the day...that day.'

I take the envelope, staring at my own handwriting. Turn it over; the tape I put across the flap for security is still intact. I hold it to my chest, a tear falling onto my wrist.

'No, Mavette.' I lift the girl's cold hand and give her the envelope. I fold her fingers around it. 'It's not mine. It's yours.' The envelope lies between us, a fragile connection.

'Thank you.' Mavette's first words to me.

I kiss her lightly on the forehead. 'One day, I hope, we will get to know each other better.'

She nods as Wahida translates the words.

'Yes,' she whispers. '*Inshallah.*'

Wahida hugs me and the two girls begin to walk back the way they came. As they reach the doors Mavette stops, hesitates and turns towards me. She lifts her head and smiles. She raises her hand in a small wave, her stick hanging from her arm.

A soft whoosh from the closing door takes them from me.

I stumble back into the chapel, allowing grief to claim me now. Precious minutes with Maha before the hearse arrives.


In London's Gower Street James is signing books. The queue snakes out of the door. People wait, they talk and laugh, oblivious to the fine architecture above them.

Maha has been here all morning looking down at him from the news-stand. She is smiling, her hair lifted by a breeze.

### Body of British Journalist Flown Home

The headline is stark and black.

'I loved your book, a first novel, it was brilliant. Please tell me you're writing another one.' The woman, her blue-rimmed glasses askew on her nose, drops her newspaper onto the table in front of him. There it is:


*...mown down by a security vehicle...28 dead in violent clashes... cover-up...a more insidious threat to democracy...*


The woman is talking, her voice too loud. 'What's it going to be about? Will it be in the same genre?'

'What?' James looks up at her. 'I have absolutely no idea.'

He slams her book shut, unsigned.

He pushes back his chair and runs. 'But I'll call it *A Pharaoh's Daughter*.' His words strafe the startled queue as he flees through the door and is swallowed by the anonymous crowds.

# About the Author

Jo Jackson was born in Birmingham. She was a nurse and midwife before qualifying and practising as a family psychotherapist. She lived in Cairo in the 1980s with her husband and children. Jo began writing thirty years ago when she had several short stories published. Work and family interrupted the creative process and she returned to it only in retirement. This is her first novel. She now lives near Much Wenlock in Shropshire.

Made in the USA
San Bernardino, CA
04 November 2017